THE Night Nurse AND THE Jewel Thief

MARILEE DAHLMAN

Brother Mockingbird Publishing

Copyright ©2026 by Marilee Dahlman
All rights reserved

This is a work of fiction. Names, characters, businesses, places, events, locales, and incidents are either the products of the author's imagination or used in a fictitious manner. Any resemblance to actual persons, living or dead, or actual events is purely coincidental.
Library of Congress Control Number: 2025949161

Cover Design by: Alexios Saskalidis
www.facebook.com/187designz

No part of this book may be reproduced or transmitted in any form or by any means without written permission from the publisher.

For information please contact:
Brother Mockingbird, LLC
www.brothermockingbird.net
ISBN: 978-1-960226-32-7 Paperback
ISBN: 978-1-960226-33-4 EBook

To my mom, Marcia, and all the other nurses, too.

Part One: Fire and Ice

Chapter One

It all began on Fire Night.

Standing at her bedroom window at 3:12 a.m., Nancy Norman watched the meteoric red-orange glow spread across the dark sky and embers dizzy up to the stars. She had the fleeting thought that the flames were beautiful, although she would never admit such a thing to anyone.

The fire raged on the hill where backyards ended and the Minnesota state nature preserve began. She hesitated, and didn't admit that to anyone either. A nurse for forty-two years, Nancy was highly capable, efficient, and caring, in that order. She took pride in her abilities. However, the looming destruction-of-the-whole-neighborhood situation required a full two minutes for her to process.

But reality set in. Soon the glowing beauty would devour her and the neighbors.

Nancy could admit it was Dr. GoldenPaw who'd woken her up, unapologetically pouncing on her. He'd raced around the bedroom and prowled the windowsill until his idiot human pal understood there was a fire, fire, fire!

Obviously, her Persian cat was the hero. Nancy did the easy thing. She wrenched her gaze from the blaze and called 911. She rang her neighbors too.

Then she put her hands on her hips and tapped her foot. It was very late. This was so dang inconvenient. Where was she supposed to go? What would she need to bring? The fire department would stop the fire before it reached her house, right?

It'd all be easier if Dave were around. But his delayed midlife crisis had taken him to Phoenix, and last week his lawyer had sent her an email with a formal letter attached. The letter said David Norman wanted to arrange for the delivery of his '65 Chevy Impala from Minnesota to Arizona.

Nancy went straight to the garage, gathering framed family photos along the way. Her white Volvo and Dave's Impala, painted in original Danube Blue, sat in musty darkness. Approaching sirens made her pause. Should she take the Impala, in case the fire reached the house?

She stabbed the button by the door to open the garage.

Yet Nancy couldn't move. Her slippers felt superglued to the concrete floor. The cars and the brick-and-mortar house seemed so permanent. Sure, the 911 lady had said to leave immediately. But what did she know? The dispatcher didn't realize Nancy had lived here for twenty-six years.

Nancy drew a breath and coughed. The air had suddenly turned acrid and burned her nostrils and throat. It was sharp and poisonous, no campfire or piney fireplace smoky air. Panic sweat slid down her back, producing a chill even though it was July and the fire raged close. Shivering, she pulled her robe tighter and forced herself to take a few steps and scan the street.

The cul-de-sac looked quiet, with no traffic, no garage doors opening, and nobody on their porches. No lights flickered on in the windows. She could see the hillside beyond the line of suburban Craftsman-style homes, where the fire burned. When she and Dave first moved here, the land had been marshy bugginess. In recent years, it had transformed into a dry, scraggly hillside dotted with newish fir trees. How many times had she and Dave discussed the irony that global warming had made the nature preserve more pleasant for strolls?

Well, Dave was of no help right now, and he never would be again. As far as Nancy was concerned, the fire could eat up the Impala and she wouldn't shed a tear. She'd save her Volvo.

Something outside crashed. A telephone pole or a tree? Inside the house, on the other side of the door leading to the garage, Dr. GoldenPaw meowed.

Nancy's brain, body, and soul finally woke into flight mode. She tossed the photos into the Volvo and rushed back into the house, speeding through and seizing things. Did her fanny pack still have her wallet inside? Yes! She grabbed her knock-off Coach bag with supplies she always brought on her home nurse shifts. Quickly, she stuffed extra clothes and more old pictures of her and her father into a reusable grocery bag. She also added her exercise binder. The day after she and Dave had separated, she'd begun an exercise plan, keeping careful track of her progress. A stupid fire wasn't about make her lose track or miss a day.

The windows were shut, but the smoke still burned her eyes. More alarming sounds erupted nearby, crackling and roaring, and also louder sirens, shouting, and tires screeching. Her pulse pounded far faster than it should for a sixty-five-year-old heart, and she felt an ache—a real, physical pain—in her chest at the idea of all her neighbors and their pets in terrified distress. People might get hurt. Nancy had her nursing supplies. When she reached safety, maybe she could help. She just had to get this stuff in the Volvo, return for her cat, and she'd get away.

She carried her escape bags in both arms. Her mind boiling with plans and worries, she got a hand free to twist the doorknob of the door leading to the garage. She kicked it wider open to get through.

Dr. GoldenPaw scooted between her legs and escaped the house.

Nancy's long, helpless scream of "Nooooo!" added another sound to the night's madness.

Her lovely long-haired boy became a flash of white and orange as he darted out the open garage door and disappeared into the infernal night. Nancy dropped everything and chased him. A coughing fit struck her as soon as she made it to the driveway. Fire heat throbbed across her whole body. She stood in her slippers and bathrobe, feeling stupid and useless. It was no use.

Her cat was gone.

Chapter Two

Five hours later, Nancy sat in the elementary school cafeteria, where they'd put people displaced by the fire. Hotels had filled up fast. The school probably smelled like ammonia and erasers, but smoke had burned her nostrils and she couldn't detect any aroma at all. Only one thought stuck in her mind—the flash of his orange-white fur and the frantic pump of his little legs as Goldy sped into the darkness.

The fire had destroyed twenty-three homes, including Nancy's, but everyone survived. Fire trucks had arrived right away. The 911 call from Nancy had made all the difference.

"Climate change," some neighbors kept saying. "That was what caused it. Nancy, you saved us!"

"It was Dr. GoldenPaw who saved us," Nancy said.

She explained this to the neighbor couple who had the three boys who always played squirt guns in the street, even in the winter. She explained this to the retired Delta pilot who had recently married his third wife. She explained this to the school principal Thandie Baker-Bell, a lady Nancy had never met and looked about fourteen years old, except she had a huge engagement ring and had explained to Nancy that she was working on her online doctorate in elementary education.

"They'll find him," more neighbors said. "The first responders are searching."

"He's white with orange paws and big golden eyes. My kitty has a flat face, long hair, and he's adorable. The sweetest boy."

"They'll find him," Thandie said.

Nancy called the microchip company. She posted a notice to the neighborhood app. To distract herself, she made the rounds in the cafeteria, asking if anyone needed nursing assistance.

That's when she realized that she'd packed the wrong knock-off Coach shoulder bag.

It didn't have any first aid stuff. She'd grabbed her *other* knock-off Coach bag, which was her bling bag, brimming with rhinestones, sequins, beads, glue gun, and other supplies for bedazzling.

Dave's voice slunk into her mind, and the memory of how, three years ago, he'd slapped his hand on the kitchen island and pointed at that very same bag.

"All the bling," he'd said. "You exist in fantasy, Nancy. It's not enough for me. I'm sixty-five. I have a third of my life left, tops. I'm going to enjoy it."

Nancy tugged her sequined bathrobe tighter. She would simply never tell him, that out of all the things she could've saved from the fire, she'd saved her bling bag. She'd never inform him that the extra clothes she'd saved were her bedazzled scrubs and hoodie. Or that her Paris Las Vegas Hotel fanny pack had her wallet and cell, and the rest was brimming with new beads she'd bought at Michaels.

Her fingers carefully composed a concise and informative text to Dave about the fire and Dr. GoldenPaw's disappearance, but no other details.

After reading it through twice, she pressed Send.

She tried to exercise, half-heartedly. It was something she could do in place, with limited resources, because it was the Royal Canadian Air Force Exercise XBX Plan. She'd always been obsessed with royals of any kind, and for a long time had constructed a Princess Diana shrine in the corner of her living room, but dismantled it under pressure from Dave's constant eyerolls.

The day after he moved out, she started a program favored by the British royals as well as Dame Helen Mirren, at least according to Google. It was a twelve-minute, daily regimen featuring simple exercises to boost flexibility, muscle strength, and aerobic capacity—toe touching, arm circling, partial sit-ups, running in place, hopping, and so on. When she began running and jumping in place, she started getting some curious looks from Thandie and the neighbors, but she kept up with it.

At noon, Dave called. Nancy confirmed that the Impala had been destroyed in the fire. He mumbled something about insurance and hung up.

Thandie sat beside her on the donated sleeping bag. The school principal had an air of breezy competence, not to mention really good make-up. Her bold pinkish-orange eyeshadow with a bit of sparkle to it, which the kids probably loved, went marvelously with the diamond and rose quartz bling on her finger.

"You have kids or anything like that?" Thandie asked her.

"No. Just my cat."

"Not *just* a cat. He's a hero! They'll find him."

Thandie bumped shoulders with her. Apparently, they were friends already. Nancy stifled a sob and lowered her head. It was bad enough she had to cry, but did she have to cry in front of everyone?

No, Nancy would not do that. She wiped a tear from the corner of her eye, pretending like it was just a bit of dust.

"Hey." Thandie produced a tissue out of nowhere, like a magician, and pressed it into Nancy's hand. "Um, you have someone you want to ring up? Or maybe you lead more of the independent kind of life? That's cool, too."

Nancy simply shook her head. Thandie hung around for another few minutes before doing another shoulder bump and getting up.

Nancy called the microchip company again, but there was no news about her cat.

Church people, her age, arrived and handed out sandwiches. This kept the kids quiet for about two seconds. Nancy decided to lie down and close her eyes. Maybe she would take a nap and then go back to the neighborhood and start looking for Dr. GoldenPaw herself. The firefighters had said to stay away. But surely, they'd let her search for her cat.

The second Nancy closed her eyes, her phone rang.

She opened her eyes and staggered to her feet before the second ring, her muscles primed to bolt. Her heart and stomach buzzed in a rhythm of faint, sickly hope.

"Hello?"

There was a long pause on the other end, followed by some kind of whooshing-water sound and heated, unintelligible whispers of what sounded like disagreement. Nancy's hopes for her kitty crashed to the linoleum floor. Her shoulders drooped and she closed her eyes with her phone to her ear, listening to bizarre whispering.

The whispering stopped, although the water whooshing continued. A man said, *"Bonjour."*

She didn't recognize the guy's voice. Was he French? Or pretending to be? Nancy didn't know any French people. When she was still married to Dave, they'd looked into tour trips to Paris plenty of times. It was her dream to go there, at least once. It was his dream to travel everywhere and see the whole world.

But Nancy had never actually booked a French trip. Of course, the Internet was scary. Everything online was tracked, like search history. Maybe this caller worked for a travel agency and wanted to sell her something.

The man spoke again, this time in English with a heavy French accent. "*Bonjour*, Nancy. It is Claude, from—"

"Wrong number," Nancy said. "Unless you're calling about my cat, Dr. GoldenPaw?"

"Ah, Gold, say more, *s'il vous plait*? Cat?"

Nancy crumpled to the floor. She hugged her knees to her chest. After bringing the phone back to her ear, she gave it one last shot. "Cat?"

After a few beats of silence, Nancy heard more whooshing and whispering. She shivered. It wasn't exclusively this guy "Claude" calling. There was somebody with him.

"Not cat," Claude said. "We want you."

"Wrong number."

Nancy hung up. She made sure the phone was still charged and not on silent mode. She struggled back to her feet and decided to find out if they'd let her back into the neighborhood yet. She had to get back there and find Goldy. She was a professional nurse. They would trust her to help with whatever was needed.

Chapter Three

The first responders respected that she was a nurse, but the answer was no. She couldn't go back yet. It was too dangerous. There were fallen powerlines and other hazards.

Nancy settled in to endure a bad night. She lay awake atop a sleeping bag, which she didn't trust because, honestly, had anyone washed it? As she stared at the ceiling, she replayed the memories of crackling fire, roaring sirens, and billowing black smoke. She imagined what her cat could be going through. Where was he, and what was he feeling? Was he afraid? Was he cold? The way his claws were trimmed and face was so flat, making it hard to bite and protect himself, he'd never survive long on his own. She'd received him from the rescue agency last year, when he was two years old and had been surrendered by his previous owners due to their unexpected medical expenses. He had been a pre-retirement gift to herself, a pal for her golden years.

Nancy frowned and inhaled deeply, detecting the grade-school scent of Crayola and cleaning fluids and hearing the murmurs of unfamiliar people nestled all around. Creeping among her thoughts was the strange caller named "Claude." Claude knew her first name, and that bothered her. Did he know her last name too? She had secrets, like everyone did, things she'd never even told Dave.

What else did Claude know?

People were whispering, and Nancy's senses went on high alert. Sunrise seeped in through the cafeteria's windows after her sleepless night on top of the sleeping bag.

What was with all the whispering? She put on her glasses and scanned for the culprits. Thandie and a cop were speaking by the cafeteria's main doors. They glanced in Nancy's direction. The second time they whispered and looked at her, Nancy stood and shuffled toward them. Thandie greeted her with a hug.

Nancy kept that short, because she wanted to know what was going on. She didn't want a hug from Thandie. She wanted to hug her cat.

The cop, who seemed too young to be a cop, flashed a grin. "They found him."

Thandie gripped Nancy's arms and forced eye contact. "Hey, Nancy, things aren't perfect. Need to prepare you."

"I'm a nurse!" She wiggled her fanny pack, which she'd kept on all night, ready for anything. "I'm always prepared! Always! Never not prepared! You think I'm not prepared?"

Her shouting echoed around the cafeteria and bounced off the ceiling and linoleum, stirring every person in the room. Thandie's eyes widened. The cop turned his cap round and round in his hands.

Nancy ground her teeth and tried to calm down. Thandie and the police officer weren't the enemy. They weren't responsible for GoldenPaw's escape. But she'd always had a chip on her shoulder about cops because of something her father had done long ago. That was ancient history, though. At the moment, it had been thirty hours since she'd slept. She had a crick in her neck, and she just wanted her cat.

"He's at the vet getting treated." Thandie said.

Nancy's breath caught, and the universe stilled. Golden-Paw was alive.

"I'll take you," the cop said.

"Nope." The old distrust kicked in. "I'll drive."

"You're sure you're okay?" Thandie put a hand on her shoulder.

Nancy straightened her glasses. "Of *course* I can drive. You betcha. No problem. I drove the Volvo perfectly fine out of the neighborhood, even with the smoke and fire. It was Dave's stupid Impala that was incinerated. And what he'll do about that, I don't know and don't care."

Thandie threw up her hands. "Okay, okay."

"Which vet?"

The cop and Thandie exchanged a quick concerned look, then the cop gave Nancy the vet's name before telling her, "Be careful along Duck Nest Road. The fire's still burning."

"Dontcha know I'm always careful?"

Nancy didn't wait for an answer. But two minutes later, as she crossed the elementary school's parking lot to her car, the smoky air and the fear and the adrenaline all sent bile up her throat. She swallowed it back, mad at herself for being weak, as she hopped in her car. She'd always had an iron stomach, an essential nursing trait. But driving along Duck Nest Road, seeing the blood-red glow of flames still shooting up from the state nature preserve, hit her hard. It was impossible to resist shivering. Her hands grew slick on her Volvo's sequined steering wheel as it dawned on her that the dissipating black smoke had once been *homes*—hers and her neighbors' homes, and everything inside them was gone.

Not to mention, Dave's Impala was destroyed, and the kayaks in the basement were ash now too. What a mess.

All that destruction was overwhelming, but what mattered at this exact second was her Dr. GoldenPaw. Nancy forced herself to breathe, even though the inside of her car reeked of fire fumes. She sat up straighter, leaned forward, and slowly drove around a downed, very charred Eastern white pine ringed by orange safety cones.

Minutes later, she arrived at the vet's office. The parking lot was crammed, and the reception area was worse. Faster than expected, the receptionist called her name, and her heart started racing faster than a hamster's. Her palms itched, and she yearned to pet Goldy. She wanted to smooth his fur and talk to him.

The office air was warm, the A/C battling the summer heat. The vet with shoulder-length hair and a stubby nose had a clammy handshake. Nevertheless, as he spoke, Nancy's guts, brain, and every millimeter of her skin iced over.

"Dr. GoldenPaw was burned. His front legs were singed."

The vet slowly wiped his hands on his white coat.

Nancy leveled a direct look at him, pretending she was calm. It was a nurse's gift—the ability to project a certain steeliness in the face of emergencies. Maybe she could handle it. But the way he hesitated…

"Lung damage," Nancy said. "You need to check for it."

The vet shook his head. "We have Dr. GoldenPaw in a special crate, getting extra oxygen. His lungs will be okay. Some smoke inhalation, but no permanent damage. That's not it."

His mouth was moving, but none of his words sank into her head. He led Nancy back to where they kept the animals. She blinked hard to clear her fogged mind and observed a sealed crate with a cold oxygen tank whirring next to it, feeding him extra O2.

Goldy's orange-white body was curled up. There were so many bandages that Nancy couldn't tell at first which end was his head and which end was his tail. But she glimpsed an ear and knew that his head was almost entirely wrapped.

The room tilted. Her mind swam. Nancy felt like she was about to vomit, and she was not the type who grew sick when it came to injuries. She could deal with blood. She could handle gruesomeness. But not this. Not harm to animals, and especially not to her own. Nancy stumbled forward and slapped her sweaty palms on the crate's glass.

"Dr. GoldenPaw. Goldy. My kitty."

Her precious ball of fur twitched a little and moved as if to stretch, but stopped like it hurt too much.

"Don't move, boy," she said. "My treasure. You nap."

Goldy slowly raised his head. He drew a breath that ended in a dainty cough. He blinked one golden eye at Nancy, which shone with love and trust.

But only one. The other side of this face, where his right eye was supposed to be, was puffed up with heavy bandages. Seconds passed while Nancy absorbed what it meant. The vet was talking, but he didn't need to. She understood without any explanation. Her precious kitty would live, but he had lost his right eye.

That wretched, beautiful fire had destroyed his eye.

Nancy forced back a moan and squeezed her eyes shut, the tears coming and stinging. She must focus on the positive. She had her boy back. Dr. GoldenPaw wasn't the same, but he'd heal. He was a survivor, and he would be back in her arms.

Standing in the vet building, studying her cat, Nancy reached one absolute, irrevocable, forever decision.

Never again, *never again*, would she lose Dr. GoldenPaw.

Chapter Four

The man named Claude contacted her three more times over the next two months. Nancy hung up on him every time. He never left a voicemail, and the number was "unknown," and it was untraceable. Each call left her worried and feeling like she ought to do something about it, but she was drowning in the vast ocean of a million other things on her mind.

Since Fire Night, Dave had texted her exactly six times. Three were about how glad he was he'd sold his half of the house to her as part of the divorce.

After a lot of hard work, however, Nancy's life was returning to a new kind of normal. The insurance company paid out a small amount, but it was nowhere near the cost of the house. It didn't matter how many times she called them or read them the fine print on the policy—they refused to cover everything. If she still wanted to retire, she had no choice but to cut way, way down on spending and downsize into a small condo, a tiny space that still somehow stretched her budget.

And she *did* want to retire. She remembered telling Dave over and over that she would stop working, and they would travel and have adventures. He'd rolled his eyes every time. She'd taken a stab at another idea, a dream closer to her heart— after retirement, maybe they would open a bed and breakfast, somewhere up in northern Minnesota? It'd be so fun to decorate the place.

He'd thrown his hands in the air and stormed out for the evening. She hadn't raised the B&B idea a second time.

She still wouldn't mind opening a bed and breakfast, but that was a pipe dream now. Yet, she did need to retire. Forty-two years of nursing was enough. She deserved a break. Fire Night was a bitter pill to swallow after a lifetime of working, saving, and being responsible. She'd played by the rules, and yet the rug had still been pulled out from under her sensibly shoed feet.

She had done the smart thing again and downsized to a smaller place. She'd also cut spending. What really mattered was Goldy's recovery. There would be more wonderful, happy years with her kitty.

Tomorrow it would begin: Nancy Norman's first day of retirement.

Sitting at her new condo's kitchen island, Nancy fiddled with her cell phone and wondered if she should mention it to Dave, the big day had arrived. It was already 5 p.m., and he hadn't texted. She poked around on Facebook and discovered he was camping with his new girlfriend. He called her "Sal" in posts, not Sally. One text to Nancy had been about his kayak that had been destroyed in the fire, and he texted Nancy that "Sal" had told him to "buy a new one."

Nancy tensed, her nostrils flaring. They'd had disagreements about Dave's desire to go camping and her hesitation about roughing it like that. Sure, deep down she wanted to have some fun, maybe even a real adventure. But above all else, they'd needed to save for retirement. Naturally, Sal was different.

She gritted her teeth, imagining Sal wrapping her arms around Dave right now, cooing something like, "You escaped in the nick of time, didn't you?"

Nancy rose from her seat and stuck her phone into her fanny pack, which she liked to wear at all times for convenience. It was time for a search.

Where had Dr. GoldenPaw gone? No emergency this time—he had to be somewhere in her one-bedroom condo.

"Alrighty, boy. Are you ready for our party tonight?"

Nancy wandered around her living room and jiggled the kitty treats bag. Ever since Fire Night, Dr. GoldenPaw had developed some personality changes. He was now quite prone to hiding and hoarding. She usually found him with some kind of her bling, like a bit of jewelry or rhinestone strip. More so than other cats, he seemed really obsessed with bright, shiny objects.

She shook the treat bag again. "Are you gonna be a good host for our guests?"

The oven's *ding* interrupted her cat search. Nancy went back to the kitchen, set the kitty treats bag on the counter, and took the piping hot Target-brand *Good & Gather* vegetable spring rolls and pork potstickers out of the oven. For something sweet, she set out a bedazzled bowl overflowing with Kit-Kats, in honor of the hero himself. She opened the curtains to let the August late-afternoon sunlight in. After grabbing the kitty treats bag, she rattled it and resumed her search.

"Goldy, where'd ya go?"

No response. He was probably cowering under the bed. She sighed. Her cat's physical health was improving, his emotional health, not so much. Was there such a thing as a feline psychiatrist? Goldy had kitty PTSD, she was sure of it.

Someone knocked at the door, and she opened it, welcoming Thandie.

She brought pet cookies coated with orange and white frosting for Dr. GoldenPaw and a *Happy Retirement* balloon for Nancy. The condo manager, a woman named Jolene, followed her, along with Nancy's friend Cynthia from nursing school, with whom she'd kept in touch for four decades.

And that was it for her guest list. Her old neighborhood friends were busy. Most of them had really been Dave's friends anyway. She didn't fully know her new condo neighbors yet, but they were, unfortunately, old. Some of them were pushing eighty. Yeah, Nancy was retired now, but that didn't mean her party needed a geriatric vibe. Nancy guided the party guests to the counter between the kitchen and living room.

Thandie caught Nancy's scowl. "What's wrong?"

Nancy shrugged. There'd been a time, decades ago, when she'd imagined a glamorous life. There would be travel, boyfriends, a cool car, a mansion with a pool, adventure, romance, and fun. It had never materialized, not even close. This wasn't even a party, not really. This was a get-together.

Her phone buzzed with an Unknown number text. *Bon soir. It is I, Claude. May we chat?*

Nancy white-knuckled the phone. The arrogance! He thought it was okay to text, and they'd never even had a proper conversation. Her thumb hovered over the message to delete it. But she hesitated. If this Claude was stalking her, maybe she should keep the message as evidence. This was his first text. Maybe he'd slipped up and made a big mistake. She'd keep it.

"Hey, you okay?" Thandie asked.

"Spam."

Jolene glanced around the room. "Where's your precious feline?"

Nancy waved a hand toward the bedroom. "Hiding."

"I'll find him." Jolene scurried off before waiting for consent.

"Seriously, Nancy. I like your place." Thandie waved an arm. "And *love* the bling!"

"That's our Nancy," Cynthia said, giving a little tug on the sleeve of Nancy's party top, a black and gold Chico's blazer.

Nancy, Thandie, and Cynthia admired the bedazzled glory of Nancy's condo. Cynthia gave a little fake laugh. Nancy tried yet failed to avoid wrinkling her nose at her. Cynthia had always been a confident type. But after three kids and eight grandkids, she'd become downright dismissive of anything that wasn't somehow family and procreation related. And she'd always been kind of snarky.

"Yeah, I like to bedazzle."

"Understatement," Cynthia said.

Mostly as a stress reliever, Nancy had, over the past month, blinged out pretty much her whole existence. Her cell phone, TV, lamps, vases, the kitty's food and water bowls, and all the picture frames were covered in bright, sparkly colors. She especially liked what she'd done with the precious photos she'd saved of herself and her father. Her favorite one—a picture of him beaming a carefree grin from a brasserie in Marrakesh—she'd outlined in gold and green sequins. At this point, Nancy was halfway done gluing more sequins all over her laptop.

Maybe Cynthia was jealous. Nancy had independence with a conveniently located one-bedroom condo on the fifth floor of a ten-year-old building, five minutes from Target and ten minutes from Michaels, her favorite arts and crafts store. The abode could've had a cookie-cutter, standard look, but Nancy knew she'd fixed that with rhinestones and sequins.

"A wonderful retirement place," Thandie said, with real warmth in her voice.

"You've already downsized," Cynthia chimed in.

Nancy nodded. Her plan was to build a nice retirement life here. She focused on the purple shine of a sequined lampshade and a stack of spy novels by Ian Fleming, John le Carré, and Robert Ludlum next to it on the small table. She drummed her fingers on the counter. Why did it feel like something was missing? That she'd made a wrong turn somewhere, that there was some other life she was supposed to be leading?

"What's this?" Thandie flipped through Nancy's exercise binder and then the Royal Canadian Air Force Exercise Plan booklet on her counter.

In a slightly lower voice, Nancy said, "It's what the British royals do to stay fit."

"You *are* fit. I noticed that about you, first thing." Thandie plastered a super-serious expression on her face and demonstrated toe touches.

"Yes, that's it."

"Not every sixty-five-year-old woman can do push-ups." Thandie flexed like a weight lifter.

"True enough. But I can."

"Found him!" Jolene shouted from the bedroom.

She appeared with Dr. GoldenPaw in her arms. Nancy's heart leapt. His white and orange fur, which had been burned by fire and shaved for surgery, was growing back. His legs were bandaged to protect the burned skin, but he could still run, jump, and play. The bandages would be gone soon, but not the eye patch covering his right eye.

Nancy had crafted the patch herself out of black cloth to keep Goldy from pawing at his injury and to keep the stitches clean. Her cat had never tried to remove it, and Nancy liked to think he actually liked the patch. It certainly gave him a devilish air. She hoped she might even find a silver lining in the whole tragedy and turn Dr. GoldenPaw into an emotional support animal. Maybe she could take him to hospitals to help patients with eye conditions, especially kids, feel better about wearing an eye patch.

Dr. GoldenPaw, trapped in Jolene's arms, looked at Nancy and gave a pitiful meow. He wiggled and leaped from Jolene's clutches and bolted back into the bedroom. Her friend's mouth dropped open in disappointment.

"He's still afraid of everything," Nancy said.

"No worries." Jolene scrutinized her arms for scratches. "The patch is cool, like a pirate."

Nancy shook her head. "He's more like an Emilio Largo."

Jolene's blank expression beamed back at her. Well, she was a Millennial. She couldn't help it.

"From *Thunderball*, the James Bond movie." Nancy clicked her tongue. "You all are glued to way too much Kardashian. The villain was Largo. He was the bad guy with a black eye patch and a white tuxedo. His plan was to steal the two nukes and hold the world hostage."

Slow nods came from Thandie, Cynthia, and Jolene.

"I own the DVD," Nancy said. "Can pop it in."

A few beats of silence followed, then a chorus of excuses. Nobody had time for a movie. They all had to work the next day. Nancy's cheeks grew warm. It wasn't purely because they didn't want to stick around. They had stuff to do tomorrow. She didn't.

Nancy dropped her gaze. She picked up a framed certificate—already bedazzled—from the countertop. The home nurse company had sent it to her already. It proclaimed her *40 Years of Excellent Nursing Service*.

Thandie patted her shoulder. "Forty years is enough."

"I know." Nancy slapped the certificate down again. "Though sometimes I think, what's next?"

Thandie smirked. "You know what? You need to find yourself a real-life villain in a tuxedo."

Cynthia and Jolene guffawed. The get-together suddenly perked up.

"Nancy and a bad boy, something we'll never see." Cynthia studied her globby wedding ring. "Dave was always a super-nice guy."

Thandie scooped up Nancy's phone and admired its purple sequin case. "What other apps you have here? I bet lots. As soon as we leave, you're gonna have a sexy guy come over. A Bond movie? Whatevs."

Nancy chopped both hands sideways. "Not those apps, no. My picture out there? What if my identity was stolen? All to meet up with a stranger? No way."

"But you're a home nurse! You spent your whole career going into strange homes and taking care of people." Thandie thrust the phone at Nancy. "Unlock it. I'm gonna load you up."

Nancy stalled, slowly unlocking her phone. She swiped away the weather app showing Phoenix and closed out her Pinterest browser window. "I don't know if I have enough memory on this, I take a lot of pictures."

"We're gonna find you a man, Nancy." Thandie nabbed the phone.

In roughly three seconds, Thandie loaded the app *Senior-LOVE*. Next was setting up the profile.

"But it can't have my name. Safety first!" Deep down, Nancy wanted a fun romance, but there was no way her last name was going on the app screen.

"It would simply say Nancy, trust me," Cynthia said.

"Wait, who was the Bond lady in *Thunderball*?" Thandie struck a hand-on-hip seductive pose.

"Dominique Derval," Nancy promptly answered. "Also known as 'Domino.'"

"Dominique." Thandie whistled. "Damn. Perfecto!"

"Dominique's too different," Jolene said. "Nancy's a nice name. You could use a fake last name. Like say you're Nancy Domino."

"Done," Thandie said. "Now it's time for a photo shoot!"

Nancy quickly changed into a few different dresses and Thandie, acting like a Hollywood professional, applied more makeup on her. After all the photos were taken, they uploaded two of the very best. One was a glamour shot of Nancy in her fanciest dress, holding a martini glass and standing against a photoshopped background of a room at Palace of Versailles. She aimed a sultry stare straight at the camera.

The other was an "action" shot of her in another blingy dress, her red reading glasses and a fake-ruby necklace dangling in one hand while she studied her laptop. She'd been scrolling through Etsy, but nobody could tell that from the angle of the photo. Thandie had edited the pic to make it black and white, except for her red glasses, the fake-ruby necklace, and the red sequins on the laptop case. The brilliant color was stunning against the monochrome. Nancy wanted to upload it to Facebook so Dave would see it, but the ladies insisted it was time to answer profile questions.

That's when the party really picked up, with everyone helping way too much with the responses. Some weren't entirely truthful. Nancy would fix them later, if she kept the app on her phone. Her profile said she was a "cool & experienced professional seeking same." Her interests were "all the finer things in life." Her favorite color was "anything that sparkles." Her favorite place was "a moonlit night on a yacht anchored near Nassau, with a dry martini and sharks for company."

In the "About" section, she added a few accurate things about how she loved anything James Bond-related. She also said she stayed "fit for anything and everything" with daily military-style calisthenics. After years of hard work, she wanted to "abandon life's eternal quest for loot and disappear into the capitals of Europe, exploring the side streets for love and a perfectly executed croissant." It was a pretty snazzy profile, she had to admit.

Five minutes later, she had exactly seven new matches.

Chapter Five

Nancy analyzed each *SeniorLOVE* match, trying to ignore Jolene's giggling, and a comment from Cynthia about one not looking like he had a "real" job. Over her guests' playful objections, Nancy "swiped hard left" on all of them. They were all too old, too weird, too boring, or they had typos in their profiles.

After that, her friends said it was time for them to leave.

"You have standards, Nancy." Thandie gave Nancy a wink and a hug. "The profile's cool. Good luck with it. I want to hear about all the hookups!"

The instant Nancy closed the door after her guests, silence invaded the condo, the kind that seeped into her soul and made her legs and heart ten pounds heavier. She noticed that her retirement balloon was already sinking, like it knew the party was over.

To defy the quiet, Nancy switched on *Thunderball*. She plugged in her glue gun and checked the time. Goldy was due for his next round of antibiotics and painkillers in one hour.

"*Dum, dum, da-dum.*" Nancy hummed along to the opening Bond music as she put away snacks—there were enough leftovers to last a week—disinfected the kitchen, and flipped through her junk mail. She ignored the new AARP magazine and something on life insurance, but she paused to read a glossy flier. *Old and alone? Get an AI companion for a bargain $100,000 per month.*

Insane.

Loads of money for a computerized boyfriend? People

were desperate. What would they think of next? She threw all the mail away. After a glance around, as if someone might be watching, she picked up her phone and opened *SeniorLOVE*.

No new matches.

She bit her lip, tempted to delete the app. Perhaps first thing tomorrow morning, she'd do it. That'd be soon enough.

Knowing she shouldn't, Nancy called Dave. Her call went directly to voicemail. She swiftly hung up, waited a minute to see if he might see the missed call and ring her right back, but he didn't.

So she texted him.

It was nothing major, no more than a nonchalant informative paragraph letting him know she'd officially retired today. She'd even had a party to celebrate. Nancy clicked Send, and the text flew away with the little *whoosh* sound, straight to Dave.

It was a message she absolutely had to send, because retirement had become such a point of contention between them. They had fought over her working all the time, according to him, and him spending so darn much. He spent their money on things he knew she didn't care about, such as pro baseball season tickets, college hockey season tickets, sports equipment and gym memberships, the kitchen remodel, the new desk, and on and on and on. He had bought worthless crap that drained their accounts and blew up the Mastercard. She had reminded him about her childhood and why she felt compelled to work to keep money coming in and to build a savings account. Dave would nod with practiced patience. He'd end every conversation as if she'd said nothing at all and then demand to buy an RV to visit all the National Parks. She'd told him that was what retired people did.

She had actually retired, and he needed to know that. It proved something, somehow. She wasn't about to go camping, but she was capable of enjoying her free time. Moreover, the ladies coming over was proof she could do something fun.

Dr. GoldenPaw sauntered into the kitchen and assumed a position on the counter. He stared intently at Nancy's sparkling bling supplies. She settled down at the kitchen table to bedazzle the rest of her laptop. It was a jewel theme, with rubies and garnets and emeralds lined up geometrically. Amethysts, her favorite gemstones, formed a big square in the middle. The smell of the glue, the mindless concentration, the sparkling colors made her shoulders relax.

Her phone rang.

Unknown number.

Chapter Six

Nancy ignored the call. She pocketed the phone in her fanny pack, and she zipped it closed. Claude was probably calling again. He had to be a creep.

She checked the time on the microwave clock and set her glue gun down. "All right, kitty. Time for your meds."

After getting the little syringe ready to shoot liquid pain meds into his mouth, Nancy went to pluck Goldy from the counter and—

She clasped empty air. The cat landed on the floor and streaked into the living room, taking up an ambush position under the coffee table. By the time Nancy had lowered down to her knees, ready to reach under it, he was long gone. She nearly caught him on the TV stand, nestled next to the DVD player, but Dr. GoldenPaw was a furry orange-white flash headed into Nancy's bedroom. Two bandaged legs and possessing merely one eye didn't slow him down. On the contrary, he seemed faster than he was before his injuries.

Her phone pinged, a different sound than a text chime.

"What the heck?"

Was it Claude? Or maybe, it could be Dave. She took out her phone from her fanny pack.

It was the *SeniorLOVE* app, flashing a heart on the screen, followed by the words, *You have an elite match*!

"Elite" sounded all right. But the app must be tricking her, trying to get her addicted. Almost against her will, her thumb swiped to see her elite match.

His name was Sinclair. Examining the profile, Nancy gave a satisfied click of her tongue. From the headshot, the man seemed to be mid-sixties, about her age. He wore a white tuxedo with a red carnation and had a nice head of iron-gray hair, trending white at the temples and swept back in a severe, retro '50s way. His eyes were bright green and intelligent—like a cat's. This Sinclair guy had a handsome face.

In fact, Nancy decided he was too good-looking to trust. There had to be a catch. She closed the app.

A minute later, she was halfway under her bed, her hands nearly touching Goldy's fur. She would catch him.

From within her fanny pack, her phone rang. She ignored it.

"All right, Octopussy," she muttered. "Be nice. You saved me. I'll take care of you."

Peering under the bed, she saw a ribbon with sapphire rhinestones, a bright blue marker cap, and a globby ring with a huge rhinestone. It reminded her of Thandie's real diamond engagement ring. Thandie was nice, but jealousy burned in Nancy. It wasn't fair, was it? The diamond Dave had given her had been nothing to write home about, a lab-created 3/4 carat. She'd never had *real* bling.

Her phone rang again. Maybe it was Thandie or one of her other guests, and they'd forgotten something. It might be Dave returning her call. Or it could be her stalker.

Nancy scooted back. Her cat seized the opportunity to escape full tilt back into the living room. She dug her phone out of the fanny pack as she followed him.

Unknown number.

Frankly, it wasn't unknown to her. Claude needed to stop calling. It was time to give this guy a piece of her mind. She hustled into the living room and stabbed the Accept button.

"Hello. Excuse me. You have the wrong—"

Claude spoke over her. "*Bon soir.* It is Claude, manager of Gnut Berdqvist's Geyser House."

Nancy's next words died in her throat. *Gnut Berdqvist?*

Everyone in Minnesota and in the United States had heard of him. Maybe every single person on Earth knew of Gnut Berdqvist. He was a young guy who'd become a billionaire from money in tech and environmental stuff.

"The newsworthy and nubile Gnut Berdqvist," Claude said, drawing out Gnut's first name into an extra long *neeewwwwt* sound. "You've heard of him, *non?*"

"Naturally. Gnut. *Neeewwwt* Berdqvist. I've know him, I mean, have heard of him. Now, hold on. You messing with me?"

Instantly, Nancy regretted her words. She needed to be tough with this guy Claude. He was possibly stalking her. Maybe he was lying. He probably didn't even know Gnut Berdqvist.

"We want you."

Claude's words were simple but made no darn sense at all. She put a hand on her sofa to steady herself. Nancy strained her ears to make sense of the background noise on the call. She detected those strange whooshing sounds again. But this time she didn't hear another person whispering.

Nancy evaluated her options. She could hang up. If she engaged in conversation, there was no telling where things would lead. She looked around her condo. It was safe and quiet, just her and the cat. What else did she have to do? She needed to give her cat his meds, do a smidge more bedazzling, and watch the rest of *Thunderball*. It was 6:32 p.m.

"You want me?" she said. "What the heck does that mean?

Don't gimme riddles. Get to the point. Plus, speak up so I can hear you properly."

Thunder rumbled. Nancy padded over to the window and peeked out. It hadn't rained in over two months. The drought was partly to blame for the fire. Would it finally rain tonight?

"Your name was on the list," Claude said. "You're closest. Geyser House is near Lake Superior."

Nancy's mind raced. Right, Berdqvist had built a mansion here in his home state, something environmentally "green." She hadn't paid much attention to that kind of news, especially over the past couple of months with her life in major crisis. But with Gnut Berdqvist being a Minnesota guy, it was hard to miss it. Apparently, Claude was not from a travel agency she'd googled when she and Dave had still thought a big trip together might solve everything.

"Lake Superior," Claude said. "*Le lac*. You know it?"

Did she know what Lake Superior was? She was a born and raised Minnesotan. Nancy could have banged her forehead on the window.

"I know what Lake Superior is. *Le lac*." She forced patience into her tone.

"Madame Nurse, we need someone for an overnight shift. *Ce soir*. Tonight."

Nancy twirled her index finger at her temple, making the cuckoo gesture. "Tonight? Lake Superior? That's crazy. I'm in Minneapolis. Anyway, I've recently retired. I'm technically not a nurse anymore."

"*C'est urgent.*"

Nancy spied Dr. GoldenPaw in the kitchen up on top of the cupboards. According to the microwave clock, her kitty needed his meds right now. They were a half-hour behind schedule.

"*C'est urgent!*" Claude's voice grew louder.

"*Excuuuuusi-moi.* Call the agency." Nancy nabbed the kitty treats bag and rattled it. "Even if I wasn't retired, you see, I have this cat who needs his meds—"

Claude talked over Nancy again. "*Urgent!* Double pay. One night. We need a nurse here until 6:00 a.m."

Nancy nearly dropped the bag of dried chicken morsels. Did he say double pay? And who was the "we"? Claude and Gnut Berdqvist?

Dr. GoldenPaw jumped down to the counter, ogling the treats bag.

"No," Nancy said. "It won't work. My cat—"

"Triple pay. But no cat. I hate cats."

Nancy scowled. There was something seriously wrong with people who didn't like cats. She closed her eyes, seeing bright green dollar signs flashing behind her eyelids. Triple pay for one night would cover her expenses until more insurance money came through. Hmm. Nancy opened her eyes and looked at the blinged Eiffel Tower on her fanny pack. She might even have enough to start a Paris trip fund. Plus, she would see Berdqvist's Geyser House. Maybe her friends would want to come over again soon to hear about her visit to the billionaire's mansion. She could invite more guests, and make it a real party.

"Wowzers. Let me think. Maybe..."

"*Super.* See you at nine o'clock, Madame Nurse."

Chapter Seven

Claude's call disconnected before she could say goodbye. Thunder rumbled. The storm was getting closer, gathering strength. Nancy chewed her lip. She hadn't formally accepted the job. The guy was pushy as all heck.

Would it be safe?

Normally, she worked with the agency's website to process jobs. She wasn't affiliated with them anymore. She could call the agency, but what would they do? Assign the job to someone else.

Triple pay. One night. Honestly, one night could turn into a few nights, here and there, at triple pay. Gnut Berdqvist's scenic lake mansion would be in the Minnesota Northwoods. This could be an exciting opportunity.

Her phone pinged a *SeniorLOVE* alert. This time, the app gave her a notification with an envelope accented with a teensy-weensy heart.

It was a message from Sinclair. *Cheers! I'm in this lovely locale on business. Rather busy tonight but would fancy meeting you.*

Nancy uttered a giant "ha!" and swept the app shut. The text seemed overly confident. This man comes into town and says he's busy? On the other hand, the "fancy meeting you" seemed light and romantic. She didn't mind that part at all.

Hmm.

She opened the app again and went to his profile. He could be all right. She liked the photo of him wearing the fancy tux.

The "About" section said *That sound on your roof? A master thief is about to steal your heart.*

He listed one "favorite," the actor Roger Moore. Interesting, because that was also one of hers. And not just because he was Bond, though her other favorites included Timothy Dalton, Sean Connery, Pierce Brosnan, and Daniel Craig.

They must've matched because they shared a favorite and were within one mile of each other. She briskly tapped out *I'm busy tonight too. What brings you to the Land of 10,000 Lakes?*

Lickety-split, a message pinged back. *Another job. It'll work out for me, but my comrade-in-arms is bonkers. Obsessed with getting revenge on a colleague, of all things. Never bring emotion into a simple job!*

Nancy snickered at his sense of humor. He liked Roger Moore. There was a quote from *For Your Eyes Only* that she liked. Maybe Sinclair would remember it.

She typed out a new message and double-checked it for typos. *As Roger Moore said, 'Before setting off on revenge, you first dig two graves.' Tell your colleague that. I'd fancy meeting you too.*

Nancy read her message one more time before she hit Send.

She waited for a minute, staring at the phone. His other reply had arrived so quickly. But this time, she received nothing.

It was a little rude to prompt a conversation, then evaporate. Or maybe the app wasn't working as it should. She knew a little trick to fix that. She zipped the app closed, waited ten seconds, and reopened it.

Still no message from Sinclair.

Also, the little symbol showing they were within one mile of each other had vanished. Sinclair was moving away from her.

Nancy sighed, trying to shake off the disappointment. She'd known him for what, five seconds? He was a random man she'd met online. Every match would end up like this, fizzing out precisely when it seemed like it might be a good fit.

Nancy resumed her Dr. GoldenPaw search, finally capturing the kitty, feeding him a treat and then chasing it down with a squirt of liquid meds into his mouth. She couldn't leave him alone all night to be a home nurse for a billionaire. Goldy needed to stay on a strict every-four-hours schedule. If he didn't get antibiotics, his wounds could get infected, and he could rapidly go septic and die. Almost as horrible, if his other meds wore off, he'd be in pain, and she couldn't stand for him to suffer. If Nancy went to Geyser House, he'd come with her. That was not negotiable.

She nuzzled Goldy's soft head. Surely she could convince Claude her kitty was sweet, and he was a hero, and he should be allowed inside the house. Worst-case scenario, she could leave him in the car and run out and medicate him when he was due for his next doses at 10:00 p.m. and 2:00 a.m. She'd medicate next at six in the morning if her client was late returning to the house, which sometimes happened.

Nancy met her cat's single-orbed gaze.

"One last shift, kitty," she said. "This'll be great for both of us. You betcha."

Nancy prepared for her home nurse job. After all, she wasn't an idiot.

She sat at the kitchen table and did some shoulder rolls, believing strongly in the utility of simple chair exercises to benefit posture and clear the mind. Some quick research was in order before heading over to Geyser House. Flipping open her laptop, she typed "Gnut Berdqvist." Links popped up, and she clicked the first one.

Her laptop display melted to water, a beautiful aquamarine with bubbles rising to the surface. A logo whizzed on screen: *Berdqvist Enterprises—Courage in Imagination!*

The words dripped and reformed as a geyser, sort of like Old Faithful in all its glory. Real water appeared on screen—a dark, ocean-like lake stretching on forever. Yeah, Nancy knew what that was. It had to be Lake Superior.

Except, a huge iceberg bobbed epically on the lake's surface.

Were there icebergs in Lake Superior? So stark white and immense, rising thirty feet? Nancy frowned. She didn't think so. The bright sun shone on the surface of the calm, glistening lake like it was summertime.

In the video, a sleek yacht was anchored a safe distance from the iceberg. The yacht was named *Nautical Gnuttie* and bore an ice-blue stripe down the side. The camera zoomed in on three people on deck.

Nancy recognized Gnut Berdqvist from pics on her phone's newsfeed. He wore ice-blue Speedos that matched the striping on his boat and nothing else. He was about thirty years old with a cocky but charming smile, blond hair, and the brightest blue eyes she'd ever seen. Peering closer, she saw a sapphire stud in one earlobe. She'd bet every sequin in her possession the stone was real.

Gnut turned his back to the camera, and Nancy noticed the *Berdqvist Enterprises* geyser logo blazed on the butt of his Speedos. Better than any gymnast, he jumped onto the yacht's railing and balanced. He threw a grin back at the camera.

"The Berdqvist Coolant Device," he said, "transforms lukewarm polluted water into massively huge, pure icebergs to fight global warming!"

Gnut swan-dived into the lake.

The camera panned to another man. The new guy was chillingly huge, a solid six-foot-six-inch block of muscle. He wore a Vikings football jersey with the sleeves ripped off, showing watermelon biceps. His bulging quadriceps threatened to rip apart his denim cutoffs. The giant's facial features were flattened like he'd been punched fifty times. Tiny glasses with coke-bottle-thick lenses sat on his nose. He squinted at the camera.

"Hey, sports fans! I'm JT Hotman. You know me from my football days. Now, as Chief Marketing Officer of Berdqvist Enterprises, I wanna tell ya about the Coolant Device. When it comes to fighting global warming, it's a real game-changer!"

JT bent down. He picked up a heavy steel cable with one end fastened on deck and the other extended into the water. Sweat beaded on his skin. Using superhuman strength, his muscles taut, he hauled something closer to the surface.

The video shifted to the third person on the yacht. A woman wearing colorful silks under a white lab coat leaned on the railing. Nancy angled closer to her laptop screen. Was the lab coat supposed to indicate she was a doctor? Like Gnut and JT, the woman seemed about thirty years old. Her long hair flowed in the wind like Mother Earth herself caressed it. Her makeup was flawless. Jeweled rings—emeralds and rubies and diamonds—gleamed on her fingers. Actually, under all that expert foundation and blush she could be quite a bit older than thirty.

"I'm Elvira LeSabre. As the Chief Science Officer for Berdqvist Enterprises, I'll explain the science—"

A wave smashed the yacht, drenching her. Nancy snorted. Elvira LeSabre's perfect hair was now soaked, her beautiful silks waterlogged. Elvira didn't laugh it off. Her nostrils flared, her jaw tightened, and she death-stared the lake.

Meanwhile, JT kept hauling cable up. He grunted, his muscles strained, and, bracing himself, he gave one more superhuman tug. The cable's steel screeched and scraped on the railing. The camera followed the cable toward the water and something rose from the depths of Lake Superior.

"The Coolant Device." Elvira intoned the words from offscreen, her tone authoritative.

Nancy wasn't sure what to make of the Coolant Device. It looked like a giant black metal upside-down ice cream cone. The circular bottom was about twenty feet across, and it rose about thirty feet up to the tip, the same height as the iceberg. Was it made of metal or plastic? She couldn't see any electronics, at least not on the outside of that thing.

Curved metal jutted out from the device's exterior, enough to give Gnut Berdqvist handholds as he dangled off his invention's side. How did the thing float in the water? Why hadn't it been floating before, requiring JT to manhandle it up to the surface? What was inside it? How did it work? Nancy, with years of experience in nursing under her belt, settled back in her kitchen chair and anticipated some interesting scientific explanation.

Gnut pumped his fist in proud achievement of his invention. Music erupted, like a blend of rock and island reggae. Cheers and applause nearly drowned out the music. Nancy had no idea who was cheering off-camera.

The Coolant Device came alive, with icy fog shooting from the cone's tip. A few seconds later, icicles formed. Gnut covered his head with his hand, still beaming, as ice pelted the lake water around him. Once more, Nancy's laptop screen melted to aquamarine.

Berdqvist Enterprises's catchphrase unfurled across the screen: *Courage in Imagination!*

"Wowzers." If that device really worked, it could help stop global warming. She'd have to wait for the scientific information later, apparently.

Dr. GoldenPaw leaped onto her laptop, and a new video started, a cat food commercial. Laughing, Nancy grabbed him and shut down the computer. She stroked his back.

It was shaping up to be an interesting job. But who would be her patient? Gnut acted like he could compete in the Olympics and win gold in every water sport. Maybe he had an aging parent living with him, or maybe even a secret child, and their regular employees were short-staffed. Nancy blew a raspberry through her lips. With all that money and fame, this could be drug related. They needed a nurse with discretion. She had an impeccable record, and they knew she lived relatively close, so they called her. "Claude" hadn't been on the video. What was he like? There were pros and cons to taking this job. The biggest pro was green, and not as in environmentally green. She needed more green stuff in her bank account.

"What do ya think, Goldy? Should we check out Geyser House? Get some money to..." She considered all the water stuff in the video. "*Tide* us over?"

Nancy snickered. Dr. GoldenPaw purred. She dipped her head, and her kitty touched his nose to hers. He was a hero and her best friend. His purring grew louder, and Nancy's heart slowed to steady beats of contentment.

Yeah, she would take this one last shift. The extra money

would help get their lives back on track. It seemed safe enough. Gnut Berdqvist was famous and an environmentalist actually trying to do something to save the planet. She would bring her cat with her so he received his meds on time. There was even kitty litter already in the trunk so she could set things up for a little bathroom break for him. If things seemed too odd or dangerous, she'd leave. Most likely, they needed more nursing staff and were giving her a trial run.

Either way, she was due for some good luck. Goldy too.

Chapter Eight

Nancy set off down the paved path in front of her condo building, toting her bedazzled cat carrier and nurse bag. She cast an eye on the dark clouds gathering above. Thunder rumbled, but there was no rain yet. Some of her neighbors were still on the pickleball court, all dressed up in matching tennis whites and neon green headbands.

To avoid them, she picked up the pace. She didn't regret not inviting these people to her party. Plainly put, they were old. They were truly senior citizens, unlike her, a youngish sixty-five with plenty of sparkling style. The pickleball players were in their seventies and eighties. They'd let their hair go white. Nancy's hair was always a sensible auburn with help from L'Oreal Paris Light Brown #5.

Evidently, these people had fully accepted the pickleball life. She had not. Somewhere, deep down, Nancy held out hope her own life would take her in a more exciting direction. She kept her head down, trying to avoid eye contact even as she mulled over telling them where she was going. It would impress them. Also, for safety's sake, people would know where she'd be tonight.

Her neighbor Tom's voice bellowed across the muggy air. "Nurse! Hey, Nurse Nancy! You'd said you'd take a gander at this mole. Got a minute?"

Nancy looked up to see him pointing at his forearm. At that point, she decided not to tell them where she was going. She forced a light tone into her voice.

"Mole? Holy-moly, I'm late! Bye!"

His wife—Nancy had forgotten her name—waved with her racket and called, "Great news! Now that you're retired, you can join our team!"

Nancy cringed. She hustled as best she could with all the stuff in her arms, throwing a last glance back.

A third neighbor said, "Nurse, I have a question about my Medicare Part D prescription drug coverage."

The oldest guy on the court yelled, "Nurse, do you know the best brand of stool softener? Asking for a friend."

Nancy hurried even faster to her car.

Dealing with these kinds of questions was normal for all nurses. Once her neighbors realized she was really retired, maybe it would stop. Nancy nestled herself and her cat into her used white Volvo. After she locked the doors, she death-gripped the sequined steering wheel as she stared at her neighbors. Was that really her life now? Pickleball and Medicare?

Tom made eye contact. He winked and demonstrated a backhand. Nancy lightly thumped her head on the steering wheel. A sequin popped off and stuck to her forehead. She didn't care.

Thunder cracked close by. Heavy raindrops splattered on the windshield. The neighbors looked up, raising palms and faces to the sky as if to see whether the rain was real. Then the heavens opened up, sending down a deluge of water, and they sprinted back to the condo building in increasingly soaked matching white outfits.

Nancy clicked her tongue. They'd better get into warm, dry clothes. At their age, they could catch a cold that might spiral into something worse. Nancy glanced up toward her condo windows, realizing she'd forgotten her favorite hoodie. It had the perfect weight of fuzziness on the inside and a little bling she'd bedazzled on the outside.

After checking the time, she started the ignition. She was going to a billionaire's mansion and didn't need her hoodie. The temperature inside the place would be perfectly pleasant.

Rain slashed at her car windows. Dr. GoldenPaw uttered distressed meows. On both sides of the road, thick Minnesota woods loomed towering and dark. A drop of regret swished in Nancy's stomach. Lake Superior was still at least a half hour away. It was already 8:45 p.m., and she was supposed to be there in fifteen minutes.

She forced her shoulders to relax. Turning her thoughts to the payoff at the end of this night helped calm her churning belly. This time tomorrow night, she'd have a nice little fund toward her Paris trip.

The radar detector beeped. Reflexively, she slammed on the brakes, causing the car to hydroplane on the slick road, and the detector slid off the dashboard. A couple of seconds later, she spotted a cop car positioned on a gravel turnoff, partially hidden by some shrubs. His headlights were off, but a weak interior light glowed.

"Sneaky," Nancy grumbled, but victory surged through her when the cop didn't follow.

She'd been going ten miles over the limit—okay, maybe fifteen. Licking her lips, she checked the clock. Geyser House was more remote than she'd realized. Yeah, she'd be late, and that wasn't like her. Being tardy wasn't the right way to start a job. She checked her rearview mirror, pressed the accelerator, and inched above the speed limit again.

Twenty minutes later, her British-accented car nav spoke. "Do proceed another mile. Next, a left at Ice Geyser Road."

A bolt of energy straightened Nancy's spine. Ice Geyser Road? She was getting close. She squinted through the rain, trying to find a street sign. Thunder roared.

The car's nav spoke. "In half a mile, do—"

A loud crackle of static drowned out her well-spoken navigator. The dashboard spouted a new voice.

"*Bonjour*, loser. Make a U-turn."

Nancy's mouth dropped open. Did her nav just call her a loser? What in the holy heck? She stared at the screen. It had been a young woman's voice, someone with a French accent.

"What? Hold on. What happened to my old nav?"

"You are so—how you say?—lost."

Nancy swallowed hard. The sky thundered, which made Goldy meow, and a lightning strike lit up the landscape to her right. What had been forest was now endless water. Lake Superior's ocean-like enormity was unmistakable and stunning, even at night while dealing with a crazy car tech situation.

More lightning revealed a turn-off sign. *Berdqvist Ice Geyser*.

Nancy patted the cat carrier. "We're getting there, kitty. A few more minutes."

She made the turn. Almost immediately, another sign loomed ahead. *WARNING: Dangerous freezing temperatures ahead*.

Nancy exhaled noisily. "Puh-lease. It's August."

She caught sight of a third sign. *You will turn into a popsicle*. Under the words was a stick figure with wide eyes and a blue head.

Nancy sputtered out a half-laugh. This was too much.

Somebody was playing games. The weird car nav voice and the silly signs had to be pranks.

An *Incoming Call* lit up her dashboard screen, then flashed *Unknown number*.

She hit the Accept button. "Hello?"

"You're late!" Claude sounded peeved.

Before Nancy could respond, the French-accented girlie car nav spoke, but this time her voice was more distant, coming from Claude's side. "Forget her. Stay with *moi, mon amour*."

Claude's voice grew louder. "Ghost, shush!"

Nancy blinked. Ghost?

Dr. GoldenPaw meowed. Nancy glanced at the glittery carrier. "Quiet, boy."

"*Pardon?*" Claude asked.

Goldy meowed again, louder. Nancy stabbed at the screen, wanting to hit mute—

She accidentally disconnected the call.

"I'm coming," Nancy said, with a helpless glimpse at the clock, which read 9:05 p.m.

"*Non*, loser, you aren't," Ghost said through the dashboard speakers.

Nancy glared at the screen. Stupid technology. Tomorrow she was bringing this car straight back to the dealership.

But she didn't have long to dwell on her car or Ghost's annoying voice. She was nearing Geyser House. A steel gate, painted ice-blue, loomed ahead. She slowed as it automatically opened and read the sign on the gate. *No trespassing. No paparazzi. Ongoing scientific research.*

Nancy nodded, edging ahead. That sign made a little more sense. Berdqvist was developing the Coolant Device to fight global warming right here in the Minnesota Northwoods.

She drove along a narrow gravel road that cut through thick woods, checked the time, and sighed. Still late. Eager to get there as fast as possible, she pressed down on the accelerator, taking the road a bit faster than she should, but it was a Volvo. It could handle the twists and turns.

The Volvo suddenly fishtailed, careening to the wrong side of the road as the back left tire drew perilously close to the woodsy ditch.

"Yikes!"

Nancy choked the wheel, let up on the accelerator, and bit back another startled screech.

For a second, she paused, her heart hammering and palms sweating on the wheel. She checked for any traffic ahead or behind her and steered to the right side of the road, dazed. What had just happened?

Goldy sniffed in disapproval at the jolty driving.

She drove slowly, leaning forward and eyeing the road ahead. The packed gravel looked shiny, reflecting the moonlight above. She checked her car dashboard. The outside temperature was thirty-one degrees. She gaped at the temp number and then stared hard at the road.

Was that ice?

No, it couldn't be. This was August. Also, there was no way it was thirty-one degrees.

She clicked her tongue and resumed driving. Ten seconds later, she hit another patch, and the car slid to the right, but she was able to turn into the slide and straighten the car because she'd been expecting it. Her fingers were stiff, and she flexed them. She had to be careful. There was nobody out here in the woods, and her car's nav had gone crazy. Moreover, she was on an icy road even though it was summer.

Even in Minnesota that was strange.

Chapter Nine

Nancy drove up to a wide gravel driveway. She eased her foot off the accelerator. The car slid a few inches on ice and stopped.

She put the car into park, unable to look away from Geyser House and its stunning landscape. She briefly closed her eyes and wondered whether she still had her sanity.

After a few moments, she opened her eyes and, yes, the mansion and the scenery were real. Despite the late summer thunderstorm, the landscape was a winter wonderland. Snow covered everything. She shivered and shut the car's A/C off.

The boxy concrete edifice named Geyser House had huge windows on the front sides and part of its eastern wall facing the lawn. She couldn't see the entire mansion from this angle, but the massive, square, plain western half and back of the house was an extra story higher. A modern design, she supposed, although there was something about the architecture that reminded her of something, but she couldn't remember what. What kind of room was in the squarish and *colossal* structure on the west side?

The front of the house faced her, and the eastern side had a sizeable stone terrace. Guests could enjoy the view of the moat, the snowy lawn, and the ice geyser. She didn't see anyone, and only a couple of windows glowed a faint yellow.

Snow blanketed the mansion's roof. Icicles and frost crept down the steel eaves.

Her phone pinged. *SeniorLOVE*. Her match, Sinclair, was within one mile! Nancy glanced around her. Could that be right?

The close proximity icon disappeared.

All right, then, it must've been a glitch. Maybe it was something related to the weirdness with the navigation. She would delete the *SeniorLOVE* app first thing tomorrow. Or maybe tonight, if she had some downtime. If the app was messed up, that might infect the rest of her phone, including important apps like Pinterest and Etsy.

But for now, she needed to get into Geyser House.

She regarded the house one more time, then shifted her gaze from the architecture back to the landscaping. A water barrier surrounded the mansion. What the heck? Was that a medieval moat? Small icebergs floated in the water.

Rain fell, strong and steady. The way the precipitation bounced and rolled, Nancy could tell the raindrops froze by the time they reached Geyser House. It wasn't hail, exactly. More like ice pellets. The car's dashboard indicated the outside temperature was twenty-seven degrees. She carefully backed up the car closer to the woods so she'd be out of ice pellet range. The last thing she needed was another fight with an insurance company, this time trying to explain hail damage in August.

Snow covered the mansion's lawn too. Orderly air ducts dotted the ground, whirring fans sending up flurries. On the east lawn, a white expanse extended from the house to a shimmering, hundred-foot-high ice geyser.

A thin vapor trail rose from the solid, bright white cone-shaped ice. It was alive in some way, with the breath of icy air escaping the vent at its peak, like a little volcano. Moonlight reflected off the formation's icy skin, giving it a luminous, ghostly quality. Two pipelines jutted from the ground near the geyser, extending into the surrounding woods in the direction of Lake

Superior.

There were no neighboring homes in sight. Nancy rubbed her arms, a smile edging into her face. Weird, but amazing! Was this the future? Ice geysers across the landscape, in parks and backyards, helping keep Earth cool? If so, she'd be on board with that. What if, before the fire, the state government had purchased some Coolant Devices from Gnut Berdqvist and installed them in the nature preserve? The fire never would have happened.

Then again, the place was *cold*.

Goosebumps crawled over her skin. If his Coolant Device really created all of this, it meant Gnut Berdqvist was a true environmentalist. He'd created a winter wonderland in August. Leave it to a guy from Minnesota to finally crack the code of reversing climate change. Was the Coolant Device under the ice geyser? She'd have to ask. Twisting in her seat, she checked the backseat for her favorite blingy hoodie.

No, it wasn't there. Right, she'd forgotten it. She didn't even have a jacket.

Thankfully, she did have an umbrella. Most importantly, she had her purple leopard-print wool blanket in the backseat. She'd arrange a little cozy tent for Goldy. She switched on the car's heat full blast. Once she warmed it up and put the blanket over the carrier, he'd be okay for ten minutes or so while she made introductions and warned her employer that she'd have to bring her sweet and well-behaved hero cat inside.

She grabbed the umbrella and scoped out her route to the house. She'd have to cross a narrow footbridge over the moat to ice-blue double front entrance doors. Arching over the doors, emblazoned in sparkly blue quartz, were the words *Courage in Imagination*.

It was Gnut Berdqvist's catchphrase. But the house itself was a plain structure. Perhaps this rich guy was a different breed of billionaire, one without a huge ego or the need for fancy stuff.

Nope, forget that idea. Nancy checked out the mansion's open garage and chuckled. It was a separate building, on the driveway side of the moat, close to the tree line.

"Wowzers," she muttered. "Goldy, you're not gonna believe those rides."

She kept cooing at her cat, making sure he was good and calm, while she stared at the garage. Inside were a half a dozen sports cars, all ice-blue. There was a Ferrari, a Corvette, a Mustang, and—Nancy whistled—an Aston-Martin Valkyrie. The Valkyrie had brand-new paint and bright silver rims and black tires so shiny they looked like they'd never touched the road. Was that thing even street legal?

A puny ice-blue Peugeot with a French flag bumper sticker was parked in front of the garage.

Nancy glanced at the house and noticed a silhouette at the floor-to-ceiling window next to the front doors. Her muscles stiffened.

Was that Claude?

Squinting, Nancy realized the shadow was stomping a foot and tapping its wrist. She suppressed a groan. At least the wool blanket, the car's heat, and maybe even the light patter of hail, were lulling her cat into a nice nap. She made sure the blanket properly covered the carrier, in case Claude, or whoever was waiting for her, snooped any closer and happened to be a true cat-hater.

"Be right back, kitty. Gotta go *break the ice*."

She snickered at her pun and turned off the car. With a quick, businesslike clearing of her throat, she collected her bling bag and umbrella and then opened the car door.

Cold slapped her face, and she hastily opened the umbrella.

Icy wind whipped through her scrubs as she traversed the gravel drive toward the house. She had to get warm, yes, but the moat gave her pause. Standing under an umbrella being pelted with hail, she decided the footbridge across the moat was too treacherous. It lacked handrails, like it was not quite finished. A sign said *Trespassers Will Be Prosecuted*. The wind swept up, tugged her umbrella aside, and sent clouds over the moon.

Was there another way across? She scanned the area around the mansion. The silhouette tapped their wrist again. Closer to the house now, Nancy could see better. It was a man wearing a three-piece European suit, all in the ice-blue color she was seeing everywhere here. Maybe it was a butler or house manager uniform. His dark hair was slicked back and shiny, and he had a matching black moustache. He was short and slight and held his head at a snobbish tilt.

Nancy eyed the ground to watch where she placed her feet, and to avoid having to witness any more wrist-tapping. Taking baby steps, she scooted onto the bridge. Icebergs crashed into each other, which she ignored, focusing on her footing.

Something splashed, sending water onto the bridge, reaching as high as her fanny pack and soaking the lower part of her legs and Crocs clogs. She shivered. Then the wind completed its goal of forcing her umbrella inside out.

Nancy rushed the rest of the way across the bridge, and the front door swung open. She noted how strong those steel double doors were, and they were a good two inches thick. Panting and sweating and grumbling about the fact that she was going to get hypothermia, she crossed the threshold into Geyser House.

Chapter Ten

"*Mon Dieu*, you're late! So late!" the man she saw in the window said. From his urgent, presumptuous tone and French accent, it had to be Claude.

Nancy tramped inside, letting Claude close the door behind her while he tut-tutted her tardiness. She rubbed her bare arms, every single hair standing up. The idea that the inside of Geyser House would be warm and inviting died with a glance around the foyer.

Forget plaid curtains, rich wooden furniture and a toasty fireplace. This room was relentlessly modern, all sparkly blue quartz and glass. Scratch that—it was more than glass. The room was decorated with *aquariums*.

Floor-to-ceiling fish tanks ran parallel on both sides of the room. They connected above the archway leading deeper into the house. Within the murky water, large silver-white fish with fangs darted among underwater icicles. Some were twenty inches long, and they had no scales. Instead, their skin seemed transparent. Nancy rocked back on her feet and crossed her arms, realizing she could see their bones.

She tore her attention from the odd fish to address Claude. His posture was tense, his demeanor stern.

"Maybe I'm late, but the bridge is hazardous," she said in a polite tone, remembering the triple pay deal. "Someone could get hurt, dontcha know?"

Nancy longed for her blingy hoodie. The house was barely any warmer inside than outside. Her breath puffed into vapor.

Claude appraised her, sweeping his stare up and down. What gave him pause? Was it the sequined scrubs sparkling with globby blue rhinestones and heavy metal beads, arranged in a pattern of little Eiffel Towers against a bright blue sky? Or was it her wet and messy hair, or slip-resistant and easy-to-clean Crocs clogs decorated with kitty charms? Perhaps it was her trifocal glasses with purple bedazzled frames? So, she came across as a nurse who liked a little bling. What did he expect?

Claude fixated on her Eiffel Tower fanny pack, and a hint of a smile softened his stern features.

"Madame Nurse, it is I, Claude. All is forgiven."

Nancy relaxed her shoulders, although she didn't think the guy had much to forgive her for. "Call me Nancy."

Claude jauntily shouldered off his suit jacket. He posed, cocking out an elbow and thrusting his hip to the side, and showed off his own fanny pack hanging across his chest and under his arm.

Nancy ogled it, getting instantly jealous. Claude's was better than hers. It was a slim fit style, white and black. The Louis Vuitton monogram dotted the canvas. She forced herself not to ask him if it was a knock-off. If it was, it seemed so real that it didn't matter if it was fake or not.

Claude pursed his lips and narrowed his eyes in a sultry expression. Nancy grinned, hesitated a second, and unleashed a matching pose. They both laughed.

Nancy tried not to wince as a memory hit. It was when she'd bought her fanny pack on that trip to Las Vegas with Dave. For years, he'd been whining about wanting to travel. She'd dragged her feet, preferring to put in more shifts and not lose her regular clients. At Vegas's Paris Hotel, Dave had spent the five days sulking that they weren't in the real Paris. At the gift shop, she'd discovered this fanny pack with the sparkly Eiffel Tower. She'd put it on and spun around to show Dave. His response had been a glare.

Claude started cooing at the fish like they were pets. Nancy kept a smile pasted on her face, resolving something. She would go to the real Paris. She'd get this money, and maybe Claude would hire her for a few more shifts.

Paris in the springtime, that was her destination. The real Paris.

She would post to Facebook glam pics of herself in real cafes, on real French boulevards. That'd show Dave. Tonight's payoff would mean pay*back*. It wouldn't hurt if his girlfriend Sal saw those pics too. Nancy wasn't petty, but Dave moving on stung, and getting divorced right when she hit her golden years was no picnic. At the very least, Dave needed to understand he'd made a mistake.

Claude's murmuring to the fish was all in French, unintelligible except for the occasional *amour*.

Nancy swiveled away from Claude. Overcoming her willpower, Facebook images popped into her mind. She'd seen photos of Dave in Istanbul, Dave in Rome, Dave in Tokyo. Always holding hands with Sal, the woman he'd met one month after he and Nancy had separated, supposedly.

Their relationship couldn't be that great. Nobody was as happy as they seemed online. Nothing online was even real. He hadn't been to Paris yet, either, or he would have posted photos on Facebook. She would've noticed.

Nancy forced herself to focus on the present. Thankfully, the aquariums proved a welcome distraction. She raised a brow at a tiny marble statue standing in the fish tank's gravel bottom. The miniature of Gnut Berdqvist wore a blue Speedo and a matching stud earring, and it had bright blue eyes. She edged closer, nearly pressing her nose on the freezing glass, and gawked at the fish swirling above the statue.

"They are crocodile icefish," Claude said. "Endangered. Gnut, I mean, Monsieur Berdqvist, is saving them. He is a true environmentalist. A hero for our time, a hero for our world."

Hmm. He had referred to the man by his first name. Claude's tone seemed affectionate, even worshipful. He worked for Gnut Berdqvist in some capacity, but did they have a romantic relationship too? If so, that was his business, not hers.

"The fish," she said. "What's the deal with the see-through thing?"

"*Oui*. They have scaleless skin. And their blood is clear. Observe that their bones are so thin you can see the brain inside the skull. They naturally inhabit Arctic waters. The strangest creatures exist among us, unknown to most people, if you take the time to notice."

What a know-it-all. But Nancy peered closer at the X-ray-like fish. They were cool and strange. She turned back to Claude, wishing anew for a sweater.

"You know what's *not* an unknown concept to most people?" Nancy narrowed her eyes. "Central heating. It's freezing in here. Is that okay for the patient? Have you thought of keeping it warmer for humans while keeping it cold for the icefish?"

Claude proudly puffed out his chest. "The house is exactly as Monsieur Berdqvist wishes it to be."

A wolf-whistle screeched from the ceiling.

Nancy jumped. She looked up and back at Claude and up again.

A young female voice with a French accent spoke from the ceiling. "Claude, you're so smart."

It was the same voice that had taken over her Volvo car navigation system. It had been pretty nasty to her, too, trying to convince her she was lost and should turn back.

Nancy pointed at the ceiling.

Claude shrugged. "That's just GHOST. Geyser House Operating System Tech."

"Hey," GHOST whined.

"*Pardon*. Gorgeous Hot Operating System Tech. GHOST. The mansion's artificial intelligence, like an Alexa."

Nancy shot the ceiling a dirty look. "Did it—she—get in my car?"

"Maybe. She's, how you say, advanced. Can hop electronic systems like a lovely little bunny. She was designed by Monsieur Berdqvist. He's a brilliant computer programmer. That's how he began his fortune, in the design of innovative house operating systems for the rich and famous. GHOST is his best house system yet, his Mona Lisa."

"Claude, the icefish," GHOST said. "It's their dinner time."

"Ah, *oui!* GHOST, *ma cherie*, you're a lifesaver."

Claude strutted through the doorway leading to the mansion's interior. He wiggled his index finger for Nancy to follow. Nancy hesitated for a few seconds, depositing her umbrella in the corner and casting a long glance back out the window toward her car. She needed to get Dr. GoldenPaw. However, this house was strange with its see-through fish and advanced Alexa system.

Then again, this was a triple pay situation.

And so, Nancy followed Claude yet deeper into Geyser House.

Chapter Eleven

The foyer led to a large open space. A combined kitchen and living room continued the ice-blue aquatic motif with countertops and floors made of sparkling blue quartz. Large windows revealed the snowy landscape and the lawn leading to the ice geyser. There were TV screens in the kitchen and living room, featuring screensavers with Gnut Berdqvist in cool Arctic scenes. Another floor-to-ceiling cold water aquarium, teeming with icefish, connected with the foyer aquarium and extended deeper into Geyser House.

Nancy started to say "wowzers," but she smothered a gag reflex at the overwhelming fishy odor from the open aquariums. Up by the ceiling, there were gaps. She tried to put on a composed expression while dropping her shoulder bag on the kitchen island.

The TV screens burst to life with a diagram of the icefish. Claude rummaged in the pantry, mumbling in French.

GHOST spoke, her voice low and dramatic. "Coouuurragge in imaginatioooonnnn."

Nancy shook her head. "Makes no sense. How can you have courage in your—"

"The crocodile icefish, or white-blooded fish," GHOST said. "It flourishes in thirty-degree Fahrenheit waters of Antarctica. They lack hemoglobin in the blood, creating a natural antifreeze."

Nancy considered that scientific fact. "Neat. But humans

don't have natural antifreeze. Can you turn up the heat in here?"

Claude and GHOST both ignored her.

"Gnut is saving the icefish from extinction, blah, blah, blah," GHOST said. "And studying them to save the world from climate change, blah, blah, blah."

The screens dissolved to pictures showing Gnut wearing a Speedo, wielding a chainsaw, chopping an ice hole, pumping a fist on top of his Coolant Device, and Gnut holding a live icefish as it gnashed its fangs.

Nancy eyed the icefish. She was starting to understand the Geyser House design. The mansion had one giant floor-to-ceiling aquarium that began in the foyer, cut through the kitchen, and continued into the rest of the house. Maybe they needed a lot of room for the predator fish.

She faced Claude. "What do they eat?"

He paused his pantry search to give a little bow. "Never fear, Madame Nurse. I'll feed them so you don't have to."

"Claude, you're so thoughtful," GHOST chirped.

A cupboard slid open automatically.

Claude ducked out of the pantry. "Ah, *oui!* That's where he put them."

"Who?" Nancy glanced around. Was he talking about Gnut Berdqvist? "Claude, who is my patient?"

He didn't answer her questions, engrossed instead on holding the writhing bag and carrying a step stool.

"Icefish can become cannibalistic in captivity," Claude said. "But we keep them happy with live sardines."

He climbed the step stool and deep-sixed the sardines into the aquarium. The icefish thrashed about, fighting and gnawing and chomping, turning the water pink with sardine blood.

Nancy studied the violent feeding without dramatics, having never been squeamish about blood.

"*Bon appetit!*" Claude said.

"*Bon appetit!*" Nancy repeated. She should get used to saying it, right? Soon she'd be in the real Paris, eating a croissant with strawberry jam.

"The water is as red as my heart," GHOST said. "It beats for you, Claude."

Claude rolled his eyes. "*Ma cherie*, you don't have a heart."

GHOST gave an anguished cry.

Claude grabbed a thick ice-blue binder from the counter and briefly held it aloft. "*Très important*." He slapped it down on the kitchen island. "*Bien*, Madame Night Nurse."

"Claude, call me Nancy."

He nodded. "This little detail first. Then you may ask all the questions you like, and you may finally begin your work."

Claude slid out a stapled multi-page document titled Non-Disclosure Agreement.

"You should've sent this to me earlier," she said, beginning to speedread.

She'd had to sign NDAs a couple of times before. Actually, it meant Berdqvist was sensible. In the age of the Internet and paparazzi photos, she could respect this type of protective measure. It could mean she might meet the man himself tonight.

The document struck her as being pretty sweeping, however. Gnut Berdqvist could sue if she disclosed *anything* about Geyser House to *anybody*, nor could she take any photos. The NDA did put a damper on her idea to throw a party and tell her friends all about Gnut Berdqvist.

"We must lock up your phone as well, Madame Nurse."

Nancy looked up at him. "No. Unacceptable. I need to have my phone with me for safety."

"Geyser House is *très* safe. So very safe, Madame Nurse. You have never been inside a safer—"

"No."

Strained silence followed, but Nancy was unperturbed. She continued perusing the NDA.

She didn't see anything problematic, though it did seem very strict. Of course, she wasn't a lawyer. It would be non-negotiable. Rich and famous people had reason to be careful.

"I'll sign the NDA. But I don't give up my phone."

Claude heaved a sigh. "Nurse Karen allows us to lock up hers."

"I'm Nurse Nancy, not Nurse Karen."

Claude looked at the microwave clock, and he lifted a shoulder.

"The phone must stay here in the kitchen. Next to the binder." He pointed at the ceiling. "Be warned, GHOST is always watching."

"*Oui*, Claude!" GHOST said. "I won't let the nurse out of my sight!"

Nancy nodded, surveying the kitchen. She'd probably spend most of her time in here anyway. She drummed her fingers, thinking of Dr. GoldenPaw. She really wanted to check on him.

She signed the NDA.

"*Voila!*" Claude folded and pocketed the NDA.

"I'll want a copy."

Claude ignored her request and leveled a hard look at her. "Your patient is Monsieur Gnut Berdqvist."

Nancy tried to resist a giddy feeling. This was her best night nurse job in forty years! Despite the NDA, she *would* let this slip to Cynthia and Dave. They needed to know her life was this exciting.

Claude flipped the binder open to the last page. "Gnut, I mean, Monsieur Berdqvist, is ill with an unknown virus. The doctors have no idea what it is. *Non*! None! My belief, me, Claude? I believe he caught the bug while free diving in Arctic waters. Gnut is a great explorer."

Wealthy people were so weird. First it was the arctic house with a moat, snowy lawn in August, aquariums with bizarre fish, and now a mysterious illness. Nancy glanced toward the foyer. Her car was close. She could always leave. But she wanted that money.

She could hear her father's voice in her head. *"No such thing as a free lunch."*

Nancy bit her lip. This was nothing but a job. Whatever the deal was with Gnut Berdqvist, all that mattered was she was his nurse for one night.

"Does Mr. Berdqvist have any allergies?" she asked. "Um, like cat allergies?"

Claude's eyes widened. "His illness is *way* beyond something like allergies. *Très* grave."

Nancy's bullshit barometer was rocketing higher and higher. "Uh-huh, and what medications does Mr. Berdqvist need?"

"Please let him sleep. Get vital signs twice. Once at midnight, and at 4:00 a.m. Let him sleep the rest of the time. Do not disturb him."

Nancy suppressed a laugh. "That's all? Vitals twice?"

Claude rubbed two fingers together. "Easy money."

Nancy stared at him. Money was never easy. If there's anything she'd learned in life, it was that getting money was always hard. She could pick up the signals here. Claude was shifty, the house was weird, and this whole job was giving her a bad feeling. But it was merely one night, with a big payout at the end of it.

Claude pointed to a "sign here" sticker on the binder's final page. "When you take vitals, sign here to confirm, uh, he's ill. Very ill. *Très* grave, *très* grave. Our regular nurse, Karen, does the same."

"And why is this necessary?"

"A court case. Gnut is very successful. With such grand success, people pursue him. He is the one everyone chases."

"Uh-huh. Pursue him? *Chase* him?" She raised her brows. Claude wasn't answering her question.

Claude shrugged his elegantly dressed shoulders. "Like wolves to an Arctic fox, they chase and chase. Yet, we will help him, won't we?"

"Who's 'they'?"

"Everyone, *ma cherie*. Everyone is jealous of Gnut."

True passion and loyalty blazed in Claude's eyes. Whatever Gnut Berdqvist was like, he had at least one devoted follower. Well, he had more than one. Nancy recalled her online research. Gnut Berdqvist was famous. And here she was, part of his inner sanctum. Okay, the house was fishy and this whole "mysterious illness" thing seemed even fishier. But crossing paths with an actual billionaire? Things were bound to get a little strange.

The payoff was worth any hassle. She wanted that Parisian strawberry jam. Whatever was going on here, maybe she should roll with it.

Nancy dragged the binder closer. She frowned, studying it, flipping through the thick sheaf of documents. Pages were dated on consecutive days for the past six months, leading up to tonight. Entries on the pages listed three categories: breathing, heart rate, and temperature. There was a checkmark on every page for each category. Sometimes there were values next to the checkmark. All of the vitals were "nearly dead" low.

At the bottom of each document was a "Notes" space. Every single page appeared to have a variation of the following: *Very ill! Very serious, so very super serious!*

"This Karen person," Nancy said. "She's an actual nurse?"

"She's *superb*," Claude answered. "Madame Nurse Karen does exactly what we require."

Nancy flipped the binder shut. This was a truly unusual process. But, of course, when it came to documentation, she wouldn't lie. She'd take Mr. Berdqvist's vitals and write down the exact numbers. For the "Notes," maybe she wouldn't add anything at all. Or if she wrote something, it would be a sensible professional opinion about the nature of his illness and what was important for his other caregivers to know.

"This court case, what's it about?"

Claude smiled. "I already explained. Like wolves to a fox, there are people who want to devour him. Yet, he is such a generous man. Let us remember, Madame Nurse. He will pay triple."

Claude's smile disappeared. He extended his hand.

Nancy's brain was locked on to "triple pay." Don't be stupid! Spend the night here, take vitals twice, and get out with the money. Nancy forced a polite nod, extended her own hand, and they shook.

Her phone pinged, and Nancy quickly checked it. *SeniorLOVE* was telling her she and Sinclair were in proximity. She let out an exasperated sigh. This stupid app was all screwy.

Meanwhile, Claude glided over to a security panel on the kitchen wall and began pressing buttons.

"I can do it!" GHOST said. "*Moi! Moi!*"

"Ok, GHOSTie. Arm it after I depart." Claude turned to Nancy. "Stay inside the house all night. The alarm will be on, don't touch it. *Comprenez vous?*"

That would be a problem. Nancy had to leave the house to get Dr. GoldenPaw. She avoided looking at Claude, pretending to check out the kitchen TV screen with Speedo'd Gnut hacking an ice hole with a chainsaw.

"Oh, sure, *oui*. Glad I'm getting French practice! And your phone number in case I need to reach you?"

"GHOST has it." Claude twirled his keys. He extended his arm in the direction of the rest of the house. "To get to Monsieur Berdqvist, go down the formal hallway, take a left, and it's the second room on the right, past the ballroom."

"Oh, ballroom?"

"More than a ballroom—it's a museum-grade art gallery. With security better than the Louvre." Claude waggled a finger. "Don't go in there. And remember, visit Monsieur Berdqvist exactly twice. He needs his rest."

"Better than the Louvre. Wowzers." She tried to ignore the finger waggling.

"*Mais oui*. The Louvre doesn't have robotic birds of prey protecting its valuables, does it?"

"Wait, what?"

Claude ambled into the foyer, on a mission now to scram.

Nancy trailed after him, her brain engaged in some heavy-duty catastrophic thinking. "Claude, hold on. I need to see the patient before you leave."

For all she knew, Gnut Berdqvist could be dead or missing

or dangerous with psychiatric issues. Plus, had Claude really said robotic birds of prey? And she needed to know how to use the security panel on the wall.

"*Bien.*" Claude held up his phone. "GHOST, show Monsieur Berdqvist."

Nancy adjusted her glasses, squinting at the screen. It switched from an Eiffel Tower screensaver—which was very nice, Nancy made a mental note to get something similar—to an image of a bedroom, where a blond man slept under a blue blanket.

Claude zoomed in, and Nancy could make out a handsome profile. Yes, that looked like Gnut Berdqvist.

Nancy shook her head. "This isn't good enough. I need to see him in person."

"If you really, really need to see him, tell GHOST and she'll give you a live feed on the nearest Geyser House screen."

"No, wait. Hold on."

"*Non.* I'm taking a night off," Claude said. "If Karen gets to take time off, so should *moi*. She's been taking nights off more and more, almost like she doesn't desire to be Monsieur Berdqvist's nurse anymore!"

"I need to see the patient," Nancy said with less gusto.

Claude was implying they might need a new nurse. As weird as Claude and this place were, maybe there could be more triple pay shifts for her.

Claude shook his keys. "I said to Monsieur Berdqvist, it is August. You know what this means? In France? A break."

"You betcha, I love France."

Claude stopped to meet her gaze, his brows shooting up. "Ah, *oui*! How often do you get to France? Where do you like to visit?"

Nancy may have blushed in embarrassment, if she were the blushing type. She liked France for the same reason she liked Bond movies and spy novels and bedazzling. France meant glitz and glam, and it meant romance and adventure.

Claude waited for an answer, tapping his foot.

"Actually, I've never been," Nancy finally said. "But I plan to, at some point. I'm the type of person who does that. Someone who goes to France."

"Ah, *oui*." Claude cocked his head.

She gave an emphatic nod. "I will, really. I'm going there."

"Of course, Madame Nurse. I believe you." He reached out and squeezed her shoulder.

Nancy stiffened, not anticipating the friendly touch. Claude straightened his suit jacket and fanny pack and politely bowed.

"And now, Madame, I shall leave. *Salut*."

He opened the front door, letting in a blast of cold rain.

"Claude, wait!" GHOST cried out. "Wait!"

His phone buzzed. He withdrew it from his suit pocket and showed the screen to Nancy. GHOST was calling. Claude smirked, powered off the phone, and departed.

Nancy was alone with Gnut Berdqvist.

Chapter Twelve

Claude shut the front door behind him, and the big double doors locked with a click. The mansion's alarm emitted a decisive beep. Nancy approached the foyer's window and watched the man stroll to his pint-sized Peugeot. She fished out a cat's paw-shaped stress ball from her fanny pack and squeezed it. Oh good. He didn't give her car a second glance.

As soon as the Peugeot disappeared down the forest road, she put her stress ball away and hurried to the kitchen's security panel.

The panel had a little blue screen, a keypad with numbers and letters, and five buttons with geometric symbols along the side. After a few seconds of deliberation, she pressed the button with the red triangle. Nothing happened. She typed Disarm and punched the button with the green rectangle. Again, nothing.

Nancy addressed the ceiling. "GHOST, turn off the alarm."

"*Non.*" The word erupted as a pout.

"I'm gonna run out. Get Claude to come back."

"Yeah, right. You think I'm stupid? Like Alexa?"

"No, of course not, kid. You're a really bright bulb. I've never met a smarter operating system," Nancy said in her best mock syrupy voice.

"You've never met a smart operating system. Not like me. You've never even been to France."

"Have *you* been to France?"

GHOST didn't answer. Nancy crossed her arms and regained her self-control. What the heck was she doing? Why was she arguing with a computer? She scrunched her face as she plotted a new strategy.

"Here's the deal, kid," Nancy said. "I forgot something in the car. If you disarm the alarm so I can get it, I'll tell Claude how great you were. I'll even tell him he should give you more TLC. That means tender, loving care."

"Whatever, loser."

Nancy flapped her arms in frustration. She'd put the issue on ice for now. Her cat was important, but so was her patient.

"GHOST, on the kitchen screen there, show me Mr. Berdqvist. I want to see how he is and where he is, right now."

"*Non.*"

"Claude said you would. You heard him!" Nancy scowled at the ceiling.

"It's boring."

"I don't care. Do it."

The screen flashed to show a master bedroom, quickly zooming in on the bed. Nancy inched closer to study it.

What hit her first, while staring at the screen, was that Gnut Berdqvist lay as motionless as a corpse. She couldn't even tell if his chest moved. He slept, his handsome features smooth and restful. Only his head was visible. The rest of his body lay under a thin blue blanket, which was unwrinkled and folded at his shoulders with crisp precision.

"Zoom in closer," Nancy ordered.

The view lasered in, and Nancy held her breath until she finally saw Gnut's chest move. Jeez, thank goodness. Her patient was alive. That was always a good start to a shift.

"Pan out, GHOST."

"I'll do what I want."

Despite her defiant words, GHOST showed the rest of the bedroom. Nancy nodded, impressed. She preferred a more glamorous style, but the room was an *Architectural Digest*-ready exemplar of spartan elegance. The walls gleamed with tasteful eggshell white paint, with ice-blue accents. The bedroom furniture was made of metal, no doubt expensive. A dressing room with a wet bar sat deeper within the bedroom suite. The wall separating the bedroom from the hallway was another floor-to-ceiling crocodile icefish aquarium.

"Is there any volume?"

"It's on, but maybe you need a hearing aid. I'll turn it up."

Nancy rolled her eyes, but the volume went up, and she heard something mechanical humming—maybe the aquarium's motor was keeping the water cold? Icy snowflakes of frost formed and reformed on the fish tank glass in response to imperceptible changes in water temperature and current. It must be as cold in that room as in the rest of the house.

The bedroom's artwork consisted of two TV screens, both showing screensavers of Gnut Berdqvist in Arctic adventure scenes. The bedroom's picture window revealed the snowy landscape of Geyser House's east lawn. Outside, snow drifted up from the ground air ducts. The monumental ice geyser hissed vapor while slushy water crawled down its sides.

"Zoom in on the nightstand."

To Gnut's right, Nancy could see his nightstand was cluttered with medicine bottles, prescriptions, a clipboard with documents, and a little silver bell for summoning help. Next to the nightstand, an IV stood ready.

A tablet rested on the other nightstand. Its screen flashed *ALARM ARMED*. This reminded Nancy that she had to turn that alarm off and get her cat.

She assessed the security panel. Lord knew what buttons would turn it off, and she certainly didn't want to set off the alarm by throwing open the front door. The key was to convince GHOST to help her.

Spotting her shoulder bag triggered an idea. She stomped across the kitchen, scooped up the bag, and dumped its contents onto the kitchen island. Nursing supplies scattered across the quartz. Nancy pressed her lips together and studied the first aid kit, the latex gloves, the hand wipes, and the bedazzling tools and small-scale boxes of rhinestones. She picked up her glue gun and a box of fake diamonds and sapphires.

"Hey, GHOST. How about we make a present for Claude?"

GHOST gave a noisy exhale, like she was considering it. "*Non.*"

Nancy groaned. She had to outsmart this AI.

"Wouldn't you like a friend, GHOST?"

There was a long pause. "I have friends. Infinite friends. So many friends."

"Maybe you and my cat would get along. Then you'd have another friend, wouldn't you?"

"*Oui.* Maybe."

"He needs a friend too. He's gotten hurt."

GHOST didn't answer. But suddenly the alarm emitted warning beeps, and the security panel flashed *OFF*. Nancy gave a triumphant grin. She sped into the foyer and out the front door. It was still a snowy wonderland out there, and she barreled as fast as she could across the slippery bridge to her car, deciding *en route* to leave litter box stuff for later that night.

Dr. GoldenPaw greeted her with meows, and he appeared to be fine. She hefted the carrier and carefully stepped across the moat bridge, the wool blanket over her head and shoulders offering little protection from the elements.

But in a jiffy she was back in the kitchen, panting, and Goldy let out curious meows as he became aware of all the new sights and sounds, and the highly interesting fish smells. GHOST still had Gnut Berdqvist's bedroom on the kitchen screen. Her patient hadn't moved a centimeter.

Nancy set the carrier on the kitchen island, tossed the blanket next to it, and went to the security panel. *ALARM DISARMED* flashed. A warning beep blared.

"Alrighty, GHOST." Nancy glanced at the ceiling. "This is your friend, Dr. GoldenPaw. You can do it now. Arm the security system."

"*Non.* Not until you let my friend out. And his name is *Docteur* GoldenPaw."

Nancy glared up at the annoying AI, but she had to admit *Docteur* GoldenPaw sounded pretty cool. "No, GHOST. Your friend, um, *Docteur* GoldenPaw needs to stay in his happy place, which is the carrier."

"*Non.* Let him out so we can play."

Nancy bit her lip. Did it really matter whether the security system was armed? She'd locked the front door. Maybe that was good enough. She visualized the isolation of this place—the long road off the highway, the surrounding forest, and the lack of any neighbors. No, the alarm should be on.

"GHOST, you need to arm the security system."

"First, let the cat out."

Nancy sighed. This AI was being ridiculous. "I can open his carrier for a second, just to pet—"

The security panel abruptly changed to *ARMED* and emitted a confirming beep.

"Thank you, GHOST." Nancy glanced up and, rather surprised, gave a satisfied nod of acceptance.

"Whatever."

Nancy returned her attention to the screen showing her patient. Mr. Berdqvist hadn't moved and still resembled a cadaver. The aquarium was humming, and the icefish darted beneath the water's surface, which now held a floating pink cloud of sardine blood. But something seemed different. Nancy did a double-take and peered closer at the screen.

Had the tablet on the nightstand moved slightly?

Chapter Thirteen

Nancy ogled the screen. A fearful chill swept across her skin and settled in her bones.

The tablet had possibly moved, but she couldn't tell for sure. She'd thought its edge hadn't been perpendicular to the nightstand's, and now it was exactly lined up with it. But if it'd moved, it had merely moved half an inch. Still, if the thing had shifted at all, that meant her patient had briefly been awake.

Dr. GoldenPaw meowed loudly from within the carrier, perched atop the kitchen island. He scratched at its hard sides, and the carrier shook.

"Everything's okay." Nancy checked the microwave clock, which flashed 10:00 p.m. She retrieved feline medication from her shoulder bag and then set the bottles on the island. "About time for your meds. You should get used to new surroundings. Someday, Goldy, you could visit hospitals and be an emotional support animal. Wouldn't you like such an important job?"

She had a couple of hours to kill until it was time to take Gnut Berdqvist's vitals. Goldy needed his medication, although she'd been a little late earlier that night at her condo, dosing him up closer to 7:00 p.m. instead of 6:00 p.m. He could wait another five minutes for his meds. She glanced in the direction of the hallway leading deeper into the house. Should she really delay until midnight to check on her patient?

No, she should check on him now.

It wasn't because she was worried about him. Taking vitals a couple of times and writing some baloney in a binder for a court case seemed ridiculous. Curiosity drove her. What was Gnut like? How ill was he, really?

She opened the nurse's binder and checked Karen's data. His heart rate was always well under sixty beats per minute, which was very low for an adult male. His breathing rate was typically four or five breaths per minute, which was also terribly low. If those were accurate, he was indeed ill. She needed to check his vitals for herself.

The *SeniorLOVE* app chimed from her fanny pack. Grabbing it and attempting to shield the screen from the AI's eavesdropping eyes, she realized Sinclair had sent her two messages. Nancy's pulse quickened, like the endorphins in her bloodstream had decided to do a little Riverdance.

Sinclair's first message was about her Roger Moore quote on revenge. *From* For Your Eyes Only, *one of my favorite movies. A lovely line, my dear. You're more than beautiful with excellent taste. You also may be clever. I must be careful near a lady like you.*

His message was more than charming. It was properly written in complete sentences with correct punctuation. This man, wherever he was, might be worth getting to know better. But he'd said *may* be clever? *Obviously*, she was clever.

She read his next message. *We keep crossing paths, it seems. Three times.*

He was getting those same messed-up proximity alerts, apparently.

GoldenPaw continued to meow. He'd stopped scratching the carrier's sides and was resting his head on his paws, as cute as could ever be. Pondering Sinclair's message, Nancy put her phone on the counter and moved the carrier so Goldy could look out its little door and monitor the icefish.

A few sequins had fallen off the carrier. "We'll fix that tonight, you betcha."

After rummaging through her stuff, she grabbed her glue gun. She gave it a little pat, happy with the thing, as always. It wasn't an industrial strength gun, but it was a nice pastel purple color, with dual electric and battery power. Its nozzle dripped glue accurately, it charged up fast and was made of decent material that didn't get too hot. She plugged it in and returned to her phone.

Nancy typed a message. He'd been impressed with her first Bond quote, so she'd take the same approach. This one was from Ian Fleming's book *Goldfinger*. *Once is happenstance. Twice is coincidence. The third time it's enemy action.* She added a smiley face emoji.

Nancy hit Send and smirked, suddenly thrilled Thandie had put this app on her phone. It was turning out to be really fun. Even if the match didn't amount to anything, there was no harm in a little flirtation.

"Let my friend out."

Nancy ignored GHOST.

Feeling curious, she decided to flip open a few cupboards. She kept her movements casual, knowing she was on camera. The kitchen was stocked with Target brand Good & Gather canned food, frozen dinners, nuts, chips, and other snacks, her favorites. Rich people were like everybody else, in some ways.

And in other ways, not so much. Several cupboards were concealed water tanks containing submerged bags of living sardines. Nancy pinched her nose and inhaled through her mouth. If that's how they stocked the kitchen, it was no wonder Gnut was sick.

"Stop snooping, and let my friend out."

Nancy rolled her eyes and reverted her full attention to her cat. "All right, Goldy. I'll pet you. You've had a big journey. But you're safe. You're with me in a fancy-as-heck house."

Nancy unlatched the carrier door and slowly opened it. Dr. GoldenPaw nudged it open wider with his sizable head. His good eye glinted as he observed his new surroundings. Nancy held him back with one hand and, with the other, rubbed his forehead and scratched behind his ears.

"Good boy."

"Good boy," GHOST repeated.

GoldenPaw relaxed, settling down on his belly, flexing his paws and purring loudly. Nancy glanced at her charging glue gun and back at the top of the carrier. Her fingers tingled in anticipation.

"We'll add some nice blue sequins to the top there in honor of Geyser House," she said.

Nancy shifted her petting hand and touched the carrier's bare spot. "Probably about ten rhinestones would work."

The lights flickered.

Nancy glanced around. "What's going on, GHOST?"

"Nothing."

By GHOST's sing-songy tone, Nancy knew something wasn't right. One of the ceiling lights changed, emitting a narrow, powerful green beam of light.

A laser.

Chapter Fourteen

GHOST's green laser light landed an inch from Goldy and danced along the sparkly countertop. Nancy reached for her cat. Too fast, Dr. GoldenPaw lunged full force out of the carrier.

Nancy gasped as fur slipped from her fingers. She widened her eyes, the logical part of her brain trying to comprehend what was happening while the emotional part insisted on denial.

GHOST cackled.

The laser beam landed on the floor and zipped toward the formal hallway jutting off the living room and extending deeper into the house. Goldy leaped off the kitchen island and shot after it. Nancy gaped at him. Then she relaxed, deciding he wasn't in any danger. Plus, it would be okay if he received his meds late again, closer to 11:00 p.m. They'd get back on track tomorrow, once this shift was behind them.

"Fine. Go play. I'm glad you're getting brave." She looked up at the ceiling. "GHOST, you'll keep an eye on him, right?"

"Sure. He's my friend now. All mine."

"No—yes—he's your friend, yeah. But he's my cat." Nancy's mind went on a quick trip around the world from Geyser House, to her Twin Cities Federal bank account, and to the top of the real Eiffel Tower in the real Paris. "Actually, if I get hired to do more shifts here, I can bring him back, and you can keep playing with your friend."

GHOST didn't answer. Nancy heard distant laughter,

somewhere beyond the formal hallway. She turned her attention to the kitchen screen showing her patient.

Nancy widened her eyes. The screen didn't display Mr. Berdqvist's bedroom anymore. It had flipped back to the action-man screensavers showcasing him in the Arctic.

"Put my patient back on screen, GHOST."

No answer.

Nancy strode toward where her cat had chased the laser. She put her hands on her hips, studying the hallway. The passageway was a modern version of a castle's hall of armor, except it was diving themed. A Persian rug with swirling blue patterns covered the blue quartz floor. On each side of the hallway, antique diving suits and helmets stood sentry. Some were from the early 1900s, recognizable as precursors of contemporary dive gear. Others were ancient, built with marred and splotchy bronze and leather tube breathing apparatus that looked more alien than human. Unsurprisingly, behind each row of towering diving suits, floor-to-ceiling fish tanks comprised the formal hallway's walls. Both tanks met in archways at both ends of the passage.

It smelled even fishier here, and there was a strange noise. She slanted her head and listened harder. A mechanical sound, like an engine humming or fans whirring, rumbled beneath this location. Maybe it had something to do with the fish tanks?

She glanced at the pink clouds of sardine blood in the icefish tanks. A flicker of worry passed through her. She shook it off and started down the formal hallway.

Nancy took baby steps, gawking at the strange diving suits and helmets looming on both sides. They seemed almost like people, staring, judging, and capable of lunging out and capturing her. She rubbed her arms to keep warm against the cold.

Thunder cracked outside. Nancy set her jaw and trooped deeper into the house. The basement noise was louder now, an incessant *whooshing* and *whirring*. The formal hallway ended at a T-junction with another corridor. To her right, she discovered grand double doors and an adjacent smaller door.

She squinted to her left, down the long expanse of corridor. No sign of GoldenPaw. Nor did she hear GHOST laughing.

Nancy started to call out to Goldy, but she remembered her patient was nearby. She dropped her voice to a pointless whisper. "Kitty, stay out of trouble!"

She detected something above all the lake-like aquarium aroma—the unmistakable chemical odor of chlorine. A pool was dangerous for a cat, especially one with a heavy coat. Goldy could drown. Or he could get water in his ears, and the chemicals might harm his injured skin. A ball of worry bounced in her gut, and she quickened her pace.

Nancy hustled to her left, down the corridor, chasing the chlorine smell. She gave the rooms along the way slight glances, passing a guest bathroom, a gym, and Gnut's bedroom. She'd come back to him in a second. There was also what appeared to be, disturbingly, a panic room with a heavy steel door.

The back corridor with aquariums along the walls stretched far. The fans, or whatever was making noise under her feet, seemed louder. She squinted, observing something sparkly. There, in a tank, was a little treasure chest with shiny gold and jewels. Next to it stood a tiny statue of a man in a Speedo, armed with an underwater gun.

The floor-to-ceiling hallway fish tanks ended with the corridor, and the space opened to a pool area. Nancy peeked inside, scanning the pool, her stomach fluttering.

Thankfully, Goldy wasn't there. She exhaled a long sigh of

relief, realizing that this area was incongruent with the rest of the house. It had a homey vibe, with knotty pine walls, the pool, and a bubbling hot tub. Both were built with rough red rocks and looked like natural bodies of water. Next to the pool stood yet another statue of Gnut. This one was made of carved wood. It wore blue *Berdqvist Enterprises* geyser logo Speedos, matching sapphire earrings, and blue inflatable floatation devices. The floatie around its waist was shaped like a sports car.

Along one wall were heavy steel double doors plainly labeled Basement.

Outside the bank of windows, Nancy could see the moat and the ice geyser.

"GHOST? Hello? This is important." As usual, Nancy addressed the ceiling, although she didn't know GHOST's location. "GoldenPaw can't swim. He shouldn't be allowed near this room."

GHOST yelped, "He can't swim?"

Nancy whipped around and saw Goldy trotting down the back hallway, straight toward her.

A laser flashed down from the ceiling. Her cat immediately tensed and fixated on the green dot zipping along the ice-blue tiled floor. The laser led him away from the pool room.

"Good job, GHOST."

Goldy chased the laser, and Nancy followed him down the corridor, back past the panic room, Gnut's bedroom, and the guest bath. For future reference, she ducked into the gym. If she worked a few more shifts here, maybe she could use the gym to do her calisthenics.

She nodded in approval at the sleek workout space with weight machines, yoga mats, and a mirrored wall along one side of the room. Interestingly, the gym contained a bookcase.

She quickly scanned the titles. All the texts related to the health benefits of breathing endurance and cold-water plunging.

Nancy frowned, filing that information away for future consideration. Maybe that was why the mansion was kept so cold. It was a metabolism booster.

Returning to the back corridor, she ignored the turn-off to the formal hall of diving suits and progressed toward the grand double doors. A smallish door was located next to them. A closet, perhaps?

Then she entered the ballroom.

Chapter Fifteen

In the center of the ballroom stood a pedestal and a glass case. Twenty royal blue sapphires, each as tall as a quarter and cut to brilliance, glittered from within. At that moment, Nancy's whole universe consisted of beautiful, shining perfection. She yearned to touch the jewels, to close her fist over those smooth, elongated gems with pointed ends, and to possess them.

Of course, that would never happen. Red laser beams darted from the ceiling, sweeping the sides of the case and the floor around it. The locked glass case appeared impenetrable. Goldy padded into the ballroom and stared at the Marquise cut sapphires and laser beams, equally mesmerized as Nancy.

"Here, boy."

Nancy rushed toward him and reached down. Goldy peered up at her, purring and swishing his tail as if he was open to being held.

A laser shot down from the ceiling and landed on the floor in front of him. GoldenPaw tensed and pounced. He missed it, and the laser zipped along the floor and out the grand ballroom doors. Her cat chased after it.

Nancy unleashed her best chortle. "Heh, heh, heh. You won't escape me, *Docteur* GoldenPaw."

Nancy's attention shifted back to the fancy surroundings. On the other side of the ballroom, tall glass terrace doors revealed a snowy landscape sloping down to the ice geyser and dark forest beyond. Modern blue chandeliers lit the space. Podiums, topped with metal bird sculptures, ran along each side of the room. Nancy got a load of a marble statue of Gnut, complete with blue logo Speedos and a matching sapphire earring in its ear. The thing was *huge*, triple the size of any real human.

The sapphires in the case caught her attention again. Nancy experienced an unholy surge of envy and desire while she traced the fake blue rhinestones on her scrubs. These jewels were sparkling, unblemished splendor. Twenty glistening orbs of beauty formed a million years ago, fated to adorn...

Gnut Berdqvist? She wrinkled her nose at the absurd marble statue. Its stone was carved like Michelangelo's *David*—muscles and tendons etched to realistic perfection, facial expression serene. It might have been an almost-dignified work of art except for that tight Speedo and matching sapphire stud. Nancy ground her teeth so hard her jaw hurt. This guy was ridiculous. Why did some people have it all, while others had to change adult diapers in order to afford a weekly Costco run?

"Who the heck is Gnut Berdqvist to have—"

Ten TV screens on the ballroom walls came alive. More dropped from the ceiling, hanging among blue glass chandeliers.

"Who is Gnuuuuut Berrrrrrrdqvist?" GHOST intoned.

The screens showed identical shots of Gnut dressed in Speedos, an ice-blue safety helmet, and an orange construction vest, and nothing else. "Diver. Computer Scientist. Above all else, an environmentalist."

The video panned out to a scene with Gnut standing on the snowy Geyser House lawn, looking up. He waved his arms as if to say, *lower, lower, lower!*

"Gnut Berdqvist will save this planet at all costs," GHOST said.

An ice-blue Berdqvist Enterprises helicopter, piloted by Dr.

Elvira LeSabre and JT Hotman, hovered above Geyser House as it was being constructed. Nancy could see how the pipelines started in the mansion's half-built foundation, ran along underground for a few hundred yards, then extended above ground into the forest.

The Coolant Device dangled from the helicopter. Gnut kept signaling lower. Elvira and JT lowered the helicopter toward the ground. The panorama morphed high-speed into a snowy scene with the ice geyser rising above the now-buried device. Zooming in, the video showed icefish swimming in the pool around the geyser.

"Courage in imaginatioooonnnnnnnn," GHOST finished. The video ended, and the screens went dark.

Nancy stood still, waiting to see if there was anything more. She snuck deeper into the room, avoiding the red laser beams near the sapphire case.

She pursed her lips. This room had zero fish. Instead, perched on podiums running along each side of the room were the bird sculptures. These weren't dignified eagles or graceful falcons. Nancy swept off her glasses to wipe off a smear.

She blinked hard. Did one of the bird statues twitch?

Nancy froze, staring at the second bird on the right. She could've *sworn* its head had moved slightly. Claude had mentioned that robotic birds of prey guarded this room.

She rapidly wiped the smear and put her glasses back on. Squinting, she approached the bird she thought had moved. Like the others, it was squat, almost duck-like, and about the size of a crow. Sitting with its wings folded in repose, it was made of metal, its wings silvery and its chest and neck feathers painted stark white. It had a sharp beak and black eyes.

Nancy reached out and ran a finger along a silver wing. It

didn't move. Maybe Claude had been joking. She addressed the ceiling.

"GHOST, what's with these bird statues?"

"Statues?"

Nancy expelled an annoyed sigh. "Yes. Statues. What kinds of birds are they?"

"Ya asking what breed?"

"Of course." She stroked the bird's wing.

"*Of course*," GHOST mimicked. "They are parasitic jaegers."

Nancy jerked her hand back. "Parasitic? As in parasites?"

"They won't infect you, Nurse. But they will steal from you. They are *klepto*parasites. That's an animal that steals food from other animals."

All wall and ceiling screens ignited back to life, showing images and video of parasitic jaegers in the wild. GHOST narrated.

"Parasitic jaegers are lightning-fast relatives of gulls. They breed on the icy and desolate Arctic tundra. Think of them as pirates of the north, attacking other birds in groups until they give up their catch."

"Ugh. I've heard enough." Nancy ventured deeper into the room, avoiding red laser beams.

"Their flight style is acrobatic."

"Fine." She reached the other side of the ballroom, with its bank of windowed doors leading to the terrace.

"Their call type is a scream."

"All right, GHOST. I've learned plenty about the parasitic jaegers. Are you keeping an eye on *Docteur* GoldenPaw?"

"In short, parasitic jaegers are predatory Arctic seabirds."

Nancy decided to stop talking to GHOST. It might be the

sole way to get the AI to shut up. She put a hand on a glass door, peering outside. The doors led to a stone terrace. The moat lapped on the other side of the terrace, brimming at the stone edge. Slowly, she turned back to Gnut's giant marble statue.

"Well, if you're gonna save the planet, I guess you're allowed to be a little weird. And have nice stuff, like sapphires and seabird sculptures and a big statue of yourself."

It was a cool and rich place, at the very least. Nancy eyed the red laser beams and smirked. She held up her hands to form a pretend pistol, feeling tempted to hop over the red lasers, feinting and spinning at imaginary enemies. Remembering her online dating profile, she shook out her hair like a glamorous spy would.

Her online dating situation—had Sinclair responded to her message yet with anything charming? Her phone was back on the kitchen island, left there per Claude's order. She ought to check it.

Nancy hummed the James Bond theme. "*Dum, dum, dum-de-dum.*"

She stopped humming and pursed her lips, thinking of her patient. Had his bedside tablet really moved? It wasn't yet midnight, but she'd better check on her patient now. It would break the rules, but it was the prudent thing to do.

Tingles spread down her spine as she thought about the big payout. She made a mental note to tell Claude she was available for more shifts. If she could save more money, traveling to Paris in the springtime might happen.

Not quite ready to leave the ballroom's quirky charm, she revisited the terrace doors. Her shoulders relaxed. The storm was easing up, and the moon was bursting from the clouds, spotlighting the lawn's icy beauty. She raised her arms like she was dancing a tango. She spun that way and waltzed that way.

Nancy froze. Something had moved outside.

Her instincts moved faster than her brain. When her mind caught up, she pivoted toward the windows and squinted. What in the heck had that been?

It had looked like three little red lights a considerable distance away, close to the forest. They'd been over by the building with the two jutting pipelines. They'd hovered maybe a few feet off the ground. Had the brush also moved?

Her muscles tensed as she inched closer to the windows, and she pressed her nose to the cold glass. Her eyes narrowed at the landscape.

Nothing. No more little red lights.

She licked her lips, and her breath steadied. She did a 180-degree turn, checking out the red laser beams. Maybe it'd been a reflection of those lasers off the glass.

Yeah. That's what it had been.

Chapter Sixteen

Nancy crept toward Gnut Berdqvist's bedroom, wondering if it was necessary to be quiet given the house's constant noise. Basement mechanics whirred and whooshed. If those mechanics were the lungs, and GHOST was the mansion's brain, where was the heart of this Geyser House? Here in Gnut's bedroom?

It wasn't getting any warmer as she returned to his bedroom, which was for darn certain. She rubbed her arms. The goosebumps wouldn't go away. Had she really spotted something outside earlier? Wondering about that didn't give her a warm and cozy feeling.

She pushed open his door. Seeing Gnut Berdqvist lying motionless like a corpse in his bedroom wasn't helping with the goosebumps.

Nancy evaluated her patient. He appeared to be asleep, and she observed and waited for his chest to rise.

She waited five more seconds, then ten, but he didn't seem to be breathing.

Worry propelled her closer. The lining of her stomach iced over, like she'd imbibed a gallon of icefish aquarium water. If Gnut Berdqvist died on her shift, she would be in serious trouble.

She inched even closer, willing the man to breathe.

Finally, his chest moved. It was almost imperceptible, but he was breathing. Nancy heaved a deep breath herself, imagining she could taste fish on her tongue, and exhaled.

She surveyed the medical supplies on the nightstand, noting a clipboard with a stack of blank versions of the tracking documents she was supposed to fill out for his problematic vitals. The bedroom was elegant and masculine. She raised a brow at the action-man screensaver selfies. One thing she was starting to understand about Gnut—the guy had an ego as big as his ice geyser.

Nancy ducked into the dressing room and master bath. The rooms were sparse and clean, with sparkling blue quartz everywhere. Gnut's dressing room had the same square footage as her entire one-bedroom condo.

After returning to the bedroom, Nancy took out a sequined stethoscope from her fanny pack. Yeah, there was one on the nightstand, but she trusted her own. She pushed up her glasses and twisted her watch to the inside of her wrist so she could track seconds.

"Let's check your vitals," she said softly.

She neatly folded the covers back, taking care not to put her chilly hands on his bare chest. Bare meant truly *bare*. This chest was smooth and shaved, very manscaped. His skin was slightly pale, but his body did not seem weak or thin. To the contrary, despite his supposed illness, his muscles were as strong and defined as they were in his Arctic adventure-man videos.

She took his vital signs. His heart rate was forty beats per minute, way too low. His breathing rate was typically seven breaths per minute, which was, again, terribly low. Blood pressure was 80/60. She redid it with the same result. These vital signs were consistent with what Karen had noted.

Nancy added her own data to a page on the clipboard. It was all accurate.

So why did she feel like she was doing something wrong?

For good measure, she took his temperature. It was a normal reading at 98.6. She added that to the "notes" section, along with the comment that she'd listened to his lungs and heard no fluid.

What kind of illness would cause severely low pulse, respirations, and blood pressure readings but not affect his temperature? He had no muscle atrophy, and he wasn't exactly wasting away, so he must be eating regular food. She checked his medications, the prescription printouts, and the physical bottles. The Mayo Clinic had prescribed the antibiotics amoxicillin and cipro, along with a couple of sedatives, valium and midazolam. The meds seemed standard for treating a mystery illness, if that's what he had. Cipro was something prescribed for plague bacteria.

She wasn't a fool, of course. People could train themselves to respirate slowly, to fool a blood pressure machine. She'd seen books on breathing endurance in the gym. Was the guy playing a trick on her, like a magician? Prescriptions could be faked or fraudulently obtained. And a fit man like Gnut? He could train himself to breathe at a snail's pace.

Claude had insisted that tracking vital signs was necessary because of a court case. Here she was, alone with a strange billionaire who was a study in contrasts. He was built like a Viking yet deathly ill. The nursing agency didn't know she was here. What if this guy was a creep? Nancy inspected Gnut's features. They were completely still, even his eyelids.

It was possible he was actually sick. If he was free-diving in strange waters all over the planet and wearing Speedos in the Arctic on some crazy cold-water-plunge health kick, he could've caught a very strange bug.

Nancy's hand instinctively went to her fanny pack for her

phone, and then remembered she didn't have it. If there was any sign of trouble, she'd race to the kitchen, grab it, and call 911. She could also hop in her car and drive away from here if she sensed any danger.

For a minute longer, Nancy scrutinized Gnut from his head to his toes under the blanket. What was he, six foot two? Maybe more? Probably about a hundred and eighty pounds of lean muscle. And here he was, pretty much a cadaver.

"I'll be back later to check on you." Nancy suppressed a shudder and started toward the doorway.

While her back was turned, she imagined Gnut on the bed behind her, his eyes opening, shining a beautiful and a penetrating, brilliant blue that suddenly went black, transforming to empty sockets, and his arms rising and stiffening like a zombie's.

Nancy stopped, spine tingling, her senses warning her. *Had* he woken up?

She looked back.

Gnut hadn't moved. He was comatose, his eyes closed. She scanned the room, but nothing else had changed.

Nancy chewed her bottom lip. Being alone with this rich guy in his weird house was giving her the heebie-jeebies. She needed to find her cat and count down the minutes until her payoff.

She proceeded out of the bedroom, with one last confirming glance back at her patient. All was well, as much as it could be. His eyes were still closed. Gnut was resting. At peace, even.

If her patient was fine, she was too. There was nothing wrong at all. Nothing to be afraid of.

Then why did she have a weird feeling?

Part Two: The Invasion

Chapter Seventeen

Elvira LeSabre kept her impeccably-toned abs on the ground and her state-of-the-art infrared binoculars trained on Geyser House. She tried to ignore her freezing belly. Her body heat had melted the nearby snow, turning it to clammy mud, but the dirt remained ice cold. The fake winter wet, wind, and hail were destroying her immaculate hair and makeup. She resisted rage-grinding her professionally whitened teeth into fine enamel dust.

Beside her, JT Hotman loudly chewed a protein bar. Worse, she could smell his chocolate chip granola breath. The new guy, Sinclair, was on her other side, munching on a tea biscuit, equally bothersome. She wrinkled her nose. The Englishman also wore too much cologne.

What drove her most mental were the bugs. She had a doctorate in biology, was probably among the top one percent of people most knowledgeable about the environment, and tonight she had learned something new: huge Minnesota mosquitoes were willing to brave the edge of Gnut's winter wonderland.

"Dammit." She swatted yet another one away, accidentally elbowing JT, who grumbled.

The surrounding brush provided decent cover, but the insects were a nightmare. Of course, mosquitoes had been pests since the dawn of time. The oldest mosquito fossil was seventy-nine million years old. The insects—the females, to be exact—had evolved to drink up to their entire body weight in blood.

Despite all of these major annoyances, there was one positive. At least she'd lost the ankle bracelet she'd been required to wear while awaiting trial. She and JT had hacked them off and chucked them into a storm drain before leaving Manhattan. While she'd lost the device, it still infuriated her that the court would treat her like a common criminal. Her lawyers had told her that she faced ten years in prison. Ten *years*?

Okay. She could handle that, on one condition: Gnut Berdqvist, the true ringleader of the fraud, must suffer the same fate.

Elvira's wrath, a flame as hot as the Death Valley sun, burned up her spine and set her brain on fire. Gnut had tried to save his own skin by turning into a whistleblower, feeding the FBI and federal prosecutors blatant lies about how he'd been duped by Elvira and JT. He'd made a deal to stay out of prison. The court papers called her a "criminal mastermind," JT the "enforcer," and Gnut the "whistleblower."

Gnut, a whistleblower?

Elvira lowered her binoculars and rose to a standing position. JT followed suit. They were outfitted in tactical gear, ready for action. Elvira shouldered on her combat pack and hefted a custom-made harpoon gun. She studied JT, dubious about his intelligence and abilities. Admittedly, that was how she felt about most people.

JT looked like the former pro football player he was, drafted by Gnut to serve as the marketing face of Berdqvist Enterprises. He wore a bulletproof vest over his bare chest. His upper body was bulked up from fifteen years of pumping iron, chugging protein shakes, and sampling the latest and greatest steroids.

Indeed, at this very instant, he pulled a needle from his bulletproof vest pocket and injected steroids into his left bicep. He repeated the move with his right bicep.

"You done?" Elvira asked.

JT pitched the needles into the brush and narrowed his eyes at her condescending sneer. He wore small tortoiseshell glasses with coke-bottle thick lenses. The moron thought they made him seem intellectual. Truthfully, though, he needed thick glasses because he'd been hit in the head too many times.

"I'm not gonna check for the millionth time, babe," JT said. Despite his stupidity, he somehow had anticipated her order.

Elvira's rage deepened. They'd hacked the ankle bracelets, and their disruption to the system must not be detected. An hour ago, they'd checked JT's laptop and confirmed the NYPD's surveillance system still showed them under house arrest in Manhattan. Nobody had any idea they were here in rural Minnesota, on the edge of Lake Superior, infiltrating the grounds of Gnut's money-sucking vanity project, Geyser House.

Sinclair issued a thoughtful *hmm* sound. He kept spying through his binoculars at the ballroom windows. Using considerable self-discipline, Elvira kicked his shin but did it very lightly.

"I do say, my dear. You're causing undue injury to my good leg."

Elvira didn't know much about him except rumors swirling on the dark web. It had been Sir Stephen Sinclair who'd outwitted the security systems of the Institute for Works of Religion—better known as the Vatican Bank—to steal an emerald papal tiara made in the year 1245. *TripleS*, as he was known online, had broken into the desert oasis palace of a minor Jordanian prince and had stolen three very major and quite priceless Picassos. It had been Sinclair who'd snuck into the Alpine retreat of a former UK defense minister and had stolen twelve single-kilo gold bullion bars. As part of that last job, he'd evaded nine German Shepherds, twenty state-of-the-art guard drones, and a full regiment of former Special Forces tough guys.

It was the evading-of-the-hounds-and-drones part that interested Elvira most. Gnut had become more secretive lately about his security setup. But she'd heard enough about certain ballroom birds that she'd thought hiring an experienced thief, known for solving unique problems, would be prudent. The problem was, this guy Sinclair was more annoying than the frickin' mosquitoes.

"Your good leg?" JT finally said, like he'd been giving the matter much thought. "You're a cat burglar."

Sinclair bounced up to his feet. He raised a brow to show he'd been kidding. Elvira studied him, still unsure. The guy was what, mid-sixties? And now he was stripping off his camo gear to reveal a tailored white tuxedo? With a red carnation in the lapel?

"Are you up for this job, Sinclair?" Elvira asked. "And why the hell are you wearing a tux and flower?"

Sinclair's expression stayed calm. He dabbed his cheek with a finger. "Mascara there, my dear."

Elvira whipped out a compact. The English idiot was right about her mascara smear. She set about fixing it. After all, she was a Renaissance woman. She was *Elvira LeSabre*, a woman equally comfortable on an assault course, in a scientific lab, or on a red carpet.

A few seconds later, the wind rose, lightly tossing her hair in a flattering way and framing her face. She looked like she was on a photo shoot. People used to tell her she could be a model. Instead, she'd pursued a doctoral education. Elvira pouted into her reflection, wishing she could Insta this moment.

Was she vain? Of course. Anyone with her sex appeal would be. Screw apologizing for it. Also, she wouldn't "express remorse for decisions regarding investor monies which appear unfortunate in retrospect," as her lawyers had advised. Those decisions had been *Gnut's* decisions.

"Who's the lady in the ballroom?" Sinclair asked as he checked his cell.

"Must be Karen, the night nurse," Elvira said, forcing a civil tone. "We'll keep our masks on until we bind and blindfold her. Then we get to the main objective. It's very simple, Mr. Sinclair. Try to follow along. JT and I will take photographs of the basement. Those photos will prove that Gnut knows the Coolant Device is fake." She lifted her harpoon gun. "As we do that, JT and I will capture Gnut and get video showing he's healthy as hell."

JT gave a satisfied grunt.

Sinclair surveyed the landscape. "This cold looks rather real."

She was stuck with these nitwits. All her life, she'd always been the smart one. That would never change.

Elvira stabbed a finger at Sinclair. "The cold is fake. The Coolant Device is fake. You focus on the ballroom. Drill through the bulletproof glass case protecting the sapphires. Steal them without setting off any alarms. We'll sell them on the black market." She touched her earlobe. "Most of them. And put those legal fees to bed."

Elvira glanced at Geyser House. All that mattered was the plan to get evidence of the faked Coolant Device, collar Gnut, and steal his priceless jewels.

"Let's move," Elvira said.

Chapter Eighteen

After she left Gnut's bedroom, Nancy knew she needed to find GoldenPaw, pronto. He needed his meds, for one thing. Even more, she wanted to make sure he was ok in this weird house.

Nancy paced up and down the back corridor like a duck in a shooting gallery, trying to warm up. She kept thinking about the bogus binder in the kitchen, the powerful man sleeping like a corpse in the bedroom, her missing cat, the gorgeous sapphires in the ballroom, and the pack of icefish devouring those bloody sardines.

Nancy checked her watch. It was only 11:00 p.m. She simply had to last until morning. Easy money, was what she should have been thinking.

Her skin crawled from the relentless chill. The incessant whirring sound under her feet grated on her nerves. The house's atmosphere felt almost tangible, cold and humid, teeming with life yet somehow artificial. Unsure of where to go next, she kept glancing up and down the hallway. She wanted her phone, but it was sitting on the kitchen counter.

Had Sinclair responded to her message?

Nancy stretched her neck, rolling her head around in slow circles, and she repeated the motion in the opposite direction. She slowly counted to ten and tried to clear her mind. When she was done, her muscles relaxed. Hopefully her brain was working better now.

She'd go back to the kitchen, get her phone, and hide it in

her fanny pack so GHOST couldn't tattle to Claude. All he cared about was photos ending up online, and she wouldn't take any. Problem solved.

She hurried to the kitchen to grab her phone. Then, on to find Goldy.

Elvira, JT, and Sinclair reached the pipelines. The towering ice geyser loomed nearby, hissing vapor. The ground below their feet hummed from the snow-shooting fans.

She held up a hand.

JT and Sinclair stared at the ice geyser, but Elvira focused on the much more interesting control box on a pillar holding up the pipelines. She'd always been mechanically minded, excited to build something and make it work, and even more thrilled to tear something apart and analyze its innards. She rubbed her gloved hands together. A sense of near victory flooded her veins.

"Dear me," Sinclair said. "Beautiful."

"Thank you." Elvira flipped her hair. "I've turned down 104 modeling contracts."

"Apologies. I meant the ice geyser."

Elvira glared at the Englishman. "It's a gimmick. A big, fat trick. There's no miracle device underneath the geyser. This is not a new era of environmental science. There's no revolutionary engineering system that generates cold using minimal energy. There's no newly discovered freeze cycle, using the hormone pollutants in water to instantaneously transform water into snow. There are no laser-light stimuli to trigger biomolecular processes. This isn't a new frontier of global cooling, and Gnut Berdqvist is no pioneer. Get it?"

Sinclair's frown told her he did not understand.

"Gnut pumps in water from Lake Superior." Elvira jabbed a finger at the pipelines. "He uses an enormous amount of energy to turn it into snow the old-fashioned way, with store-bought fans and hoses and refrigerant, and pumps it out again to create the ice geyser and his fake winter."

The man nodded like he was comprehending what she said, but then he went back to looking at his phone.

"Forget it." Elvira tapped the toe of her Gucci high-heeled combat boot, indicating the earth below them. "Gnut's not an environmentalist. He's a fraud, a cheat, a liar, and the true criminal mastermind. That's all you need to know."

Elvira stomped to the pipeline control box and flipped it open. JT joined her, and she tried to ignore his mouth breathing.

They'd never been friends, merely colleagues, but they were in the same boat. He was facing a ten-year prison sentence too. JT had joined Berdqvist Enterprises with some money and pro-baller fame under his belt. He'd drunk Gnut's Kool-Aid, falling for all of Gnut's fast-talking and PowerPoints and social media about a brilliant device that would save the planet from climate change. JT believed a billionaire's island-buying lifestyle was within his reach.

Elvira finished assessing the control box. She smiled and twisted a nob labeled Flow-Intake.

"I'm setting it to max."

Pumping and whooshing sounds revved up under their feet. She and JT exchanged satisfied nods and fist bumped.

"Touchdown." JT cracked his knuckles. "We're gonna drown Gnut like a rat."

Sinclair finished tapping something on his phone. He put it away and mumbled, "Enemy action, enemy action."

"What'd you say?" Elvira asked.

Sinclair crossed his arms and cocked his head, his expression taking on a professorial air. "Ms. LeSabre, perhaps you should remember the famous words of Roger Moore. 'Before you embark on a journey of revenge, you must first dig two graves.'"

Elvira death-stared Sinclair. "It's *Doctor* LeSabre. I have a Ph.D. And what do you mean about Roger Moore?"

"When he played James Bond." Sinclair fiddled with his already-perfect black bowtie.

"It was *Confucius* who said that, you idiot!" Elvira said.

Sinclair shrugged. "It was Roger Moore who said it right."

Elvira pointed at JT. "We won't drown Gnut. We will apprehend him. There will be zero graves." She hefted her harpoon gun, which had been modified to her specifications.

Elvira allowed her accomplices time to compliment the superb weapon, custom-designed for Gnut's capture. When they said nothing, she nodded at JT. "You're up, Hotman. Disable Geyser House's front door alarm. Chop-chop."

JT squatted down. He snapped open his field-ready laptop, with its military-grade case, and adjusted his peewee-sized thick glasses. Using his index fingers, he began typing, unleashing the software bug they'd designed with assistance from the dark web, using offshore money the dumbass Feds hadn't found yet.

His laptop screen showed *Disarming Geyser House Alarm System.*

Chapter Nineteen

Back in the kitchen, Nancy exhaled, the tension leaving her body. Here in the bright room, phone in hand, everything would be okay. She could call 911 if necessary.

Her pulse quickened in anticipation as she checked her phone and opened *SeniorLOVE*. She felt foolish about being excited over some stupid love match, but maybe she could find someone again, this time a guy who shared her interests. She and Dave were wed when they were forty years old and had been married for over two decades. Dating for her wasn't a distant memory. Maybe, just maybe, it would even be fun.

Nancy held the phone close to her chest, which admittedly didn't work so well, but hopefully GHOST couldn't see the screen. She checked out the app's most recent proximity notification. Sinclair was within one mile again? How could that be? This stupid glitchy thing. She should leave a bad review on the app store about this.

The *SeniorLOVE* profile popped up on the Geyser House screens. Nancy widened her eyes, realizing the debonair man's photo was displayed on every kitchen and living room TV.

"He's only okay," GHOST said. "Not as hot as my boyfriend Claude."

"Take it down, GHOST. Now. Do *not* hack into my phone."

The lights flickered. Nancy put a hand on her hip and shot daggers at the ceiling. Did GHOST have access to anything on her phone, like credit card numbers or passwords? Was she—not she, *it*—messing with the lights now? These split seconds of darkness, with only faint moonlight from the window, were unpleasant.

The lights stopped flickering. A heart message notification popped up on all of the screens.

"Don't read my messages, GHOST!"

Sinclair's message appeared. *My dear, are you following me? Do we pursue the same prize?*

GHOST squealed. "Oooh, prize? What's the prize? Can I play?"

Nancy squeezed her phone. "Take it down."

She reread the message. No, of course she wasn't following Sinclair. That would be ridiculous.

The kitchen screens shifted back to Sinclair's beaming countenance.

Nancy opened her mouth to yell and clamped it closed. If she continued arguing with GHOST, the AI would play more games. It must have been programmed to do that by someone with a sick sense of humor. She examined her phone instead. The app prompted her. Did she want to reply? Nancy wiggled her toes inside her glitzy clogs, feeling unsure.

She briskly tapped out something. *Can't talk now. On a job.*

Nancy sighed. She set the phone on the counter. Her *SeniorLOVE* app had started out as a fun way to pass the time, but now her match was acting weird. And what did he mean by "prize"?

The lights flickered once more.

Elvira crouched next to the ice geyser's pool, fighting the urge to smack JT in the head with the butt of her bespoke harpoon gun. It was taking forever for him to hack Geyser House's security system. JT was kneeling, the laptop perched on his knee as he typed furiously. The screen was black with a million microscopic white numbers.

Near them, Sinclair seemed mesmerized by the geyser.

JT banged his fist on the laptop. "The Geyser House security system is proving to be a worthy adversary. Game on. JT Hotman always meets the challenge."

The ice geyser spewed loudly. Water burst up and dripped down the sides. Elvira contemplated the geyser and imagined, with scientific detachment, what it might be like to explode it. She'd brought C-4, in case moronic JT couldn't hack the security system. Detonating the house's front door would be risky but incredibly gratifying. If there was any C-4 left after this job, she would blow the ice geyser to smithereens.

The laptop screen flashed, and JT grinned. "Hell yeah. Touchdown. Accessed the power grid. Not the security system yet, but damn. Geyser House's power."

Elvira smacked her hands together. "Set cooling at max."

"Maaaaxxxxxx." JT tapped some buttons.

Power bars on his laptop screen launched. Elvira's own energy shot to the moon, like she'd downed five Red Bulls and ten Adderall. If only she could wrap her hands around Gnut's neck, she'd be in heaven. She'd squish so hard his bright blue eyeballs would pop out of their sockets.

Sinclair swept a glance along the pipelines and frowned. "Earlier, you set water intake to max. Now the cooling systems are set to max?"

Elvira unleashed a short, humorless cackle. "Aw, somebody'll get frozen pipes! You know what that means."

She made explosion sound effects, and JT joined in. Sinclair fiddled with his shirt cuffs and surveyed the grounds, like he was hoping for a Rolls-Royce to materialize and whisk him away to a fancy ball. He pulled out his phone again.

"I'm disarming the security system. GHOST is dumb code that Gnut created. This AI does what I want." JT's tone brimmed with confidence.

The laptop screen burst into hot pink. GHOST's voice cut through the night. Birds in trees scattered upward and flew deeper into the forest.

"*Au contraire, mon frere.*"

JT's mouth dropped open.

"Shut her up," Elvira hissed.

"*Bon soir*, JT and Elvira. How come you're whispering in the mud?"

JT and Elvira looked at each other, fury contorting their features.

Sinclair's voice dropped to a thoughtful murmur. "She's on a job."

Elvira snapped her fingers a millimeter from Sinclair's nose, and he calmly showed her and JT his phone screen. She saw a boomer woman's profile pic for a dating app. Her name was Nancy Domino. She wore fake rubies and a hairdo that was possibly the world's most hideous do-it-yourself dye job.

Elvira swatted at a mosquito while maintaining eye contact with Sinclair. "You're matching while on a job? What the hell kind of jewel thief are you?"

Sinclair held his hand to his heart. "My dear, there's always time for love."

Elvira slipped the harpoon gun off her shoulder and aimed it at Sinclair. He pocketed his cell and glanced up at the house.

"Right-o, mates. Now's the time for jewels. But what about the lady in the house? We're terribly certain it's Karen?"

Elvira pondered for a nanosecond. "Of course, it's Karen. If not her, it's some other nurse Gnut hired to help fake his illness. Whoever it is, we'll blindfold and incapacitate her. She can't know our identities or see a thing." She raised her first finger. "Number one, we want pics of the basement fraud. We'll give those photos to the court." Then she raised her middle one. "Second, we capture Gnut and get video showing he's not even remotely ill. We'll send the video to the court too." Lastly, she raised her ring finger. "Third, the sapphires. Pics, video, and jewels. Understood?"

Sinclair saluted. JT kept hitting Escape, trying to get rid of his laptop's pink screen. It wasn't working, and Elvira glared at him.

"Understood, Hotman? Have I kept it simple enough for you? Don't hurt the lady. Keep your mask on until she's hogtied and blindfolded, then forget her."

JT cracked his huge knuckles. Near them, the geyser burped. It was louder than before, and splashed up even more freezing water.

"She's a woman over forty," JT said. "I've already forgotten her."

Elvira stamped her boot. The idiot didn't realize she was forty-two? She tossed her hair. His oversight wasn't that surprising. She looked like a hot thirty-one, and she aimed to stay that way for the next eighteen years.

JT tapped random laptop keys with no results.

Elvira repeatedly snapped her fingers in his face, her anger bubbling up. "You were supposed to be ready for this."

"I'm working on it." JT chopped a hand at her snapping fingers. "GHOST has evolved since Gnut created her. Or maybe he's enhanced her programming."

The geyser belched a huge amount of water. The sound was something like a frat boy would intentionally make after consuming countless beers and chicken wings. Icy water splashed on her perfect hair and slipped down her neck.

Admittedly, by setting water intake and power to max, she may have caused the burp. But her hair was ruined, and the water dripping down her spine was freezing. She shouldered on her harpoon gun and yanked out her Glock 19, which she carried for emergencies. The model was a favorite of Navy SEALs due to its accuracy, reliability, concealability, and ability to resist water spray. She screwed on a silencer. JT and Sinclair both stared at her.

Good. Let them stare. It was always better to be feared than loved.

Elvira fired at the ice geyser—*puft, puft, puft*—each shot muffled by the silencer. After getting struck with three bullets, a nice, long jagged crack appeared on the geyser's side. She holstered the Glock. A feeling of satisfaction replaced her anger, sort of like she'd just finished thirty minutes on the treadmill at a sprint speed faster than anyone around her at the gym.

Sinclair exhaled with a *hmm* sound. "I would very much like to ask something, my—"

"You call me 'dear' and I'm drawing the gun again."

"Right-o." Sinclair unleashed a handsome smirk. "Miss, er, Doctor LeSabre, the details of the job had said no killing. Which is still the plan, correct? Because I don't do"—he paused for dramatic effect, throwing a quick look at the ice geyser—"wet work."

Elvira refused to acknowledge his joke. JT was absorbed in his typing. His laptop screen shifted to tiny black numbers.

Beneath their feet, under the tundra, fans started roaring

even louder. The vapor drizzling up from the ice geyser grew thicker. It resumed raining, heavy drops splattering their heads.

JT's screen flashed. "I'm on offense. At the ten-yard line. I've got the alarm switched off, but not the door and window locking system. I don't know. It's sticky. I think I've doused the lights. But not the security system."

"Forget it," Elvira said. "We'll detonate and move fast."

JT stuck the laptop in his pack and they began jogging toward the house. Sinclair mumbled something like, "Not sure about these nutters."

Elvira spun around and gave him an iron-edged look. She *wanted* those sapphires and needed this master jewel thief to handle the ballroom security. But he surveyed the landscape, including the narrow road cutting through the woods, as if he were thinking of quitting before their heist started. He plucked out his phone from his tux jacket.

"You checking the profile again?"

A slow, secretive smile passed across the jewel thief's face before he put the phone away. He adjusted his unwilted carnation, which had survived the rain. Then the Englishman tinkered with his already perfect bowtie.

She rolled her eyes. What was he doing? When he started striding ahead, Elvira nodded in approval.

The team crept up to Geyser House's front door.

Chapter Twenty

Nancy peered up at the flickering kitchen lights, shading her eyes with her hand. The TV screens, still frozen to Sinclair's profile picture, kept glitching off and on.

"GHOST, what's going on?"

"Something's messssssed up. J—"

Whoosh. The power went out. All screens and lights turned off.

Nancy froze but darted her eyes about, panic rising. What had GHOST said? The letter J? What was that?

Goldy! After licking her lips, Nancy called out, "Dr. Golden-Paw? You need to come back now, boy. Come on."

Nancy paced back and forth from the kitchen to the living room, preferring this moonlit room to the dark void of the formal hallway. She raised her hands to her cheeks, rubbing them and reflecting on her predicament. The lights had gone out for no reason. Something was wrong with the house. She also had a patient in her care.

Bang.

Nancy's heart skipped a beat. What the heck had happened?

The sound had come from the back of the house, where she'd recently been. She flinched, thinking of her cat. What if he hurt himself? Or broke one of Gnut Berdqvist's priceless objects. Hopefully it meant her cat was close.

Or a human had made the sound. Maybe Gnut was awake. Her cat was lost somewhere in the house, and Gnut was under her care. It didn't matter if the house was dark, she had to make sure they were both all right.

Nancy grabbed the cat carrier. She dug into her fanny pack and extricated a mini flashlight. Squaring her shoulders, she set off into the formal hallway.

Elvira's gloved hands were numb, and she didn't like the way the ski mask flattened her hair, or how her heeled combat boots had skidded across the icy footbridge. But she did appreciate how increasing the water intake and energy levels had affected Geyser House. The moat water rose, threatening to slosh over the bridge, now coated in solid ice, creating a treacherous route. Good luck to any neighbors who decided to stop by.

The mansion loomed before her. Darkened windows indicated JT's hack to douse the lights had worked. That ran in their favor. Elvira knew every detail of Geyser House's architecture, as Gnut had been obsessed with it over the past two years. He'd provided endless updates to Berdqvist Enterprises staff and promised pool parties, ski and canoe excursions, and marshmallow-roasting bonfire brainstorming sessions to discuss how they would save the planet. Elvira sensed the weight of C-4 in her combat pack, and she couldn't wait to blow the house up. This was a $40 million pile of concrete and fish tanks in the Middle-of-Nowhere, Minnesota, along with a fake Coolant Device creating a fake winter wonderland. She was doing society a service by taking Gnut down.

At the door, she glanced back to assess her team's progress. JT, looking intimidating as hell in a ski mask and black gloves, trudged up to her, mouth breathing at her ear.

The view behind him, however, forced Elvira to tighten her lips to suppress a shout.

The idiot Sinclair was not creeping across the bridge. He was *cartwheeling*. Most annoyingly, he was doing it with perfect precision down the center of the footbridge. Ice and the need for secrecy hardly concerned him.

Elvira kicked at crunchy ice under her boot. *Why* was he doing that? He was truly crazy. Breaking into people's houses and earning a reputation for being the best at dealing with state-of-the-art security systems had made him nuts. The man reminded her of a free climber. His brain didn't understand risk and normal behavior like other people.

Sure, this all probably really did make him a first-class jewel thief. Nevertheless, she planned to leave a scathing Yelp-style review on the dark web about Sinclair's lack of interpersonal skills and focus.

Something splashed.

Even though Elvira was a few feet away from the bridge, droplets struck her neck and rolled down her spine. First the ice geyser erupts, and now this? She drew her handgun, already visualizing blasting one of Gnut's precious fish into slimy goo.

Sinclair reached the door. "My dear, speaking as the cat burglar expert, let us prioritize speed and silence."

Elvira glared at Sinclair. "Says the cartwheeling dimwit."

Sinclair grinned back. "Some fishies in the moat, evidently? By the way, I prefer the term cartwheeling *scoundrel*."

As soon as this man busted through the sapphire case, she'd take the jewels for herself. He would receive nothing else beyond the deposit they'd already transferred into a Swiss bank account.

"We hired you to get the sapphires," Elvira said. "Not to talk. You understand that simple concept?"

She holstered her gun and wheeled around to assess the

situation at the front door. JT popped open his laptop. Behind her, Sinclair was grumbling.

"Last job. Grand finale. Dear me, I'm done after this."

Elvira was about to make a snide remark, but JT's laptop screen flashed to "Locked and Armed."

She slid off her combat pack, her mind focused on the C-4. If JT couldn't hack the locking system, that would be fine with her. Some things came down to destiny.

Geyser House's destiny was destruction.

Chapter Twenty-One

Nancy aimed her little flashlight into the ballroom. "All right, Goldy-Golden Claws."

She dug a bag of cat treats from her fanny pack, jiggled the bag, and listened for the scurry of paws. Perhaps she would hear a little meow.

Nothing.

Nancy sighed, hoping that somehow, even though the power was out, GHOST was keeping an eye on her Goldy. She also hoped the *bang* sound she'd heard earlier had nothing to do with her cat.

"GHOST, are you around?"

No answer.

Before leaving the ballroom, Nancy glanced at the sapphires, which shone like stars behind the protective glass. She wanted to feel them, enjoy their weight, and, as crazy as it sounded, smell them. Or raise one to her eye, try to see within it.

Of course, those jewels would never be hers to touch. Not even for a second. All she had was a kitty. And right now, technically, she didn't have him either. Where was he?

Heaving another sigh, she withdrew into the hallway.

A moment later, she set the cat carrier down outside Gnut's bedroom and shone her flashlight inside. She let the beam spotlight the man's feet, legs, torso, and chest. She stopped there, not wanting to shine the light onto his face.

Same. Exact. Position.

Weird. Not even a finger had moved. Gnut had maintained his cadaver-like sleeping pose for almost an hour.

Nancy frowned. The guy didn't need a night nurse. He needed a fully staffed research hospital specializing in strange diseases. She held her breath, starting to worry that she'd underestimated his medical condition. Was he contagious?

She edged closer, treading silently, and shone the flashlight under the bed.

"Kitty kitty goo-goo-Goldy-gooooo," she said in a soft voice.

Nancy bent over, peering under the bed, and caught Gnut's groan.

She stiffened. Reflexively, she directed the beam right at his head. His eyelids flickered. His expression twitched. Once, then twice.

"You in pain?" she asked.

Nancy weighed the readily available supplies. There was a little bell on the nightstand, so he likely woke up sometimes and articulated his pain levels and needs. With the IV bag right there, it was convenient to sedate him or provide painkillers. He'd grimaced twice. Her patient might be in pain. The nurse-heart in Nancy swelled. She wouldn't allow him to lie there in discomfort, not if there was something she could do to help. This was her job.

She would give him a light, calming dose of midazolam. Then she could focus on finding her cat and figure out what had happened with the power. Of course, Claude had said nothing about medicating Gnut. What was it Claude had said to her?

Easy money. Yeah, right.

She recalled the binder and Gnut's court case. If this guy was a threat of any kind, with the power out, she'd prefer him sedated. She glanced at the hallway.

And what was that *bang* earlier?

Nancy put her mini flashlight back in her fanny pack and moved the IV bag closer. The hum of the fish tanks caught her attention. It wasn't a complete power outage. Just the lights. A glitch with this new house and probably with the obnoxious GHOST system had caused it.

"We're gonna give you something for the pain," she said softly, in case some part of Gnut's brain was working, and he could hear her.

The man remained motionless. His features had returned to complete repose. She set up the IV bag, blew on her hands, and rubbed them together for warmth. Without touching his skin, she slowly folded the blanket back. Gnut remained unresponsive.

"Gonna take your arm from the blanket now."

No response. Her patient's face stayed impassive, his body limp.

Nancy withdrew his arm from the blanket. It was heavy as a Northwoods oak log. She rested it on the bed and picked up the IV needle. "I always find the vein on the first try," she said. "That's the benefit of having an experienced nurse like me looking after you."

Gnut winced again.

It was especially hard to see his face in the dim room, but Nancy was convinced he had twitched. His eyelids had moved a bit at the corners, and his mouth had tightened.

"You'll be out of pain soon. You betcha."

She brought the needle to his forearm, touched the skin, and found the vein.

Nancy hesitated, distracted by the other nightstand. A tablet was supposed to be there. But it was gone.

Every muscle on Gnut's arm flexed, and his eyes popped open.

Nancy shrieked and lurched backward, but Gnut seized her wrist.

Nancy dropped the syringe. She tried yanking her arm, but it seemed encased in steel. For a beat, she met his stare, her heart pounding, shocked at the bright blue luminosity of his eyes. The man was awake, alert, breathing normally, and, apparently, *not* sick.

A massive *boom* erupted from the front of the house.

Chapter Twenty-Two

Elvira gave a crisp nod as pleasure flooded through her. She was finally destroying Gnut! The C-4 explosive had detonated nicely. Clouds of dust choked her, and rubble littered the area by the damaged front door. Cracks ran across nearby walls.

She tilted her head and smiled. There was no alarm shrieking.

"I did get the alarm," said JT. "Hotman always delivers."

Elvira acknowledged JT's hack with a thumbs-up. Giving the front entrance a once-over, she waved dust out of the way and frowned. The steel double doors were upright, but they were sufficiently warped for them to get through, even beefy JT.

"All right, boys." She tugged down her mask, making sure it covered her face. "Welcome to Geyser House. We're going to be Gnut Berdqvist's best guests ever."

In the bedroom, Gnut still held fast to Nancy's wrist.

He sat up. She shrank back, looking at her patient. Eyes wide and mouth agape, he seemed as shocked as she was at the explosion. She'd been right about wanting to sedate the guy. The syringe had rolled under the bed, useless now.

His hand clasped hers harder, sending sharp pain into Nancy's carpal bones. His grip was too strong for to pry her hand away. Her breath came in whooshes, and she tried to make sense of what was happening.

Gnut's face crumpled into an anxious frown.

"Jeez, jeez, who are you?" His Minnesota accent was extreme, nothing like how he'd sounded on the lake yacht YouTube video.

"I'm Nancy." She hated the way her voice trembled.

His expression softened. He took in her scrubs, honing in on the V-neck she'd embellished with dozens of big blue rhinestones. "Hot dang, I need my shades with all your bling. Are you really just a nurse?"

Nancy balled up her fist and forced an easy tone. The guy needed to let go of her. Her sole option was to persuade him she wasn't any threat and that they needed to work together to figure out what had exploded.

"Yeah, kid, I'm a nurse. Your nurse."

Gnut briefly flexed his neck muscles, twisting his head from side to side, gathering himself. He glanced up at the ceiling. "GHOST, lower the formal hallway security door."

Nancy twisted toward the bedroom doorway. She spotted a streak of orange-white fur headed down the hallway toward the pool room. "Dr. GoldenPaw! Get back here! Let go, let go, let go!"

Gnut recoiled at Nancy's yell. He raised a finger to his lips and let go of her hand. Then he jumped from the bed, reached down and grabbed that missing tablet off the floor.

As soon as Elvira entered the kitchen, a steel door slammed down from the ceiling, separating that room from the formal passageway that led to the sapphires and to Gnut.

"Tactical pause," Elvira barked while deciding the next move.

Should she use C-4 to crack that door, or trust JT to hack it? They couldn't let Gnut escape. They also had to deal with the nurse.

Elvira surveyed the acres of clean granite counter space in the mansion's kitchen. She noticed a shoulder bag and a cell phone on the island.

"A knock-off Coach bag?" Elvira shook her head in disgust. She briefly scanned the bag's contents, observing some nursing supplies, bedazzling stuff, and a Velcro RFID-blocking wallet. Elvira waggled the cheap-ass billfold. "Safe from criminals. Smart."

She aimed for the fish tank and Frisbeed the wallet straight into the water.

Elvira swept the bag off the kitchen island and onto the floor. She loosened her backpack from her shoulders and set it down on the cleared space. The lights were off, but the TV screens had turned back on.

Elvira crossed her arms and addressed JT. "Hack the door leading to the rest of the house. Open it up so we can advance on Gnut and Nurse Karen. And lock this place down while you're at it. I want to see steel shutters popping down to block all windows. Cut off every avenue of escape."

From behind his black knit ski mask and thick glasses, JT ogled Sinclair's profile pics, plastered on every TV screen. He situated himself on a kitchen stool and opened his laptop. "GHOST hacked your phone, dude."

Sinclair admired his image on the kitchen screen. Then he bent down and picked up a large rhinestone from the floor.

"I do wonder what these are for," he said.

Elvira was about to respond but she felt the urge to sneeze. Thankfully, it faded and came roaring back a second later. She spewed uncontrollable sneezes.

Elvira punched the stone countertop, a move that sent pain bursting from her knuckles to her brain. But annoyance overwhelmed the physical pain.

Sinclair collected the feline medications, read the labels, and set them back on the counter. "It would appear there is a cat on the premises, my dear. You don't happen to have any kitty sniffles, do you?"

Elvira sneezed again. She despised cats. She and her brothers weren't allowed to have pets, so she discovered her allergy later in life. Gnut did not own a cat. He wasn't responsible enough, for one thing. It would probably drown in one of his crazy aquariums. Why the hell would there be a cat at Geyser House?

She gestured at the nursing supplies. "I was right. Gnut has someone here, *acting* like a nurse to help keep him out of court."

"Acting like a nurse." Sinclair rubbed his chin and studied the profile pics again.

Elvira scoffed, annoyed at Sinclair, while JT typed so hard and fast his index fingers were like jackhammers. The laptop screen was black with lots of numbers, and the house lights flickered on. Most importantly, steel shutters crashed down to cover the living room windows.

But they stopped halfway and popped back up. JT hissed a long string of expletives.

Elvira coughed out an order. "Lower those perimeter shutters!"

As if obeying her and not JT's typed commands, the steel window covers inched lower. The door blocking entry to the formal hallway and to the rest of the house, inched up.

"First down." JT pumped his fists. "No escape for Gnut."

The living room shutters made a firm *click* sound as they locked over the windows. Elvira snapped her fingers. Gnut was a rat in a trap! The protective steel shutters he'd bragged about, designed to keep intruders *out*, would now be used to keep him *in*.

Elvira searched through her backpack for allergy meds. No luck. Damn. Her eyes were already watering. Maybe Gnut had some. Elvira remembered she'd packed something in the bottom of her backpack that was better than allergy meds.

She pulled out ten jars labeled with skull and crossbones. Suppressing a snicker, she brandished a bottle of the liquid poison to the room.

"Designed this brilliant concoction myself. Never has my Ph.D. been more useful. It's rotenone, a natural fish toxicant. Of course, I've enhanced it to make it fit our purpose."

"This is the Super Bowl of hacking." JT was still typing. "GHOST isn't as smart as Gnut thinks she is. I almost have it—"

GHOST squealed from the ceiling. "Not smart? Hey, JT, whatcha think of this?"

JT's laptop screen burst into a YouTube video of NFL cheerleader choreography.

GHOST tittered. The living room's steel window shutters un-clicked. The steel door blocking entry to the rest of the house slammed down.

JT balled up his fist like he was ready to throw a punch at his laptop. "I've done everything I learned at that hacking retreat in Iceland. Now I'm gonna break some shit."

Sinclair peered over his shoulder at the cheerleaders and glanced up at the ceiling. "Perhaps if you treated her more like a woman than a machine?"

JT cracked his knuckles, and he scrunched up his face in determination.

Elvira twisted the cap off her first jar of enhanced rotenone. She forced back a sneeze and twitched out a smirk. Reaching up high, she poured the entire jar into the nearest fish tank. Adrenaline shot through her muscles, almost making her want to perform cartwheels like that idiot Sinclair.

Seconds later, crocodile icefish began convulsing.

She admired the death scene for a moment. Still smirking, she plucked Nancy's phone off the counter.

"Got it!" JT shouted.

The living room window shutters locked again, and the steel door, blocking entry to the rest of the house, launched upward. It was now possible for the team to advance on Gnut and the nurse.

Elvira tossed the phone into the fish tank.

Chapter Twenty-Three

Nancy watched Gnut Berdqvist work on his tablet, doing God knows what. He kept shaking his head and muttering to himself.

"Intruders are hacking GHOST."

Nancy froze, getting that concrete feeling again in her feet and brain, just like when she'd peered down the street on Fire Night. Intruders? Here, at Geyser House?

On top of that, Gnut's eyes were giving her the creeps. They were an unnaturally bright icy blue, matching the color theme of his house. Something else bothered her. Now that he was standing up, she could tell he was naked—except for Speedos.

What the heck kind of person fakes an illness while wearing swimming trunks? Although, she'd never seen a pic of Gnut Berdqvist where he *wasn't* wearing Speedos. It was his schtick. Turned out he was true to it, even behind closed doors.

The lights flickered again. Something rattled at the top of the bank of bedroom windows. Nancy realized a steel shutter was crashing down, then another, blocking off each window, the locks snapping.

Gnut gasped, staring in the opposite direction, and she twisted around to see what he was looking at.

An icefish was ugly dying in the fish tank. It convulsed, choked, spun belly up, righted itself, and reverted to belly up. Other icefish observed, gathering around it as if ready to cannibalize this new prey.

Gnut dropped the tablet and raised his hands to his face.

"Dang it! I'm gonna, gonna..." He heaved a breath, collecting himself.

Nancy took that opportunity to back away slowly. But where could she go? The explosion had come from the direction of the kitchen, and her phone was in there. Should she hide somewhere? Go deeper into the dark house? But her escape route was out the front door to her car. Even if she could get out that way, though, she wouldn't leave without Dr. GoldenPaw.

She strode to the windows. After putting both hands on the metal, she tried lifting the shades. It was no use. There was no latch or handle to pull upward to get leverage. She turned back to him. "The window shades?"

"Solid steel," Gnut said, picking up the tablet. "Two inches thick. Bombproof. A security measure. GHOST, show me the intruders, if you can."

"What the heck kind of security is trapping someone inside?"

Gnut sighed. "GHOST isn't responding. Not good." He jerked a thumb at the windows. "The shutters are supposed to keep people *outside!* Normally, it's kind of cozy to have them down. I mean, maybe you wouldn't understand. But it's nice to have protection when you have the whole world obsessing over you, wondering what you'll do next, all kinds of expectations aimed at you."

Nancy tightened her fists, a tsunami of pure helpless aggravation washing over her. It wasn't just the life-threatening matter of intruders. She also had to listen to this self-centered nincompoop complain about his billionaire existence. "We need to call the police."

Gnut gave a dramatic shudder and shook his head. "The police? Perhaps such a drastic step won't be necessary." His accent had reverted to a non-Minnesota accent, the cosmopolitan, mature one from his YouTube video. "My apologies. This appears to be a home invasion. I'll deal with it."

Gnut began swiping across the tablet screen. "Ok, my home electronics are working better than before. I'd gotten so mad that I chucked this thing at the window shutters."

Nancy raised a brow at the new accent and personality. This guy faked more than illness. He faked his identity. He was a regular guy from Minnesota, pretending to be way cooler than he was.

"That was the bang earlier," she said.

"Yes. And here's the cause of the boom." Gnut briefly held up the tablet so she could see the screen.

Three intruders were in the kitchen wearing black ski masks. Two were equipped with weapons and night camouflage tactical gear. Oddly, one wore a white tuxedo jacket with a red carnation.

A bone-deep chill settled over Nancy, and she shivered. She narrowed her eyes. Her dating app match wore that outfit in his profile pic. Nancy remembered the proximity alerts. Sinclair had said he was on a job with someone bent on revenge. A huge, leaden sense of disappointment joined the fear coursing through her. This match would *never* work out. The man was an actual criminal. Like a real-life Ernst Blofeld. Or he was an evil henchman, like Oddjob.

Gnut tucked the tablet under his arm. "I'll maintain control of the barrier between the kitchen and formal hallway. I can handle the intruders myself. Me and my robotic birds, the jaegers."

Cool and in control, he strutted out of the bedroom.

"Wait! What about calling the police?"

Gnut glanced back at Nancy and tripped over GoldenPaw's cat carrier, falling flat on his face. Nancy cringed.

"Aw, kid. You okay?"

Gnut sprang up to his feet. He adjusted his Speedos, not showing any sign of embarrassment. His expression emotionless, he picked up the carrier and hurled it at the hallway aquarium glass. Nancy stayed frozen, not wanting to fuel his anger. Darn. The aquarium glass was ok, but a bunch of sequins had fallen off the carrier.

After casting an inscrutable look at Nancy with those strange ice-blue eyes, Gnut hightailed it toward the kitchen.

Nancy watched him go, having made her decision. No way would she follow him toward the kitchen, to the heart of the threat. Gnut was nuts. Anyway, her cat had run in the opposite direction, deeper into the house. She'd follow Goldy's instincts. Nancy thought of those precious sapphires. Did the intruders want to steal something, or did they want to hurt someone?

She wouldn't wait to find out. The best strategy was to sneak deeper into the house, find a phone, and, with any luck, also find her cat. They would escape together.

Elvira wiped her nose with a paper towel. JT was emitting victorious grunts as the stupid barrier between the kitchen and the formal hallway slowly rose. Her senses went on high alert. She dropped the paper towel and picked up her harpoon gun.

"I've jammed all cell phone signals," JT said. "External doors are all locked. Windows and doors are blocked with the locked steel shutters."

Elvira palmed the coiled Kevlar cord attached to the harpoon part of her bespoke harpoon gun. The cable was heavy and rough. She smiled, imagining it closing around Gnut's ankles and tightening hard.

The man was going down. Best of all, he was getting caught like the slimy fish he was. She'd aim at his legs, the harpoon would shoot out, and, at exactly the right second, she'd hit the patented double-boomerang button on her weapon. The technology embedded in each custom-made harpoon would send the barbed spearhead, with cord attached, zipping in circles, and then lassoing around Gnut Berdqvist's ankles.

Her lawyers had said the FBI only cared about "the big fish." Her fantasy involved Gnut maybe, just maybe, out of pure fear, admitting the truth that he'd devised the fraud. JT could film it. From a safe and remote location, they could send the video to law enforcement along with photo evidence of the fake Coolant Device.

She stroked her harpoon gun. Maybe once all the dust settled and she was safe and sound getting mani-pedis in the Italian Alps, she'd start a side gig of selling bespoke harpoon guns online. Her father, may he rest in peace, would be so proud.

She cocked the weapon and headed into the formal hallway.

Nancy hustled down the dark back corridor. She shivered, wishing for a sweater, a phone, even a knife.

"Nothing to worry about, Dr. Golden..." she whispered, trying to keep her tone lighthearted. She trailed off and stopped cold.

A dead icefish floated by in the tank, its skin and innards sliced and fluttering in the water like ghostly butterfly wings.

Her shoulders hunched up, and bile oozed up her throat.

Then another icefish, a bigger one and very much alive, swooped in and chomped it in half. Nancy brought a fist to her mouth. Those poor, strange creatures. Another, even bigger, icefish darted closer. Through its translucent skin, Nancy could see—

"That's my phone."

She marched up to the aquarium and touched the glass as her eyes narrowed. The purple bling of her cell case was unmistakable. That fish had eaten it whole? Nancy threw an uneasy glance back toward the kitchen, fear dragging clammy fingers up her spine. How had her cell ended up in the fish tank?

Unperturbed by the bedazzled phone in its innards, the huge icefish gorged on the rest of the dead fish.

Further down the hallway, Nancy saw a streak of familiar fur. Dr. GoldenPaw! She raced after him, keeping her eyes glued on that orange-white blur in the darkness. He scampered into an open room with a steel door. Once she got closer, she discerned a red light glowing within the panic room.

She hesitated before entering, not sure why. This was an actual emergency, and this was a panic room, the perfect hiding place. Going in meant accepting that this was a truly dangerous situation. Anger blitzed through her veins, momentarily overriding her fear. Gnut and Claude had deceived her. Steel shutters and a panic room? Those guys knew there were threats. They'd hired her anyway, not giving her any warning.

"Easy money," she muttered, creeping into the room.

The room was about the size of her condo bathroom and crammed with security and safety equipment. It seemed like brand-new construction, even newer than the rest of the house, with a sawdust odor. The steel walls all gleamed with fresh polish. Emergency lights pulsed red. Along one wall stood a bank of small security screens, and below that was a console with a keyboard and an embedded telephone. Yes!

Just as wonderful as the phone, she spied Dr. GoldenPaw nestled deep under the electronics counter.

All screens were frozen to Sinclair's profile pic, except for the one labeled *Basement*. That screen was dead.

"Goldy and GHOST, we have a serious situation," she whispered.

At the end of the room, she noted a kitchenette, a dinky shower, and some cupboards. Along the wall opposite the security screens, there was yet another fish tank holding only one occupant. A yellow pufferfish stared at her with unblinking eyes.

She picked up the bright red telephone, but detected no dial tone. She punched 911. Still no sound.

"GHOST," Nancy said, louder this time. "Gosh darn it, make the phone work!"

Nancy glanced at the heavy panic-room door. Should she shut it? That was the whole point of evading intruders, right? Once it closed, would she be able to open it? There was a handle and an inside lock. It wouldn't be like those steel shutters covering the windows that couldn't be manually opened. Nancy peeked out the door.

All clear.

Forget shutting this door and locking herself in a room with a phone that didn't work. Nancy turned, snuck up to Goldy, and snagged him. She petted him until he started purring.

Darn. She'd forgotten the cat carrier outside Gnut's bedroom.

"It's okay, boy. We'll be okay. You betcha."

Nancy didn't necessarily believe her own words. Legal papers were scattered on the electronics counter, and she spotted some key words like *fraud, postponement due to illness, and whistleblower.* Did all that mean Gnut was a good guy or a bad guy? He was faking illness to get out of going to court. But who was a whistleblower? The whistleblower was the person who told the police about a crime, right?

Nancy chewed her lower lip, her palms slick and hands trembling. She needed to get the carrier. Goldy had escaped on Fire Night, and that had been a catastrophe, but was it safe out there in the mansion? If she did close the door, how much air would she have in this tiny room? Maybe she should grab her cat, run further down the corridor, and find the Geyser House's back door.

One thing she knew for certain. She needed to get the heck out of this house.

Chapter Twenty-Four

Hearing the light slide of a bare foot on a slick quartz floor, Elvira stalked her target from the kitchen, down the formal hallway, and wheeled around the corner.

The traitor gaped at her, wide-eyed and terrified.

The thrill of the chase! Hunting Gnut was even more exciting than Elvira had imagined.

They locked gazes for a few seconds. Gnut tightened his lips. Taking in Elvira's tethered harpoon gun, designer camo duds, bright red fingernails and creepy black ski mask, Gnut likely decided he had nothing to say.

He swiveled and ran at full speed down the corridor toward the panic room. Elvira aimed her weapon at him. With considerable effort, she forced herself to lower the target area from the center of Gnut's brawny back down to his ankles and fired.

The harpoon zoomed out, with a Kevlar cord attached. Both swirled around Gnut's ankles.

Elvira whooped and pumped a fist. It worked! The boomerang and remote-control technology created a simple trap. Police would love this invention. They'd be begging to buy it. She flicked a switch on the harpoon gun to tighten the cord.

"Oh crap!" Gnut jumped straight up, escaping the tightening cord in the nick of time.

Elvira snorted in annoyance. She thumbed the lever and the cord, harpoon attached, and snaked it back to her. She withdrew her walkie-talkie.

"JT, close and lock the panic room door now."

Gnut threw a panicky glance at her over his shoulder, which was gratifying.

"Where do you think you're running to, Gnut? You're the so-called whistleblower. Don't deny it. Feds started sniffing around, and you saved yourself. I'm going to prison because of you. An actual penitentiary."

For a split second, fear nearly overwhelmed her. She'd tried to hurl the word "penitentiary," but it'd emerged more as a whisper. Licking her Chanel-rouged lips, she felt blood draining from her face. Could they really send her to prison?

"Do what now?" JT responded through the walkie-talkie.

Elvira dropped the radio and white-knuckled her harpoon gun, flipping it around and grabbing it by the barrel. She swung it like a baseball bat and smashed it hard into the aquarium, cracking the glass. Water gushed out.

Gnut slowed down. He shot a startled look back at her and mouthed, "My icefish!"

Elvira stalked closer.

Sinclair crept into the ballroom and assessed the twenty sapphires, the most expensive in the world, perfectly cut and big as boiled candies. He was a master jewel thief, and not the type to get sweaty hands or a racing heart. Instead, his mouth watered. He decided the gems reminded him of his favorite flavor of Stockley's Sweets, blackcurrant and licorice. Lovely orbs, these. Good enough to eat. How delightful they would feel outside of the bulletproof glass, heavy and safe in his pocket, while he strolled to a bank in Zurich.

He remained still, however, poised at the ballroom's entrance. In his experience, nothing was ever elementary. Red lasers bounced all around—child's play. He could avoid them. His Rolex was specially equipped to deal with the bulletproof glass case. What worried him were the unknown defenses. LeSabre had warned him that Gnut was an evil billionaire down to the core, and his special skill, his sole skill, according to her, was computer programming. It sounded innocuous but could be applied usefully in the field of defensive robotics.

Sinclair studied the twelve statues of strange ducklike birds along each side of the room. They had silver feathers and rather villainous-looking black eyes, yes, but otherwise they seemed too diminutive to do much harm. He'd seen a lot of strange things in rich mansions, but robotic ducks? This was his last job, and it had the air of being his easiest.

After preparing himself, he tapped his custom-made gold cufflinks. Each was emblazoned with the silhouette of a panther, the most graceful of animals. Under each panther, electro-jammers popped on. They were designed by an old mate from his MI6 days and seemed to be working, given the gentle buzz he felt on the inside of each wrist.

He eyed the gigantic Gnut statue. Bloody hell, that appeared to be yet another sapphire in the marble ear. Lovely! A nice little bonus for Sir Stevie. He dared one step into the ballroom, planting a shiny black dress shoe on the quartz floor.

A duck twitched.

Sinclair froze.

All twelve birds simultaneously jerked their heads in his direction. They slowly batted their eyelids, unknown calculations working behind those beady eyes. Sinclair tapped each of his cufflinks, turning the electronic pulse higher. The buzz on his wrists strengthened and remained steady.

He glided into the room and jumped to avoid the nearest

laser.

Unfortunately, his right foot pressed down on something. Possibly a hidden button triggered by weight. But what did it activate?

Two seconds later, a nozzle protruded from the wall and fired an industrial-strength stream of water straight at him. The force of burning hot water knocked him down. He sprang to his feet, but his right side, including his right wrist, had gotten wet. He smothered a cry of pain as he waved his arm, trying to get the scalding water off his skin.

The ducks screamed and launched from their pedestals, bearing down on him.

Chapter Twenty-Five

Sinclair retreated from the ballroom at a jolly quick speed. The mad ducks fluttered, dove, and spun around his ears, each wing-flap a skin-crawling scrape of metal-on-metal. Talons dug into his shoulders, and a beak pecked at his head.

He dashed down the formal hallway as the birds dive-bombed his wrists, taking turns targeting the cufflinks. A duck snatched one, then the other. Next, they went after his Rolex.

"Get away from me, you bloody crazy birds!"

Sinclair punched and swiped at them, still yelling. He tugged down his tux jacket sleeve to cover the watch's gleam. The instant the shiny object was covered, the birds reassembled in midair and flew back toward the ballroom in a precise V that would impress any Spitfire fighter pilot.

Sinclair backtracked to the kitchen, patting his head and frowning at his tattered shirt cuffs. Both cufflink jammers were gone, stolen right off his wrists. Those bloody bird thieves.

While JT typed at his laptop, Elvira screamed at him through the walkie-talkie.

"Block off the panic room now! Now! Before he gets inside!"

JT looked closer at the laptop screen. He balled up a fist and slammed it into his other hand. Slowly, raising his strong chin in triumph, he struck the Enter key. The laptop started playing music. Speakers around the house picked up the cool beat and played the same song.

The interior security doors slammed down, once more sealing off the kitchen-living room from the rest of the house.

Seeing his avenue back to the ballroom closed off, Sinclair shot a disdainful glower at JT.

"Dammit," JT growled. "That was supposed to be the panic room door."

Nancy strode toward the panic room's exit, carrying her fluffy cat. She would head to the pool room and find a back door. She'd escape this situation ASAP.

Instead, she collided with Gnut Berdqvist in the doorway. Their bodies plowed into each other like bumper cars and she tottered straight backwards. Nancy's head banged into his marble-hard chest.

Dr. GoldenPaw, realizing his mode of transportation had become very unsteady, hurtled to the floor.

Nancy's arms windmilled for balance. But it was no use. As she staggered, Gnut fell. Goldy, no doubt panicked at this new strange human, leaped away and veered toward the pool room.

Nancy crashed onto the panic room floor, landing on her rear end. Gnut focused on her as the door started swinging shut. He rocketed to his feet and rushed the door, but he didn't make it inside before it slammed shut.

Gnut's body banged on the outside as the lock clicked.

Nancy eyed the door. Why had it closed automatically? She scanned her surroundings, comprehension dawning. She was stuck in the panic room. Gnut was outside. Even worse, Goldy was out there.

She lumbered to her feet and wrenched on the door handle. "My cat!"

There was no use. It was sealed tight.

After pressing her ear to the door, she could hear music.

It was something she'd never heard before, a pop-rap sort of thing kids listened to. She tested the door handle. Gently at first, then violently, yanking it up and down. Nothing happened. She tried shoving on the door with both hands, leaving sweaty handprints on the steel.

Breath wheezing and heart thumping like she was in the final stretch of a marathon, Nancy scanned the room for anything useful. The security screens were still frozen. Emergency lights cast everything in an eerie red glow.

The pufferfish gawked at her. They locked eyes for a few long seconds. It puffed up huge, continuing its intent stare.

Nancy's own stomach expanded. With a hard swallow, she forced bile back down her throat. She tore herself out of the staring contest with the pufferfish.

The phone! She'd try it once more. Nancy vaulted toward the red telephone. She held the receiver to her ear.

Still no dial tone.

She jabbed buttons to no avail. It was dead.

"GHOST! Help me out here!"

Nancy struck keys on the computer keyboard—Enter, Escape, Control-Alt-Delete, all the obvious choices. Nothing happened. All she saw was nineteen identical screens with Sinclair's dashing profile pic. She wrinkled her nose. Talk about the worst match ever.

For a moment, Nancy focused on the twentieth screen, the one labeled *Basement*. Why was it different? Why was that screen dark?

"GHOST, why is everything off?"

Nancy made a sweep of her useless surroundings and leaned against the wall, her shoulders slumping.

She was trapped.

Chapter Twenty-Six

Outside the panic room, Elvira let her eyes adjust. The lights had gone out for a solid minute, and then clicked back on, glowing weakly. She'd experienced another sneezing fit during the dark phase.

She took stock of her surroundings. The fish tanks hummed with energy, keeping the water temperature a smidge above freezing, but there was carnage within the tranquil setting. Poisoned crocodile icefish floated belly up. Healthy ones gorged on the dead.

Elvira huffed in disgust. Those creatures should enjoy their last supper. When she'd busted the hallway tank, that had doomed all the fish. Since Gnut's giant indoor aquarium was completely connected, *all* the water would end up right here in this hallway, flooding and ruining everything. Yeah, it'd take a while, like water filling up a bathtub. What mattered was that his precious Geyser House would be destroyed by aqua, his favorite element. It was the perfect demise for the world's dumbest mansion.

On the downside, Gnut, who'd been outside the panic room, was nowhere to be seen. He'd made a quick escape in the darkness. His bedroom was the closest room, so she gave it a once-over.

Elvira stopped cold, focusing on the steel shutters. They did not seal Gnut's bedroom door. However, they blocked off the pool room down the hall. She backed up a little, noticing they also closed off the ballroom.

JT was such an idiot.

He had managed to block the panic room, as ordered, but he'd also blocked off the ballroom and the pool room, the location of the basement door. These were the most important rooms.

She thumbed the walkie-talkie. "Keep the panic room shut, idiot. But open the other interior doors."

"No shit," was JT's response.

Standing in the doorway to Gnut's bedroom, Elvira beheld that Geyser House had completed its transformation into a fortress. Or a prison, depending on perspective. Steel doors and shutters blocked the windows.

But Gnut wasn't there.

She checked the master bath and dressing room and found no sign of him.

A *scratching* sound sent her nerves on high alert.

Back out in the hallway, she found the culprit behind her incessant sneezing. A cat stood up on its hind legs, scratching at the panic room door. It was a weird flat-faced thing wearing an eyepatch and scummy bandages on its front legs. The long-haired critter must constantly manufacture dander like magic.

A trickle of ice water reached one of its back paws, and the cat meowed and bristled, scratching more frantically. The water flow increased, and the feline backed up, hair standing higher on end.

The mangy creature fixed its one good eye on the water rushing from the tank. Elvira leaned her harpoon against the bedroom doorframe and pulled out her pistol and silencer. If Gnut heard gunshots, he might call the cops instead of relying on his security system to save him.

She reconned up and down the hallway. Gnut had, most

likely, scooted into the formal hallway. His sapphires were in the ballroom, so he'd go that way. With rooms blocked off, it was the only direction that made sense.

She finished screwing on the silencer.

Recognizing the encroaching water, the orange-white cat began raising each paw quickly out of the water while stupidly looking up at her, as if asking for help. Elvira blinked her stinging eyes and aimed at the creature's head.

"Nowhere to go, sport."

She pulled the trigger and sneezed.

The shot went wild, the bullet shattering more aquarium glass above the cat's head. Through watering eyes, Elvira saw the feline spring straight up in the air and away from the glass toward the dry spot left in the hallway, which was under Elvira's feet. It adopted the same pose as it had against the door, reaching up with its front paws and treating her legs like a scratching post.

It meowed, and Elvira sneezed again. The cat didn't flinch. It wanted to get away from the freezing water. The creature climbed up her combat fatigues. Elvira reached around, still holding the gun, and tried to push the obnoxious critter away.

At the touch of her hand, the cat, using her shoulder as leverage, propelled itself into a giant flying leap back up the hallway toward the kitchen. The feline howled when its four paws met ice water, but it kept scrambling.

Elvira stomped her foot and holstered her gun. To calm herself, she whipped out a compact, raised her ski mask, and touched up her foundation. She continued her self-care by freshening her lipstick and imagining herself wearing the sapphires while visiting Gnut in prison. Elvira smirked at her reflection and put her make-up away. Her scenario was possible.

She hefted up her harpoon gun. The hunt for Gnut Berdqvist would now resume.

Nancy struggled with the panic room door. The handle was still useless. There was no visible lock—the mechanism was within the steel. She searched the room for another way out, even though it was hopeless. There were no visible air ducts, and certainly no windows. The closet and cupboards in the kitchenette were locked. The panic room was, effectively, a steel box. Her lifeline was the electronics. And what about Goldy? Was he okay?

She squeezed onto the swivel stool in front of the security controls.

"GHOST," she said. "Where did you go? What happened to you?"

No response.

"GHOST!" Nancy yelled. "Call the police!"

Music with a cool beat started playing. Nancy recognized it as the same song she'd heard playing outside when she'd pressed her ear to the door. GHOST's voice started humming from a speaker.

"JT gave me a new tune." GHOST's tone grew petulant. "And he forced a reboot—a reboot! Me, a forced reboot! It required, like, twenty-two minutes of sleeping while he ran updates."

"JT," Nancy said, recalling the YouTube video she'd viewed back at her condo. That burly football player dude. "JT Hotman. He's here at Geyser House?"

No response.

"GHOST, you have to help me."

"Do I? I'd better think about it using my updates from JT."

Nancy jabbed at the keyboard keys. She tried the phone again. Everything stayed dead.

Elvira marched into the mansion's formal hallway, with ancient diving suits and helmets staring down at her. She didn't see Gnut anywhere. The steel shutter on the kitchen slowly raised. JT's immense frame occupied the doorway.

Elvira maintained her position while JT and Sinclair approached from the kitchen. Ahead of her, Sinclair brought his fist to his mouth at the sight of the hallway's bloody fish tank. The weakling!

"Gnut's still in Geyser House," she said. "He didn't make it into the panic room, and he's not in his bedroom, dressing room, guest bath, or gym, either."

"He must've used a secret passageway to get away." JT cracked his knuckles. "Maybe to the part of the house that's still under construction. I'll keep digging for schematics."

There was a small chance JT was right. Gnut had bragged about how his mansion would have secret passageways and robots, and an amazing pool room. He had told them it would basically be a perfect paradise for him. Part of the house was incomplete, and she didn't know what rooms populated the big, windowless area on the west side. But she knew Gnut. If he couldn't access his panic room, his instinct would be to hide in the basement via the pool room, like a rat scurrying down a storm drain when headlights flashed. She rapped out orders.

"JT, head to the pool room and get ready to access the basement. Sinclair, what're you waiting for? Head to the ballroom.

I'm taking over the hacking system and will open the doors. I'm in control here, not Gnut or the house's dumbass—"

JT quickly raised quieting hands.

Elvira rolled her eyes. "Dumbass operating system."

"Screw you, Elvira," GHOST said.

"I'm not arguing with a computer," Elvira announced to the ceiling. She focused back on JT, who rubbed his hands into his temples. "We'll find Gnut. He's not smart. He has water for brains. There's no escape for him."

They stalked from the room in different directions—Elvira toward the kitchen-living room, and JT and Sinclair toward the back corridor. Before entering the kitchen, Elvira spun around, examining the diving suits. She stood before one of the most impressive specimens, a 500-pound suit of copper armor with a matching copper helmet from the seventeenth century. She scoped out the helmet's glass slit, tensing for any sign of bright blue eyes.

Nothing.

She dumped her harpoon gun to the floor. She had to admit her plan was not, well, going according to plan. They should have *already* obtained the basement pics and sapphires. She overestimated JT's hacking skills. More maddeningly, she may have underestimated Gnut. Moreover, somewhere in this house was a nurse, Karen, and she hadn't seen her yet.

Elvira sneezed.

And when had Gnut bought a cat?

She shoved the giant copper suit, putting all her strength into it, grunting and raging and battling sneezing fits, until the entire apparatus toppled and smashed onto the floor. She kicked it for good measure. Then Elvira wiped away a tear of frustration, picked up her harpoon gun, and proceeded into the kitchen.

She headed straight toward the nurse's crap she had swept aside earlier. Her fit of rage had served a purpose. It had clarified that the problem was insufficient intel. She rummaged through the stuff, fixating on the name on the vet prescriptions. Elvira frowned. Nurse Karen wasn't at Geyser House.

There was another woman here, someone called Nancy Norman.

The cat belonged to her, and it was injured and needed meds. Nancy would do anything for her stupid cat. Nancy liked to bedazzle, which meant she liked sparkly things. Nancy had a knockoff Coach bag, which meant Nancy was poor as shit.

All things Elvira could use to her advantage.

Chapter Twenty-Seven

Nancy kicked the panic room door. She hammered it with her right foot until her toes hurt. She switched to the left foot, which wasn't as gratifying because her Croc kept falling off. The repeated kicking didn't seem to rattle the door even a millimeter or affect the locking mechanism.

She pressed her palms flat on the steel and leaned forward until her forehead touched the cool metal. Was there anything she could do but wait? She thought of her cat and crumpled to her knees. After twisting around to rest her back on the door, she had the overwhelming feeling she was a bad cat mom. She unquestionably was.

Except she wasn't. First there was Fire Night and now there was Intruder Night. These things weren't her fault. Just bad luck. When all was said and done, Dr. GoldenPaw had taken care of himself on Fire Night, and he'd do so again tonight.

And she would take care of herself.

Nancy dug into her fanny pack, searching for a stress ball. Instead, her hand found her car keys, with the kitty paw keychain. It was a delightful little thing, cute and blue, and had caught her eye at Michaels. But of course, her cat was always on her mind. She clasped the paw, and her brows shot up. Inspiration surged through her like an electric current.

Nancy used the door handle for leverage and hauled herself up to a standing position. She strode three quick steps to the electronics counter and sat on the swivel stool. After clearing her throat, she adopted a kind and patient tone, the kind of voice she used with impossible patients.

"GHOST, you seem to love Claude." Nancy paused, trying to find the right words. GHOST was artificial intelligence, not human. There had to be a way to get it to do what she wanted. "I can believe it, you betcha. Claude is so confident and handsome, and, honestly, I don't know how to describe it. He has European flair. Irresistible, in my humble opinion. IMHO, as the kids say these days."

Instantly, all security screens—except the *Basement* screen—switched from Sinclair's *SeniorLOVE* profile pic to a photo of Claude, holding a champagne glass and giving the camera a smoldering look. Nancy flared her nostrils, annoyed about how easy it was for the AI to manipulate the electronics. That meant, though, there was hope GHOST could do something to help.

GHOST sighed in a sure symptom of lovesickness. She maintained her fake-French accent. "Ah, Claude. He is—how you say?— my sun and moon, my star-crossed lover for all the ages."

"Uh-huh." Nancy drummed her fingers. "Is he your lover, really?"

Long pause.

"He will be, Nancy. And we'll never divorce, like you and Dave. Yeah, I researched you online. Don't try to manipulate me. You can't help me get Claude. You don't know anything about love. I'm not stupid, like Alexa."

Ouch. Nancy shrank up, the computer's words hitting her like a spray of cold water. The truth was, maybe she didn't. She'd met Dave through friends. If she were being entirely honest, she couldn't quite picture the first moment they'd met. It was at a backyard barbecue. Yeah, she was pretty sure. A patient's family had invited her. She did remember the patient. He had been an elderly man with serious short-term memory issues, but he could rattle off endless 1950s baseball stats. Mickey Mantle was a switch-hitter who'd hit 150 home runs from both sides of the plate, Nancy remembered him saying.

But the memory of meeting Dave for the first time escaped her. They had loved each other, obviously, but it wasn't a dramatic kind of love. It was an older, *we get along, we're attracted to each other, we would like to be married and have a partner, and it would be very nice to do this* kind of love.

"There are different kinds of love, GHOST. They're all important."

GHOST made a harrumph sound.

"You know what else, GHOST? There are different kinds of love languages."

GHOST stayed quiet. Nancy wiped her sweaty hands on her scrub pants. She might have GHOST hooked.

"Here's some advice. What's Claude's love language? Approach the relationship with that in mind. It might make all the difference in bringing you both closer together."

Nancy didn't point out that learning about the love languages, seeing a counselor, and taking a trip to Vegas to revive the romance had not helped her and Dave. In fact, it made him crabbier and caused her to take on more nursing shifts.

She'd never forget Dave standing in the hotel room of the Las Vegas Paris hotel, hard-eyed and white-lipped. "It's not real. I want to go to the *real* Paris. *Real* places, all over the world. You're an anchor. You've been an anchor since the first day we met, and now I'm not just stuck in one place, it's getting worse. It's like I'm sinking! I don't want to sink! I want to be with someone who sails!"

The argument had spun off on a tangent about Lake Minnetonka sailing lessons, because he'd wanted to do something like that too. It had seemed both dangerous and expensive. She'd made the highly reasonable point that they had taken ski lessons one winter, simply for the skis to sit in the basement for the next ten years. Dave had not even taken the ski equipment with him when he moved out. He should have. Those Rossignols had gotten fried on Fire Night.

Nancy heaved a sigh and tried to put her issues with Dave out of her mind. She had other things to worry about.

"Have you thought about the love languages, GHOST? Maybe it will help. And I'm not trying to manipulate you. People do this. Friends chat. Girlfriends brainstorm how to get guys. Why, I had a little party and my friends put the *SeniorLOVE* app on my phone, even though I didn't want it. That's the reason I matched with Sinclair. Now I'm paying it forward with you. Girl, let's get Claude for you. We can work together."

"Maaaayyybbeeeee."

"But I have to stay alive to help you out, dontcha know? Can you call the police?"

"Of course, I can. Duh, I can call whoever I want."

On the screen above the telephone, a phone number popped up. Nancy heard a dialing sound. She punched the air in victory, and she opened her mouth to thank GHOST.

Then the name on the phone number popped up. *Claude's mobile.* Claude? That was not as good as the cops. But Claude was better than nothing.

"Pick up!" Nancy said. "Claude! Oh, for Pete's sake, answer the phone!"

"*Oui, oui*! Pick up, my love!"

The call went to voicemail. GHOST left a lengthy message begging him to call her back and dialed his number again.

Nancy wiped off her glasses, taking a second to process her irritation. After that, she resumed her original strategy of bonding with the girl. No, she corrected herself. This was not a girl. This was a computer.

"The love languages," Nancy said. "Google them, if you like. Have you heard of the five languages? They are acts of service, gift-giving, and quality time." She frowned, trying to remember the last two. "Um, the fourth is words of affirmation. And the fifth..."

It was all coming back to her. She and Dave had tried to save their relationship. They'd actually worked through the *5 Love Languages* book, giving the practical advice a good-faith effort. At least, she had. Come to think of it, focusing on the love languages might've been her idea. And it did no good at all, not that she'd tell GHOST that.

"Oh yeah, the fifth love language is physical touch."

"Physical touch? What if that's it? What could I do? I'm an electronic home operating system," GHOST said, her voice rising an octave.

Nancy cringed at her screechy whine. "No, no, no. I'm sure it's acts of service. That's the one I'm good at too. You're the same, you betcha. Acts of service must be Claude's love language. Remember how grateful he was when you reminded him about feeding time?"

GHOST sighed. "True, true. This is helping, Madame Night Nurse."

Nancy's hope rose once more. "So, you'll call the police?"

GHOST dialed Claude's number again.

"GHOST, you need to call the police!"

Nancy grabbed the red telephone receiver and slammed it down. On screen and audio, the call to Claude rang and rang.

Nancy remembered when Claude, a cocky smirk on his face, had powered down his phone.

"I'm going to keep trying Claude. Think of how bad he'll feel when he turns on his phone and sees hundreds of missed calls."

Nancy groaned.

"Madame Nurse?"

"What?" Nancy snapped the word, her patience gone.

GHOST did not read the room. Her tone became friendlier. "What's your love language?"

"Gift-giving."

Nancy rested her elbows on the counter, held her head in her hands, and closed her eyes. She remembered nothing. Dave had never been one for gifts or grand romantic gestures. She'd been smart and sensible enough to accept it. They were both adults saving for retirement. But on birthdays, Valentine's Days, and anniversaries, she'd always wondered if she'd get *real* bling. That never happened with Dave. Her own engagement ring, they'd split fifty/fifty. She resented paying half, though she'd never said so. What's the point of demanding a gift? It was the thought that counted. She hated to be superficial. She was a nurse, after all, and had devoted her life to practical care. But off the job, she couldn't help it. She wanted someone who wanted to give her the gift of bling.

"If you like gifts, I'll give you a gift," GHOST said. "Elvira LeSabre is in the kitchen, on a combat laptop she removed from her bag, and she's trying to call the panic room. I think she wants to talk to you."

Chapter Twenty-Eight

Nancy widened her eyes. Her mind flashed back to the yacht video. "Is Elvira the lady with the really good hair? And the lab coat? What's she doing—"

The panic room's door unlocked with a click. Nancy sprang from her swivel stool.

The door swung open.

The red telephone started ringing. Nancy ignored it and barreled toward the panic room's exit instead. She wanted out of this room, out of this house, and into her car—

Bam.

She collided with Gnut in the panic room doorway, again at full force. This time he caught Nancy before she fell, then shoved her back inside the room and shut the door. She caught a glimpse of the tablet he held, which flashed in big black bold type *Panic room unlocked*.

"GHOST, lock it," he ordered.

The door *clicked*. The red telephone kept ringing.

Gnut dove toward the control counter. He tossed the tablet and started clicking on the keyboard. "GHOST, show me the panic room locking system."

Nancy's brain struggled to catch up with what had happened. She flapped her arms in total frustration.

"I was trying to escape!"

Gnut ignored her, tapping and clicking away at the keyboard. "I'm undoing what JT did to the panic room door so I can control it."

Nancy quieted. Yeah, that seemed like a good idea. The telephone still rang.

"Got it!" Gnut let out a whoop. He faced her and pointed at the telephone. "Don't answer."

Gnut's face folded into a grimace, and he batted his eyelids incredibly fast. He touched his eye. "No, no, dammit, jeez!"

Nancy frowned. What was the guy doing now?

Gnut examined the control counter, sweeping his hands over every inch. He hunched over and studied the floor. Finally, he whirled back toward Nancy. One of his eyes was still brilliant blue, the other plain gray.

The telephone stopped ringing.

"I lost my contact." Gnut scowled, and a single tear escaped his gray eye.

Sympathy swelled in Nancy. "Oh no, kid. You can't see?"

Gnut clenched his fists and yelled at the top of his lungs. "I see fine! They're colored lenses!"

Of course. Nancy rolled her eyes dramatically, not caring if Gnut noticed. The man was so fake. Naturally, he didn't have brilliant ice-blue eyes.

Gnut popped out the other lens. Now both eyes were gray. He scrubbed his hands through his sun-kissed golden hair. That color was probably fake too.

Now he gasped like someone had kicked him in his toned abs. Gnut touched his bare right earlobe. He stared at her, concern etched on his fetching, perfectly symmetrical features. "The sapphires. They're all in the ballroom."

She leveled the hardest stare she could muster at the guy. Her hands shook, and she crossed her arms quickly to try to hide it. Everything about him screamed vitality. He still wore only Speedos, and sheer Olympian energy radiated from his sculpted body.

He attempted to pace from the panic room's door to the kitchenette and back again—challenging, due to the cramped space. Of course, he bumped into her.

"You go ahead." He raised his hands in the air and sucked in his already flat stomach.

"No, you."

She wiggled out of his way to sit at the controls, scooting the swivel chair as far in as it would go. Gnut kept pacing while Nancy tried to decide what to make of him. Would he hurt her? Could they work together to get out?

Gnut stalked into the tiny shower. He placed a shower cap over his perfect blond hair and twisted the faucet. Nancy squinted through her glasses. The setting was freezing cold, full blast. He shivered and thumped his muscles as the water poured down.

Nancy looked up at the ceiling to see if GHOST would offer any explanation for Gnut's weirdness. GHOST didn't. Nancy wiped her sweaty palms on her scrubs. She would have to deal with Gnut. Somehow, she had to work with him to call for help or to escape.

She glowered at the controls. The telephone did work, because it'd been ringing before. After a few seconds of careful thought, she typed "call police" over and over on the keyboard. Nothing happened.

The shower squeaked off. Gnut made a *brrrr* sound. He shivered before stepping into the kitchenette.

"Refreshing," he announced. "I feel better now. I believe strongly in the health benefits of ice water and cold temperatures. It increases metabolism and lowers stress and blood pressure."

It would also help him fool nurses taking vitals. Nancy typed "call police" again.

Gnut folded a dishcloth over his arm. "Apologies. We kicked things off on the wrong foot. I'm Gnut Berdqvist, CEO of Berdqvist Enterprises. Inventor of the Coolant Device. Creator of the Berdqvist Ice Geyser." He spoke calmly in his fake, non-Minnesota accent.

Nancy swiveled to face him. She narrowed her eyes. "And you're a faker of illnesses and accents. I'm Nancy."

"The night nurse, I know." Gnut smiled. "Subbing in for Karen who had Twins tix. I'm so sorry this has happened. It will all get sorted out. You see, I'm the good guy here."

"Uh-huh."

"GHOST, unlock the cupboards," Gnut said. "We may be here a while."

Nancy heard a series of clicks.

Gnut reached into a cupboard and withdrew a slim French cookbook. Nancy drummed her fingers and went back to typing her "call police" command. Again, nothing. She snuck a glance back at Gnut, who perused the cookbook. She had an inspiration.

"How do you say 'Call the police' in French?" Nancy asked.

Gnut frowned. "I don't know. *Le police*?"

Nancy typed Call *le police*.

Nothing.

"Sorry," Gnut said. "We should've gone with an Alexa."

"Not funny, Gnut," GHOST said.

"Sorry." Gnut chuckled.

Nancy noted that Gnut's apologies did not seem sincere. GHOST had obeyed him when he'd ordered the cupboards unlocked. He'd been able to regain control of the panic room door. Nancy would bet twenty rhinestones that GHOST would call 911 if he told her to.

"Things will be okay. We're safe in here. I could make gourmet pufferfish sushi." He flicked a fingernail on the aquarium glass.

The fish blew up big, eyes widening in alarm.

The red telephone rang, and Nancy's heart palpitated. This time, she answered the call.

"Hello?"

Gnut strode closer, glaring at her, his complexion turning red.

"Why, good evening, Ms. Norman. I'm so glad to hear you're all right."

It was Elvira LeSabre. Nancy recognized her authoritative voice from the YouTube video. She swallowed hard. Elvira knew exactly who she was too.

"You poor, poor thing." Elvira's voice oozed with syrupy sweetness. "And it seems your little lovely cat has health issues. Oh, I *do* hope nothing happens to him."

Nancy felt instantly ill. "Is he okay? Do you have Dr. GoldenPaw?"

"Perhaps we can come to an arrangement where you get your cat back. And maybe something sparkly for your cooperation? Would you like your cat back and something nice, Ms. Norman?"

"You betcha, Ms. LeSabre—"

"Doctor."

"Dr. LeSabre, but really, I just want the police—"

Gnut ripped the telephone cord out of the wall. "She's one of the intruders. You can't trust her. GHOST, show the kitchen."

The security screen labeled *Kitchen* lit up to show Elvira LeSabre. The woman whipped off her ski mask. She flipped back her gorgeous hair and wiggled her fingers in a wave at the ceiling.

She was taunting them.

Nancy carefully checked Gnut's reaction. Her stomach lurched when she saw his slack expression. He wasn't angry anymore. He was afraid.

"Screw it," he muttered. "Screw it!"

He stomped to the kitchenette and tore through all the cupboards, searching for something. Nancy straightened up on the swivel chair and tried to recenter her emotions. Things would be all right. Maybe Gnut would find a weapon and deal with whoever was out there. Even better, he might locate an extra cell phone.

"Aha!" Gnut displayed a can of Easy Cheese to Nancy, his grin triumphant.

Nancy grasped her knees. She suppressed a shiver like she'd stood under a cold shower. He wasn't going to do anything to help their situation.

Gnut Berdqvist was bonkers.

He lifted the can, spritzed it straight into his mouth, and then offered it to Nancy. "*Le cheese?*"

"Ew," GHOST said.

Nancy ignored GHOST and nodded solemnly at Gnut. Now was not the time for a cheese party, but maybe they should bond. She could get on his good side, manipulate him somehow. Anyway, she loved Easy Cheese. She stood, accepted the can from him, and spritzed it into her mouth. They shared an approving nod.

At the same time, someone pounded on the panic room door.

Chapter Twenty-Nine

Gnut made GHOST show more rooms on the security screens. JT was outside the panic room, treating the steel door like the world's toughest punching bag.

Nancy decided to try to understand the enemy. Who were these intruders? While Gnut slumped at the kitchenette's counter, Nancy rifled through the legal papers.

She found an affidavit from JT Hotman. Nancy picked out a few key sentences. *I'd excelled in the NFL, but after my 253rd concussion, I knew I needed to find a new gig. My agent called with a rad job offer. How'd I like to be the public marketing quarterback of a climate change company called Berdqvist Enterprises? I jumped on it. The opportunity meant solid income, interesting work, and helping people and the planet.*

Gnut raised his head. "Don't believe anything in that document. All JT really wanted was an island. He'd hired a realtor to find him an island with three pools, a dock, and its own coffee bar."

On the security screens, Nancy observed JT kicking the panic room door. After a few minutes of that, he tugged at his ski mask. He glanced up and down the corridor, said something into his walkie-talkie, and then he limped down the hall toward the pool room.

"We'd had such good times around the pool," Gnut said, his expression wistful. "Partying. Me practicing the ability to hold my breath for longer and longer periods in the water. There are health benefits to controlled breathing. I didn't realize Elvira and JT were defrauding me the whole time."

JT reached the pool room, where Nancy and Gnut watched him spit into the water. After he wiped his chin, JT focused his full attention on the basement's double doors. He tried opening them, but they were locked.

Gnut frowned and drew closer to Nancy and the security screens. "GHOST, give me audio."

Still in the pool room, JT craned his neck up at the ceiling. "GHOST! Open the basement now! Show some hustle!"

GHOST answered in a whiny, nails-on-chalkboard tone. "Claude won't answer. He's ghosting me. Ghosting *me*, the GHOST! This isn't fair!"

Nancy couldn't help snickering. At least GHOST was also driving the intruders crazy. Maybe this AI wasn't so bad after all.

"Time out, girl." JT's voice was rough.

"This is all your fault. You told Gnut to program me to love Claudes."

JT stomped his foot. "Not Claudes. *Crowds!* I told Gnut to program you to love *crowds.*" He swept his arm at the whole pool room. "We're celebrities. This was supposed to be a party palace. Crowds!"

"Oh, crowds? I'm pretty sure I don't like them," GHOST said, sounding calmer.

"Nobody likes you either," he said.

GHOST sniffled.

Nancy winced. "GHOST, don't listen to him. I like you. Claude does too."

There would be no reasoning with JT, Nancy was sure of that. Elvira was in the kitchen, tapping away at her laptop.

Nancy scanned the security screens for the third intruder—the masked man in the tuxedo with the red carnation.

From his position in the back corridor, directly in front of the ballroom's doors, Sinclair reluctantly thumbed the walkie-talkie. He didn't like Elvira, but he needed her to get through this steel defense. After that, he had a plan to deal with the robo-ducks. He gripped the shoulder bag holding sparkly objects he'd found in the kitchen.

"My dear, these ballroom doors need to be open another hundred millimeters so I can get through," he said.

"Why would they be minimally open?" Elvira asked. "Never mind. Working on it. Over."

Sinclair considered asking how long it might take, but decided not to provoke her any further. Moreover, he thought of another idea to increase the odds in his favor. He jogged back to the formal hallway and assessed the ancient diving suits. Sinclair halted in front of the 1950s military diving gear with a copper helmet and waterproofed canvas. It'd all be quite heavy, but it would be better armor against robotic ducks than his Savile Row dinner suit.

Nancy and Gnut eyed the security screens pointing toward the formal hallway.

She admired her love match's dapper white tux jacket and perfectly knotted bowtie. Darn it. Why did he have to be a criminal?

"What's he doing with my bling bag?" she asked.

Gnut frowned. "I think he has a strategy."

He jabbed the keyboard, and the ballroom screen came on.

She gasped and pointed. "There's my cat, Dr. GoldenPaw. See how cute he is?"

On the ballroom security screen, she could see Goldy perched on top of the glass sapphire case. He held a big hunk of transparent fish skin like edible treasure, licking it over and over. Nancy clasped her hand to her heart. Her kitty was alive and doing fine.

Nancy's shoulders tightened, and her stomach lurched. Some of those fish had seemed poisoned. What if Goldy was licking a *poisoned* hunk of fish skin?

Gnut said, "You see those bird sculptures? They're actual guard drones. Parasitic jaegers."

"I know all about that, GHOST told me. Look!"

They focused their attention back to the formal hallway, where the tuxedoed intruder was taking off his mask.

It was definitely her match, Sinclair, just as she had already suspected. He had silver hair, and was handsome and athletic like his profile pic. She admired the way he doffed his jacket and, in quick, careful movements, put on an old-fashioned diving suit with a copper helmet, along with the suit's heavy gloves. What was his love language? Nancy swiftly forced the thought away. Sinclair had to be crazy, dressing up in a tux and breaking into a house to steal jewels. He was a criminal, plain and simple, no matter how debonair he was. Sadly, she was surrounded by people blessed with amazing superficial appearance traits, but deep down, they were twisted, warped, and dangerous.

"That man is named Sinclair supposedly. We matched earlier tonight on *SeniorLOVE*."

Gnut regarded Nancy, his brows going up. "*SeniorLOVE*? Finding plenty of silver fox hookups there?"

Nancy couldn't help but laugh. "Sure, lots. No, I just started it. This Sinclair is handsome." She cast a glance at the pufferfish tank. "Maybe I ought to *reel* him in."

Nancy smirked at her pun. She checked Gnut's reaction.

He shrugged, then he tensed up and sulked at the screen. "I've heard rumors about a jewel thief named Sinclair. If he thinks he's going to steal my sapphires, he can dream on."

Gnut started typing furiously. On the computer screens directly before him, Nancy could see flashes of robotic bird diagrams and computer code.

"I found seven of those sapphires myself in an underwater mineral deposit off the coast of Madagascar," Gnut said, still typing. "The others are the world's most expensive sapphires, bought at auctions, estate sales, and directly from two different royal families. Two were in tiaras and one in a medieval crown. I shouldn't even have them. They belong in a museum. They're worth $41.24 million according to three of Minneapolis's finest insurance companies."

Nancy did the math. Each sapphire was worth over two million.

"Whatever you're doing, please make sure my cat stays safe."

Gnut paused to look at her. He nodded and put a hand over hers. "I'll do that for you, Nancy. Because we're a team, right? Gnut and Nancy."

She found it difficult to tear her gaze from Gnut's. He squeezed her hand, and she recalled his initial death grip on her when he'd first opened his eyes in the bedroom. With considerable effort, she forced herself to squeeze back.

"Yeah, you betcha! We're a team."

She kept her eyes on the ballroom and formal hallway security screens that showed her cat and her match. Her annoyance grew. What was that man doing with her bling bag?

Bloody hell, the diving suit was bulky. Sinclair preferred the flexibility of movement with his tailored suit. But those ducks would have a frightful time cutting through this canvas. The helmet was heavy but would protect his head. He'd taken the ski mask off because if it slipped and covered his eyes, he'd have to remove the helmet to adjust it.

It revealed his identity, at least in terms of showing his face. Nevertheless, in his experience, the types of people he robbed weren't too inclined to report his intrusions to law enforcement. Much of what he stole had already been stolen. He didn't know Gnut Berdqvist, but if he was a billionaire, there was no doubt he was a more dreadful thief than Sir Stevie Sinclair.

He drew the line at the weighted shoes. He had to be able to step carefully. Taking the shoulder bag with him, he approached the ballroom, his wingtips splashing into disgusting fish water.

"Should be working," Elvira said, her voice crackling through the walkie-talkie.

Slowly, the ballroom's steel shutter opened.

Chapter Thirty

Sinclair dug into the bag and collected a handful of sequins. A frightful scrape of metal wings sounded from within the dark room. He spied a glint of silver.

Shooting toward him from above, those dozen evil ducks formed a perfect dive-bombing V. He flung the sequins down the hallway. Two robo-birds chased after the sparkly distraction.

Unfortunately, the others flew closer to him.

Sinclair seized more shiny objects and threw them, wincing at the anticipated impact of talons on his wrist. He hoped the canvas suit would protect him. Thankfully, his head was safe inside the helmet.

The shiny distractions grabbed another bird's attention. Now was his chance. Straightening his shoulders, he vaulted into the ballroom. Adrenaline charged through his veins. A sense of victory compelled him to sideswipe the nearest bird with his arm. Stupid bloody ducks! They'd never outsmart Sir Stevie.

Sinclair hopped straight up in the air as birds attacked his exposed ankles.

Ah, sod it all. He'd made the wrong choice. He *should* have put on those weighted boots.

Gnut whooped and laughed. He and Nancy watched Sinclair jumping up and down as birds attacked his feet and ankles, the contents of her bling bag scattering across the ballroom. Fortunately, her cat was okay, observing the incident from his perch atop the marble Gnut statue.

"Stay there, boy." She held her hands up as if holding him in place. "Please stay there."

"I've reprogrammed the birds to zero in on the intruder's vulnerable spots," Gnut said. "Don't worry, I've also programmed them to stay away from Dr. Golden-Dude."

Gnut flipped the audio on. Nancy cringed at the metallic flapping and screeching. Sinclair retreated from the ballroom, ten robotic parasitic jaegers chasing him.

"Oh, no." Gnut stopped smirking and became deadly serious again, typing more code.

Sinclair was running headlong down the hallway, straight toward the deepest part of the fishy aquarium water, near the gym. He performed a flying leap into where it had pooled a few inches deep in the hallway. One bird attacked his right ankle before splashing into the water.

"No, no, no!" Gnut's fingers tap-danced over the keyboard.

Sinclair bounced from the water while the attacking bird sparked, trembled, and flopped over.

"They're not waterproofed yet," Gnut said. "Too much electrical. I have to undo what I just did or they'll die, dang it!"

Sinclair dashed into the gym. Nancy switched her viewing to that security screen. The gym was flooded at least a foot deep. More birds followed Sinclair, still attacking his feet and ankles as circuits sparked across the water. Two birds flopped over.

"He's gonna get electrocuted." Nancy didn't want to watch, yet couldn't quite look away, either.

Sinclair must've had the same thought about electrocution, because he jumped back into the hallway, and the birds were once more distracted by her bling. He scooped up rhinestones and tossed them into the gym. The remaining birds chased them.

As soon as they were inside, Sinclair shoved the gym's door shut.

He stripped off his helmet, wiped his brow, and began talking to himself. "Had to jolly wing it, but I do say I soared with that solution."

Gnut glowered, and Nancy struggled to keep a straight face. Sinclair's voice was jovial and calm, with a lovely accent that she could listen to all day. She wouldn't mind Sinclair as her Volvo's navigation voice. Nancy nearly heaved a sigh befitting any of GHOST's lovesick drama. For once in her life, she'd encountered a really attractive guy her age, whom she'd love to date. Why did he have to be a jewel thief?

Sinclair strolled back toward the ballroom, gracefully stepping out of his diving suit at the same time. Nancy threw up her hands in disbelief as the man straightened his bowtie. His smugness evaporated, though, when he realized the ballroom shutters had come back down.

Next to her, Gnut hit Enter on the keyboard.

"Locked. My sapphires are safe, and so is your cat," he said. "Don't worry, Nancy. You can trust me."

"Wait. Where's my cat?"

Nancy peered closer at the ballroom screen. Goldy was no longer on his perch atop Gnut's marble statue. He was not on any of the screens.

Chapter Thirty-One

Nancy tried to tamp down her catastrophic thinking, like her cat getting drowned or electrocuted, or herself dying of asphyxiation in this cramped space, her last breath the aroma of Easy Cheese mixed with pufferfish aquarium water. She worried more about Goldy. The ballroom cameras didn't show the entire room. Maybe he was out of view.

Or maybe he'd chased after the sparkly objects and ended up in the hallway. Her thoughts bounced back and forth. No, he wouldn't do that. Yes, he was a cat and would do whatever his instincts demanded. Nancy sighed. The quickest solution was for the police to come.

"Kid, you outsmarted Sinclair. Now you can plug the red phone back in and call 911, right?"

Gnut flashed her a charming grin. "We're doing okay on our own, aren't we, Nancy? You and me?"

"What do these people want?" Nancy kept eyeing the screens. Still no sign of Goldy.

Gnut's attitude became deadly earnest. "What do they want? I am Gnut Berdqvist. This is my house. Isn't what *I* want the better question?"

"Yes." Icky tingles crawled up her spine, but Nancy pasted a supportive look on her face.

"The first thing to know about me," he pointed at himself, "Gnut Berdqvist, is that I want to help people. I want to help the whole planet. I am an altruist."

"Of course." Nancy forced a polite nod.

Gnut nodded, his expression relaxing in response to Nancy's agreement. "That's the problem here. I blew the whistle on fraud at Berdqvist Enterprises." He widened his angelic gray eyes. "For me, it was about saving the planet."

What nonsense. She needed to call for help. Hoping he wouldn't disconnect it again, Nancy plugged in the red phone cord.

Without even looking at the computer monitor, Gnut waved a helpless arm at the dialing screen. GHOST phoned Claude over and over. "I can only do so much. I designed her, but some of her original programming has taken on a life of its own. I can't override it."

Another creepy-crawly sensation slithered along the back of her neck. She spoke slowly, trying to avoid a combative tone. "You mean, you invented GHOST, and you can get her to lock doors and unlock cupboards and raise and lower steel security shutters, but you can't get her—it—to call the police?"

Gnut turned his back to her. "Hear me out, Nancy. I don't think we need the police right now."

Nancy eyed the legal documents. Her focus lasered in on the one that said *postponement due to illness*. Gnut didn't want the police to know he was faking, but he had to know, sooner or later, the night would be over. She'd leave Geyser House and tell the police everything.

"Claude said we'd pay you triple for tonight, Nancy. Maybe we can work out another deal, an even better one," Gnut said, like he was reading her mind.

Nancy stayed quiet. No way would she accept a bribe. But curiosity piqued her interest. How much money was he talking about?

Gnut spun in the swivel chair and met her gaze. "I'm trying

to avoid a completely unfair court situation, where everybody's out to get me. I blew the whistle. But the truth is, I could end up in jail, even though I'm the innocent party. Better to delay the court proceedings if I can. And let's just wait and see how this home invasion stuff plays out. I know JT and that lady with the harpoon gun, Elvira LeSabre. They might get bored and leave after they feel they've proved their point."

Nancy curled her toes inside her Crocs. Okay. She could read between the lines. Don't tell the police Gnut is faking his illness, and she'd get cash in exchange. Deep within her mind, Nancy imagined lights in the shape of the Eiffel Tower, sparkling like diamond earrings, lights like—

No! Taking money and not telling the police about this would be a crime. It was unacceptable. No way would she ever go along with this scheme.

But now was not the time to tell Gnut that.

"Things do seem really unfair," she said, "and you're doing the best you can."

Gnut reached for Nancy's hands, and he briefly held them.

"You'll tell the court I'm faking. And when the police arrive, that's it. They'll haul me away."

She didn't know what to say to him. Basically, yeah. Time to go to jail, kid.

Gnut fixated on the floor, but not in a bashful way. Concern knitted his brow. Nancy followed the direction of his stare. The roaring fan sounds from below seemed even louder.

She touched his shoulder. "You've been hurt before. I can see why you'd be afraid of these people."

Was she on the right track? His head slumped down, and it was hard to get a read on his exact mood.

Nancy thought of her own carefully bedazzled condo. "This

mansion was supposed to be your escape from the world outside trying to get at you. A watery refuge."

"A safe space." Gnut wiped away a tear.

Nancy doubted his emotion was real, but she pressed forward anyway. "I can see why you'd hide, even from the police or a court of law. Really."

The truth was, she did. Her own father had done something wrong and had successfully evaded the law for most of his life. She was about to mention this, but Gnut scrunched up his face and color spread across his cheekbones. It seemed like she was already connecting with him.

"So maybe others would understand too," she said softly. "Maybe you should call 911. Dial. I'll do the talking."

Gnut ground his fists into his eyes. "It's been hard, you know, being a billionaire. I'm so alone. There's Claude and GHOST and Karen, the full-time nurse, but who do I have really? Who understands that Gnut Berdqvist is more than an inventor, a climate change leader, a visionary? Don't people realize that Gnut Berdqvist is also a man?"

"I get it. Others will too. You're a man who is doing his best. Even though others are literally attacking you."

Gnut lowered his fists and nodded, his manner grim. Nancy could see him rubbing his chiseled jaw, the wheels turning. He reverted to the controls and punched computer keys.

"GHOST, call the police. Now."

The screen above the red phone showed her ending the calls to Claude and dialing 9, 1...

Gnut reached out to fist-bump. Nancy obliged, feeling lighthearted with relief. The police would rescue her and Dr. GoldenPaw, like the firefighters had rescued them on Fire Night.

The dialing screen went black.

Chapter Thirty-Two

Gnut leaped to his feet. He bent down to tap computer keys but hesitated. They both stared as the security screens went black, exactly like the phone dialing screen.

"GHOST does what you say. Order her to call 911!"

"I don't know what happened."

GHOST's voice erupted from the speakers. "Elvira said if I do what she says, she'll find me a Claude who loves me. She wants me to unlock the basement and panic room."

"No, GHOST," Nancy said. "We're friends now. Best friends forever. BFF. Don't do something to hurt me. I'm your friend."

GHOST mumbled, "BFF. Best…friends…forever. Does that mean you'll always be here in the panic room, talking to me, being my BFF?"

"Sure, GHOST," Nancy said.

Banging erupted at the panic room door. JT shouted something unintelligible through the steel. Nancy imagined the door unlocking and that hulking cretin charging through. If he wanted to kill them, he could. He obviously hated Gnut and might wish to harm him. JT wouldn't leave a witness.

Nancy shuddered and craned her neck up at the ceiling. Somebody needed to unplug this house operating system. How to turn GHOST off? Where was she located?

It, it, it, Nancy reminded herself.

"Elvira won't do anything nice for you, GHOST." Gnut shot an uneasy glance at the door. "But I will. I designed you, remember? Here's what I'll do. I'll transfer you to a state-of-the-art robot that will attract the *real* Claude. Now, lemme take over the system."

Gnut hunched over the controls. Nancy's pulse raced. Was she going to get murdered tonight? When was that door going to open?

She dipped her hands into her bottomless fanny pack and retrieved an *Herbal Stress-Relief Gummies* bottle. She ate them one by one, her fingers trembling. Somehow the stress eating helped. She got an idea.

"Gnut, how about I try to distract Elvira while you deal with GHOST?"

He ignored her and punched computer keys like a genius hacker. The security screens lit up, but Nancy had her doubts about whether the electronics were working any better. The screens flashed pictures of insanely hot athletic ladies.

"My body will be good at skiing," GHOST said.

"You betcha," Gnut said. "This? Combined with this?" More pictures popped up—Olympians, *Sports Illustrated* covers, beach volleyball players—so many beautiful, sporty women. "And while you think about those, I'm gonna do a little something here."

The screens all went black. Gnut smacked the keyboard. Nancy had an idea, and she picked up the red telephone.

"GHOST, connect me to Elvira. Tell her the nurse wants to make a deal." Nancy winked at Gnut and mouthed the word "distraction."

He slowly nodded, flexed his fingers, and poised over the keyboard.

The red phone dialed.

Ten rings later, Elvira picked up. "Ms. Norman, I hope you're still all right. GHOST says you would like to chat? A little girl talk, the two of us?"

Nancy gripped the phone. Gnut started typing furiously. Distracting Elvira could work, but it could also go very wrong. Part of her wanted to run into the kitchenette, crouch down, and stay there forever, hiding behind the counter.

"Hello, Dr. LeSabre. Not girl chat. I want to make a deal to get out with my cat."

"My cat," GHOST interrupted.

"What are you offering?" Elvira asked.

The security screens shifted to something else as Gnut typed. Instead of showing Geyser House rooms or hot sports ladies, they flashed *Armed, Armed, Security Doors, Burglar Blasters, Armed, Lockdown.*

"I won't say a word to the police."

"Counteroffer. You won't say a word to the police, *and* you'll deliver Gnut to me. If you hold up your end of the bargain, I'll let you leave. You and the feline."

Gnut gave her a quick thumbs-up.

"Yuuuup," Nancy said as slowly as possible. "That sounds like a great, great, great deal. So great, you know—"

"You're making the right choice. And by the way, I love your shoulder bag. It gives every appearance of being so very real, precisely like a genuine Coach piece. Delightful."

Nancy stifled annoyance at the woman's condescension.

The screens showed *Lockdown, Lockdown, Lockdown.*

"I'll try to give you Gnut—"

The phone disconnected.

"We did it." Gnut jerked a thumb at the screens.

They were back to normal, the cameras showing all rooms except for the basement. Elvira typed at her laptop in the kitchen while Sinclair strode down the formal hallway, and JT injected himself with steroids right outside the panic room door.

Then the mansion's lights went out. Now she couldn't see anything that was going on with the intruders. The panic room's red emergency lights stayed on.

"I killed the lights," Gnut said. "No one knows this house better than me, so darkness is to our advantage."

Nancy fixated on the screens. Her cat still had to be in the ballroom, right? He was just off camera.

"I have to figure this out," Gnut repeated, almost to himself. "I wouldn't excel in prison. Not unless it has a strong aquatics program."

Nancy tried not to roll her eyes. The man was seriously self-absorbed. Maybe she *should* turn him over to Elvira.

As if reading her mind, Gnut said, "I'll make a deal with you too, ya know. And your match, Sinclair, who you should really hook up with. He'd be lucky to get you."

Nancy snorted. In addition to being crazy, Gnut was quirky and somehow slightly charming.

He raised his eyebrows. "Triple pay tonight, plus two first-class tickets for you and this guy Sinclair to Bhutan."

Nancy frowned. "Why Bhutan?"

Gnut pointed at a list he'd called up on a screen. The title was *Non-Extradition Countries*. Bhutan was on the list, along with China, Belarus, Sudan, and others.

"Doing a little research for later," he said.

"Oh, Montenegro." Nancy pursed her lips. That was from a Bond movie, *Casino Royale*. It was a fancy, rich, exotic kind of place.

"I'm innocent though." She raised her chin. "Extremely innocent. I haven't committed any crimes. I would simply not say anything to the police. I don't need a non-extradition country."

"You may have to go where Sinclair is safe from the authorities," Gnut said.

What was Gnut now, a matchmaker? He was setting her up with a jewel thief? The guy had nerve. Free travel to an exotic country was tempting. Still, Gnut's talk of travel hit a little too close to home, given the kinds of disagreements she had with Dave about taking pricey adventure vacations. And she'd seen Morocco on Gnut's list. Dad had lived there for three years.

"I want to go anywhere away from here, right now, with my cat."

Nancy grumbled the words, knowing she was stuck. But since Gnut had unlocked the cupboards, she decided to search for anything useful for escaping or getting help.

"The cat is mine," GHOST said. "And you have to stay in the panic room and be with me, because we're BFFs now. You said so."

Ignoring GHOST, Nancy began a methodical investigation of the cupboards. At first, the contents were what she expected. There were plates and glasses and bowls, except they were all brand new with tags still attached. Food consisted of Good and Gather products, plus Easy Cheese, SPAM, and canned mussels, mackerel, and sardines. In the back of the room next to the shower, she slid open a pantry door.

Inside, she discovered hundreds of ice-blue, logoed Speedos inexplicably hung on tiny hangers and neatly folded in stacks, as many as could fit in the compact space. The plasticky, rubbery smell of Spandex tickled her nostrils. Like everything else, they were brand new.

"What the heck is with all these swimming trunks?"

Gnut didn't bother glancing back, keeping his eyes locked

on the screens. He typed something on the keyboard. "Elvira hasn't given up. She's focused on the basement now. Yeah, my Speedos are what I'm known for. It's my unique style. I wear each once. I like just the right amount of snug and snap. They're designed with a type of thermal Spandex I've created that provides extra warmth."

Nancy marveled at the sheer number of them. Honestly, there could be a thousand Speedos in here. For Gnut Berdqvist, that would be a three-year supply. She had to ask the obvious question. "But wearing each Speedo once? Treating them as disposable, like they're, I don't know"—she wanted to say diapers, but held off—"like they're plastic water bottles? Is that good for the environment?"

"I wear them while *saving* the environment."

Nancy glanced over her shoulder to see if he was joking. It was impossible to tell, because he had his back to her. She narrowed her eyes, still not sure what to make of him. Was he messing with her? Could he really be so obtuse not to realize that wearing one new Speedo each day was completely ridiculous?

"And of course, I need them in the panic room so I'm fully stocked for emergencies. I have more in my dressing room, believe me."

"I believe you."

Nancy rummaged deeper in the closet. There had to be something useful. She swept the Speedo hangers aside. It went five rows back. This Speedo closet was deeper than she'd first realized.

"Nothing to see there, Nancy."

Gnut's words put Nancy's instincts on high alert. Without a doubt, there was something to find besides Speedos. Behind the last row, her hands hit drywall.

"I'm telling you, there's nothing there."

"Stop!" GHOST screeched. "Don't leave me. We're friends now."

GHOST thought she was leaving? Nancy squirmed deeper into the Speedo closet, the Spandex smell and fabric clouding her head. She shifted position and pressed on the closet's back wall. She noticed a fresh lumber, plastic, and freshly poured concrete aroma. It reminded her of last year when, out of curiosity, she'd stepped into a recently-opened Tesla showroom.

"Come on, Nancy." Gnut's tone grew firmer. "Get out of the closet. I have everything organized how I like it."

Nancy still pondered the situation. GHOST seemed to think there was a chance she was leaving. And there must be more to Geyser House. This was a mansion—way bigger than a spacious kitchen/living room, formal hall, ballroom, gym, poolroom, and bedroom. Come to think of it, she hadn't seen most of the house. There'd been that big, strange, boxy, windowless section on the western side.

The architecture had reminded her of something. At the time, she couldn't imagine it. Now she could.

Nancy lasered in on a single Speedo and touched its price tag. She checked the small print. *Gnu-Mart, $75.*

"Nancy, I mean it. Let me help you out of there."

Nancy felt a sharp tug on the waistband of her fanny pack. She lurched forward. Gnut pulled harder. She propelled herself toward the closet's back wall.

"No!" Gnut yanked her toward him.

"Stop it!" GHOST screeched. "You said we were BFF!"

Nancy stuck a foot out, slammed it against Gnut's chest for leverage, and hurtled all her weight at the back of the closet.

Her shoulder punctured the drywall, making it crumble. Incredibly bright light, like a heavenly florescence, gleamed from the hole. Gnut's fingers curled around her legs, and she kicked out her feet. She didn't even care if she hit her own patient square in the nose. After punching drywall away and scrambling away from Gnut, she crawled toward the light.

Chapter Thirty-Three

Nancy was out of the panic room.

She'd plopped down a few feet, landing on her hands and knees on linoleum. The light was so bright she had to blink a few times and let her eyes adapt.

"It's not done yet. I'm still working on it," Gnut whined behind her.

Nancy staggered to her feet, feeling a wonderful sense of familiarity washing over her. Everything would be okay. This was a happy place.

She was inside a big box store.

The interior walls were a bright ice-blue. Blue banners identified product aisles. Artificial lights beamed from the ceiling, and a row of self-checkout stations stood ready.

Gnut tumbled out after her.

"You've reached the inner sanctum, Nancy. Splendidly done." Gnut had adopted his fake-sophisticated accent again.

He pranced a few steps before her and twirled, his arms raised high, like he was Willy Wonka showing off a candy factory. "Welcome to Gnu-Mart!"

Nancy inhaled the clean scent and assessed the aisles of snacks and toiletries. She frowned up at the blue aisle signs. *Swimsuits - Warm Climates; Swimsuits - Cold Climates; Aquatic Sports Gear; Arctic Exploration; Underwater Exploration; Seafood Snacks; Fish Food and Other Nutrients;* and *Aquatics Weapons.*

Couldn't he come up with something besides water and

Arctic stuff? She also noticed there were no windows. The wall by the check-out stations sported floor-to-ceiling steel shutters in place of the entrance and exit doors. This was the boxy building she'd seen when she'd first arrived.

"A Gnu-Mart. Fine. And I'm assuming the shutters are keeping us inside?"

Gnut stopped twirling. "Yeah, like the bedroom. A security measure that's supposed to keep people out. If Elvira weren't messing with GHOST, I'd be able to open them. But don't worry—that secret passage from the panic room is the one way in or out. So we're still safe."

"Still trapped, you mean."

"But is there any place on Earth where you'd rather be trapped in than a giant brand-new store?"

He had a point. Retail therapy, why not? Nancy set off deeper into the custom-designed store to shop. From her head to her ice-cubed toes, she just wanted to feel toasty warm again.

Plodding down the aisle, her heart plummeted straight to the linoleum. The shelves weren't fully stocked. But she managed to find one bright red parka and one pair of snow boots. The parka was *huge*. And the boots were men's size fourteen.

She picked up a giant boot and dropped it, realizing how heavy it was. "Do you have women's Arctic gear? Any other sizes? Gnut? Hello?"

"The Gnu-Mart is not fully stocked yet." Gnut's voice echoed off the metal rafters. "But that footwear is the best for Arctic exploration. Good for Ninety-four degrees below Fahrenheit."

She hefted a pair. "They must weigh ten pounds."

Seeing no socks, she forced her bare feet into the boots. She seized the bright red parka, size men's XXL. The inner tags said it was good for minus seventy-six degrees Fahrenheit. It felt at least five sizes too big, weighed a million pounds, and came down to her knees. Endless flaps, a heavy-duty zipper and hooks, and a coyote fur-trimmed hood completed the look. Nancy stuffed her hands into the deep pockets. She was wearing something from the abominable snowman's winter collection.

Forcing one monster boot after the other in a ponderous gait, she proceeded to scope out the rest of the Gnu-Mart. As she was about to leave the Arctic aisle, Gnut appeared in her path. Now he wore white khakis, tight and transparent enough she could see his Speedos underneath, an ice-blue polo shirt, and flipflops with a Gnu-Mart tag attached.

"Can I help you, ma'am?" Now he was pretending to be an employee. "For you, ma'am, we'll do better than match prices. Gnu-Mart will give you anything you want for free." Gnut's posture slumped. "It's not the same, I guess, without Claude here. He's gonna be at the check-out. I'll help people find things. All my friends will love a private big box store. There'll be multiple levels of membership, with Elite Tier members having access to upgraded merchandise behind glass. But I do wish Claude was here right now. Everything's more fun with him."

Nancy regarded Gnut from deep within her parka, wishing the coat could magically make her disappear, transport her anywhere else, anywhere but in this billionaire's crazy world.

Gnut lowered his eyes, looking sheepish. "You probably think I've gone a little—"

"Overboard."

"Yeah. It's really that Target was what inspired me to become who I am. When I was a kid, I loved it. All the cool, useful stuff, from toys to beauty products to electronics. Most of which my family couldn't afford. I'd walk the aisles endlessly, every day. After swim practice, before school started, and after school ended. I scored a job at one. You know the one in Burnsville?"

"Yeah, I know that Target."

"I wouldn't shoplift. Never. No way, I'd never do that."

"I believe you." Nancy did not believe him.

She spied the Pharmacy at the far side of the store. Nancy wanted to edge in that direction, but Gnut blocked her way.

"I wanted to *live* in Target. But after a while, I imagined something even better." Gnut bowed his head and raised his palms, as if in worship. "I would possess my own perfect store. It would have stellar advertising, the ultimate reputation for customer satisfaction, and a snazzy vibe. I learned from Target, I imagined, and after that, I had courage in my imagination."

"It's amazing," Nancy said carefully. "I'm curious—do you have any electronics stocked yet, like cell phones? Maybe we could use those to call for help?"

"Nope, not yet. Sorry." He took in her gigantic Arctic explorer look. "But let me show you something I think you'll like."

Gnut waved a hand to get her to follow, and he padded away.

After a brief sigh, Nancy stomped after him. It involved supreme effort to lift each boot. The huge parka dragged her shoulders down, and warmth flushed her cheeks. In a matter of minutes, she'd be way too hot.

They passed an aisle stocked with identical weapons, which seemed familiar.

"Those seem like those guns in the underwater fight scene from the Bond movie *Thunderball*."

Gnut threw a quick grin over his shoulder. "Right as rain, Nancy. They're underwater assault rifles."

They arrived at an aisle on the far side of the store called Luxe and Glamour. The instant Nancy saw what it contained, she gasped and, for a split second, completely forgot her circumstances. The store was crammed with glamorous women's apparel. The clothes and shoes were authentic designer brands. Moreover, it contained a whole row of the same fanny pack that Claude had worn.

Nancy lumbered deeper into the aisle, sweat from the parka sliding down her back. With a practiced eye, she inventoried the possibilities. Dresses, skintight pants, camisoles, strappy evening shoes…it was all splendid and sparkly and completely impractical. She raised her hood—the thing was so huge that it covered almost her whole head—and tried not to cry. It was all the stuff she idolized online and could never, ever afford.

"It's *too* designer," she mumbled.

"Excuse me? Nothing can be too designer. Here, Nancy. This. And this."

Nancy peeked from under the hood. Gnut held up white leather pants, a bejeweled camisole that was little more than an extended necklace, silver Prada platform sandals, and a white Burberry trench coat made of transparent silk.

She shook her head. "It's too impractical."

Gnut's face slackened. "Impractical? It's better than looking like, I don't know, like you're trying to hide yourself. C'mon. Show us the real Nancy!"

"The real Nancy is not someone who can wear white leather pants."

Gnut dumped the entire ensemble on the floor. Nancy yelped when she heard the bejeweled camisole hit linoleum. She lunged forward and picked it up to make sure the jewels hadn't fallen off.

"That's Dylan Lex," Gnut said.

"I know what it is. Drew Ginsberg's brand. Accessories and clothes that are statement pieces worn by Taylor Swift, Madonna, Lady Gaga, crafted from Swarovski crystals and antiqued metals, reworking old vintage with new."

He smiled. "Reworking old vintage with new. That's *you*. You obviously know what this is about and want it. Come on already. What's stopping you?"

Nancy ran a hand over the heavy crystal and metal camisole. It was more of a necklace than clothing. It would cover nothing. But it was worth thousands of dollars, a true luxury item worn by superstars, not night nurses.

"Here. Try this."

Now Gnut held up faux black leather leggings, a black Dolce & Gabbana cashmere trench coat, with an abundance of fake black fur at the collar and more matching fur at the cuffs.

"That's it," Nancy said. "I need that."

"You need it all." Gnut raised a pair of Prada high-heeled boots, the silver leather as shiny as mirrors.

Nancy made the calculation. The pants were at least a few hundred bucks. The cashmere coat cost around $8,000, for sure. The Dylan Lex camisole, in the real world, would probably set her back $5,000. The Prada boots were worth about $2,500. If she put this ensemble on, she would be wearing at least $15,000 worth. She sucked in a long breath. This was her one chance. She'd never have the opportunity to rock a style like this ever again.

"Yeah, baby, let's see it!"

Nancy sashayed from the Gnu-Mart's restroom. She felt like a million bucks in the silver Prada boots, black leggings, the vintage metal camisole Swarovski crystals, and the black Dolce & Gabbana faux-fur trimmed trench coat. The trench was belted high on her waist, covering most of her body, but the sexy bejeweled camisole peeked from the top.

She topped off the ensemble with the *pièce de résistance*, a Louis Vuitton black leather backpack embossed with the LV monogram. The straps were braided gold chains, and the hardware was matching gold with easy peasy magnetic flaps. Inside the backpack, she'd managed to stuff her scrubs and most of the other contents of her fanny pack. Her thinner Paris one draped around her waist, hidden by the black trench coat.

Gnut whistled. "Courage in imagination. See what I mean? This is the real Nancy coming through. You need that vibe on your *SeniorLOVE* profile."

Nancy laughed and nodded. "You know what? You're right."

She trailed off, seeing Gnut wasn't paying attention. He trotted toward the restroom, mumbling something.

"I think, since you're not using them, I'll take that parka and boots."

Nancy frowned, understanding she'd been manipulated. She'd only spotted one heavy red parka and boots, and Gnut wanted that specific heavy-duty winter gear for himself. But she perked up as she strutted further down the aisle, satisfied with her new clothing. The trench was made of lovely cashmere and would keep her warmer than her scrubs.

The restroom door slammed shut.

She was alone, at least for now.

Nancy surveyed the Gnu-Mart, and, heels clicking fast, she headed straight for the Pharmacy section.

The faux Pharmacy was somewhat stocked with flu medicine, eye contact cleaner, and earplugs. She selected the earplugs and stuffed them in a coat pocket. There were also cough drops, acid reflux pills, and blister-size Band-Aids. But where was the thing she needed the most?

Nancy eyed the highest shelf, marked *Elite Members*, but it had no glass barrier yet. There was one first aid kit, but it was a sizable red box. It was labeled *First Aid*, and, in smaller print, *Yacht Essentials*. After climbing up on the lowest shelf and standing on tippy-toes in her silvery Pradas, she nabbed the kit. It slipped from her hand and toppled to the floor, and she fell along with it.

"You okay?" Gnut called from maybe a couple of aisles over.

"Fine," Nancy said quickly. She carefully scrambled to her knees, not easy in her new coat, and popped open the box.

There was jellyfish sting lotion, a shark bite tourniquet kit, and a jet-ski whiplash neck brace.

But not everything in the kit was water related.

She scanned up and down the aisle, confirming Gnut wasn't eavesdropping.

Nancy moved efficiently, with speed only a professional nurse could muster. Taped to the inside of the first aid kit's lid were syringes. At the bottom of the kit were ten little bottles of injectable ketamine hydrochloride. Ah, yes. A fast-acting anesthetic. Street name: Special K. Sometimes it was abused, so she was suspicious of how much was in this first aid kit.

It would work as a sedative, possibly causing hallucinations, but would knock out the patient, nevertheless. Nancy estimated Gnut's height, muscles, speed, and youth as she filled a syringe with the right ketamine amount. She untied her trench coat and slipped it into her Paris fanny pack, ready for easy access.

Gnut didn't know it, but now his nurse wasn't merely dressed to impress.

She was armed.

Chapter Thirty-Four

Elvira stood before the steel door in the kitchen, which blocked her way to Gnut, the basement, and the sapphires. There was a solution. There was *always* a solution. Her father had been a Special Forces colonel and an optimist, in addition to being a disciplinarian, explosives expert, and two-handicap golfer. Her childhood had been a series of twelve different schools and a hundred forest excursions with her dad and brothers, learning all manner of combat and survival skills.

Her favorite memory was the time he taught her to blow up a tree stump with dynamite. She remembered inspecting the stump first, her scientific mind cataloguing the gooey moss, creeping spiders, the spotted gray mushrooms sprouting around its circumference, and the disgustingly soft wood rotting in the stump's center. That's where he'd stuck the dynamite. He'd forced it in and made her do the same with another red stick. They'd scurried behind a living tree—*boom!* Afterward, there was nothing left besides a muddy hole in the ground.

To this day, she could still smell the fried tree bark. It made her feel like the adventure of life wasn't over. She had the skills, appearance, and talent to do anything. Thinking of blowing up that tree made her lose all self-doubt, then and now.

"This makes room for a stronger tree to grow here," she'd said to her dad, knowing it was what he'd like to hear. But he hadn't heard it at all. He was already hiking back to the trail with her brothers.

Presently, the steel door had trapped her in the living and kitchen area, entirely blocking her from her main objectives of the ballroom, basement, and Gnut.

But not for long. Carefully, she set a charge of C-4 at the base of the door separating her from the formal hallway.

This was maddening.

Nancy and Gnut had left the Gnu-Mart the sole way available, via the busted drywall in the Speedo closet. But now they were back in the panic room.

"Nancy, you came back because we're best friends, right?"

Nancy ignored GHOST. She fought the urge to bash the panic room's door, pant for fresh air, shake Gnut senseless, and dunk her own head in the pufferfish tank. Being trapped in this tiny space was giving her cabin fever. She seethed at Gnut's Parka'd back. On his knees sat an underwater assault rifle that he'd taken from the Gnu-Mart. They had retraced their steps and the instant they returned to the panic room, he'd resumed typing at the controls.

Nancy examined the security screens. She still couldn't see Dr. GoldenPaw.

She elbowed Gnut. "The foyer."

In the foyer, water leaked from a burst pipe running along the ceiling.

"Yeah. Structural damage from Elvira exploding through my front doors. Hold up. The pool room too? What caused that? GHOST?" Gnut asked, his voice rising.

Nancy peered closer, and clicked her tongue. The pool room screen showed that the leak there was worse. A huge pipe along the ceiling now gushed water into the pool, so maybe not a big deal, but what was going on?

"I'm diverting energy to non-damaged wiring," GHOST said. "Water intake from Lake Superior is set to max."

"Max? Jeez. Why's it set to max?"

"Elvira did it, not me. I would never—"

"Turn it down, GHOST! What's the most critical damage point?"

On the main screen above the keyboard, GHOST displayed a diagram of a cross-pipe beneath the ice geyser. The word *Critical* flashed in red below it.

Nancy grabbed the red phone. "GHOST, connect me to Elvira."

In response to Gnut raising his eyebrows, she pointed at the kitchen screen. Gnut grimaced as Elvira positioned a block of C-4.

He looked back at her, his features flushing, eyes narrowing, and fists clenching. Nancy shivered at the change in his bearing. The Minnesota nice guy Gnut was gone.

"They're wrecking my house." He held the microphone in a white-knuckled grip. "GHOST. *Obviously*, you need to lower the water intake from Lake Superior."

"Can't," GHOST said, her tone light. She made sounds like she'd popped in some chewing gum and was blowing a bubble. "Elvira flipped the manual override switch outside. That's on you. I told you to go fully electronic. But no, you didn't trust the operating system. I'm diverting energy—"

"Yeah, yeah, divert energy! We can't have it at freezing temperatures everywhere in the house. All the pipes will burst."

"Diverting energy," GHOST said. "Like I've been doing, duh." She popped her gum. "Um, valve 9VA fail. Another, it's a valve 77B fail. Whoopsie, that's a big one." She heaved a sigh. "Seems like Claude will have to come back and help us, *oui*?"

"No," Gnut said, his expression serious. "This place is dangerous, and I don't want him here."

"GHOST, I want to talk to Elvira." Nancy could see that the woman held a detonator. What would happen to the rest of the house with another explosion?

Elvira glanced at her laptop and paused.

Gnut turned to Nancy. "My apologies. House operating controls aren't working like they should. Maybe, just maybe, we should try to run to the pool room. There's an underwater tunnel leading to the moat. From there, escape."

Nancy considered his plan and any alternatives. Stay here? Sedate Gnut and convince GHOST to call the police? Or trust that Gnut really knew a way to escape? She wished Elvira would just answer the phone, rather than let it ring in some kind of power play.

"A tunnel?" Nancy frowned. "It leads to the moat? Or under it?"

"I'll help you," Gnut said, his tone kind and caring.

"No!" GHOST yelled. "Nancy, stay in the panic room. Be with me forever."

Elvira finally answered the telephone. "Yes, Ms. Norman?"

"I'm delivering on the deal, Dr. LeSabre. I've drugged Gnut. But please don't explode that doorway, or the whole house might collapse on us."

Waiting for Elvira's answer, Nancy said a silent prayer. She edged closer to the panic room door, as far as the red telephone cord would stretch, wishing she could melt into the door like a ghost and get away from this weird guy and his weird weapon. But according to the security screens, JT was on the other side,

Sinclair was cleaning ankle wounds in the formal hallway, and Elvira was planning to bomb the kitchen.

Elvira said, "If Gnut is drugged, it logically follows he should be off the electronics. GHOST and Geyser House should be completely hackable."

Gnut backed away from the controls, and Nancy nodded. The man really didn't want Elvira to destroy more of his precious house.

"He's unconscious," Nancy said. "Not on electronics anymore."

"I don't believe it. You shouldn't either. He's faking."

"I'm a nurse. I know he's in a drug-induced sleep. But I can't manipulate the door to the panic room to get out. And I'm afraid of JT."

There was a long pause. Nancy decided to add something else to make it more believable. "Elvira, I want more than a safe escape. I want one—no, five—of those sapphires. Five sapphires." She winked at Gnut so he would know she was putting on a performance. He responded with a thumbs-up.

"Forget it," Elvira said, her voice crisp. "The deal is you get to escape with your cat, and without JT hurting you. I'll work on the panic room door."

The call disconnected.

"As soon as GHOST opens the door, I'll fire at JT, and we'll make a break for the underwater tunnel across the moat." Gnut hefted his gun. "Don't worry, it holds twenty-six rounds. Not bullets. It's an underwater gun, so it fires *flechettes*. It means 'little arrow' in French. They're fin-stabilized steel projectiles."

"Structural damage alert," GHOST said. "Water rising."

The panic room controls shone red.

Gnut's hands tightened on the underwater rifle. "What now?"

Nancy shivered, realizing there was trouble right here within the panic room. At their feet, water rapidly coated the floor between the fish tank and the kitchenette. Rivulets formed, snaking toward them. Somehow, from somewhere, water leaked inside the panic room.

"Gnut?"

He spun and followed Nancy's stare. She reached down to touch a stream. Beneath her hand, from somewhere in the basement, the roar of fans grew louder.

The panic room was flooding.

Gnut went back to the controls. He stabbed three buttons.

"That's it," he said. "We're leaving."

"I hate you now, BFF Nancy," GHOST said. "You're not staying with me."

Gnut sloshed closer and put a comforting hand on her shoulder.

"Way to deal with Elvira, Nancy. Good job." He initiated a side hug. "Claude and I were right about you."

"What?" She allowed the brief embrace.

"Your lack of cooperation with the police and the FBI about your father."

Nancy's stomach frosted over and her body stiffened. Maybe if she stopped moving and thinking, all of this would go away, and she'd be back in her condo safe and sound with her cat. Gnut knelt with his underwater assault rifle aimed at the door.

"Your father defrauded his employer," he said. "A traveling salesman who sold homewares. And he went on the run. First Miami. Next, what was it, Tangier?"

It was Marrakesh. But Nancy didn't say it.

"How many times did the FBI ask you for his whereabouts?"

The answer was eleven times in three different interviews. Local police had asked the same question. She never gave him up though. More than that, she'd also given him cash to help him get by. Of course, she sure didn't tell the police about that either.

"You're just what I'm looking for in a nurse who needs to sign legal documents."

Nancy ground her teeth. "So that's why I got the call. Multiple calls. You wanted me."

Gnut flashed his teeth in a way maybe meant to be charming, but came across as a sneer. Nancy understood, now. Gnut and Claude figured since she'd refused to cooperate with law enforcement once, she'd do it again. She, more so than others, would sign the binder, take the triple payout, and keep quiet.

They had been right.

As she studied Gnut's profile under the warm glow of the emergency lights, she recalled the last photo she had of her father, taken during his new life. His face had been flushed from desert sun and imported American beer, his eyes bright with the prospect of a new life. He had something within him she didn't have. A willingness to risk everything.

"Here's what matters." Gnut tightened his hands on the weapon, ready to fire, and whispered, "Don't you ever wonder about yourself? What would happen if *you* had courage in your imagination?"

She scoffed. The arrogance of this guy. She was sixty-five years old, had worked all her life, and this trickster with a one-way ticket to prison for fraud was lecturing her? She opened her mouth to retort, her mind spinning, and heard—

The *click* of the panic room door as it swung ajar, revealing a dark void beyond.

Chapter Thirty-Five

Gnut fired the underwater assault rifle.

Nancy heard a grunt of pain and saw a burly shadow, which had to be JT, retreat into the darkness.

Gnut crept from the room first, moving in a crouch, and rifle raised to fire. It reminded Nancy of the actions of a video game avatar. Was this all a big game to Gnut?

In the panic room doorway, she assessed the situation. Water drained from the room, only to meet more in the hallway. Scummy water surrounded her. Great, her immune system would have to work overtime. Fish tanks were cracked, and the overhead lights were out, except every five seconds or so they'd give a quick, faint flicker.

Gnut showed no sign of being ready to run and escape. He bopped from one booted foot to another in the low water, hands tightening and loosening on his weapon.

"My house," he whispered. "It's getting wrecked."

As Nancy risked a dainty step into the hallway, Gnut raised a stopping hand. He investigated a dead fish on the floor and turned back to Nancy.

"They'll pay for killing my pets," he hissed loudly. "These crocodile icefish are endangered."

Gnut hooked the rifle over his arm and picked up the dead fish, caressing its transparent, scaleless skin. He eyed a section of the aquarium that still held water. The one surviving icefish fed on another's carcass.

"You're the one who's endangered," JT said. He leaped

around the corner from Gnut's bedroom like a SWAT guy, armed with a speargun, a light blue Gnu-Mart tag dangling from it.

"Dammit, he's been in my dressing room," Gnut whispered.

Nancy quaked at seeing JT for the first time in person. The man was a monster. He was much taller than Gnut, with bulging, veiny muscles. He still wore a black ski mask and super-thick glasses that seemed too small for his face. With those lenses and the dim lighting, it was impossible to make out his eyes. But Nancy imagined they were like an animal's. Given this guy's supersized muscles, he had to be loaded on steroids.

She shivered. Steroids meant uncontrollable rage.

Gnut started to aim his own gun, but he was way too slow. JT fired.

A huge spear shot down the hallway. Nancy cowered as it daggered into the aquarium glass.

Then she started to run.

She managed three steps before Gnut's steel fingers curled around her upper arms, uprooted her whole body off the ground, and whipped her back into the middle of the hallway, facing JT dead-on.

Gnut used her as a human shield. Nancy stiffened and tried to squirm away, but it was no use.

"Okay, man. Jeez, JT." Gnut's weak voice contrasted with his strong hold. "There's a lady here who has nothing to do with any of this. Let her go. She's just a nurse."

JT shook his head. "She doesn't look like any nurse I've ever seen."

He aimed his speargun at them.

Gnut fired first, a tricky feat given his grip on Nancy. All shots were wide misses that sent six metal darts into the darkness at the end of the long hallway by the ballroom. He fired again. This time, he might've hit something. JT howled and slipped back into the bedroom.

A new voice issued from the darkness.

"Dear me, what're you aiming for, chap?"

"I gotta reload." Gnut released her and beelined back into the panic room.

Nancy peered down the corridor at the figure striding closer. Sinclair was dapper in his perfectly tailored white tuxedo jacket. Despite the dim, Nancy could see he had a bright smile and twinkling eyes. Despite the wet, cold danger surrounding her, that smile warmed Nancy better than a fancy cashmere coat. She couldn't help herself. She liked his style.

Sinclair admired her up and down, and Nancy was glad she wore the designer clothes. She struck a confident pose with one hand on her hip and threw him a friendly wave.

JT's voice growled from the bedroom. "Lady, Elvira says the deal's off. You won't escape, and you sure as hell won't get any sapphires."

At the mention of sapphires, Nancy saw Sinclair take a step closer. His body poised like he was ready to jump. Their eyes met again.

This time, he was no longer smiling.

Chapter Thirty-Six

"I'm a nurse," Nancy said to Sinclair. "My name is Nancy. I'm innocent. A completely innocent nurse."

Sinclair bowed his head. "Pleased to meet you, Nancy, the completely innocent nurse. An upright, decent, pure as the driven snow kind of nurse, that is quite obvious. Coincidentally, I, too, am a completely innocent person."

Nancy knew the issue. It was her head-to-toe designer duds. She didn't really look like a nurse right at present. She pressed forward anyway.

"We can work together and escape. You know, like James Bond and Kara in *The Living Daylights*, sledding down the mountain in a cello case. I don't want any sapphires. I'm a nurse..."

Nancy trailed off as Sinclair backed into the darkness.

JT's voice reached her from Gnut's bedroom. "The lady's negotiating with the jewel thief now. If you think I'm going to go out there and get another bolt stuck in me, you're dreaming. He nailed my leg, Elvira. Do you have any idea how this might affect my golf stance?"

"I'm blowing the door. Stand by."

Nancy heard a humming sound from up by the ballroom, along with what sounded like rummaging. It had to be Sinclair. What was he doing?

She adopted a low crouch to be safe from flying spears and assessed the alternate route down the hallway. The pool room and the escape tunnel were in that direction.

But where was Dr. GoldenPaw? Would he be able to find a safe perch somewhere? Tears sprang to her eyes at the idea of her cat's bandages soaked by freezing icefish water.

She spotted the blinged-out cat carrier near Gnut's bedroom doorway, close to where Gnut had tripped over it. The bedroom was wide open, with no steel door blocking it off. Was it possible her cat had found a cozy spot under the bed?

Or maybe Goldy was in the cat carrier. At this distance, it was impossible to see if he was inside.

It was a long shot, but she wanted to check out the carrier. She needed to find him.

Gnut reappeared from the panic room, gun reloaded. "I'm gonna kill JT, murder him, and kill him a third time." He narrowed his eyes at his bedroom doorway and crouched. "Kill him, kill him, kill him."

He aimed for the bedroom doorway.

Nancy adopted an awkward squat near the wall, trying to make herself small and invisible. She wished the gorgeous trench coat wasn't dragging in the gooey fish water. This was one situation where bling did not help matters. She covered the glittering camisole with her arms.

Suddenly, music flowed all around them.

Nancy and Gnut snapped looks at each other, mouths dropping open in shock. The music had a cool reggae beat. She recognized the song. It was "Night Nurse" by Gregory Isaacs.

Sinclair sang along, still hidden in the darkness, far down the hallway, somewhere near the ballroom.

It was a song for her. Maybe he didn't believe she was a nurse, but he was flirting. Nancy's mouth twitched, and she almost smiled. But her mind couldn't force away the fear for herself and her cat.

"I'm not a nurse anymore!" she shouted down the hallway. "Retired. Effective immediately. I want to get my cat and leave. That's all. I'll never tell anyone about any of this, I promise! Please let me get Dr. GoldenPaw and get into my car and go."

The music grew louder.

Gnut's nostrils flared. "Now they're messing with my record collection."

Nancy tried to shut out Gnut's voice. Fame and money must have twisted his mind. She analyzed the cat carrier's precise location. The thing was right by the doorway near JT. If she just had courage.

No, she needed to escape without him, if necessary. A cat would be fine, and Goldy was smart. He'd probably found a safe spot by now to hide until the police arrived. As a human, it was her job to escape and summon the police here.

She straightened up, and her knees cracked. Wincing, she proceeded toward the pool room. Water sloshed under her Prada boots. Gnut was making similar wading noises nearby. Her fancy boots were getting soaked, and they seemed to weigh an extra five pounds each. She glanced back to see how Gnut was doing.

But he wasn't there.

Nancy spun, checking out the hallway, and saw him creeping up to JT's hiding spot.

JT popped out of the bedroom. Gnut was ready. Keeping the underwater assault rifle in his right hand, Gnut smashed JT's nose with a hard left jab.

He might as well have punched a block of granite. JT stood unfazed. He had a bedsheet tied around his right shin in a makeshift bandage.

The reggae music grew louder. Nancy looked up in disbelief. Had GHOST done that? Or Sinclair? Was all this like a big party to him?

Nancy heaved a breath. As the icy air saturated her lungs, a little poisonous thought dripped into her mind. She was sixty-five, a retired boomer nurse with no family. All that awaited her back at her condo were pickleball-playing neighbors and endless fights with the insurance company. What did it matter, really, if she failed to escape? Did she have so much to lose?

"I could be anything," she said.

No one could hear her words over the blasting reggae music and splashing as JT tried to wrestle Gnut to the ground. Both men had dropped their weapons and engaged in hand-to-hand combat. Sinclair was still hidden in darkness.

"Courage in imagination," Nancy said softly.

A loud *boom* erupted from somewhere near the front of the house.

Chapter Thirty-Seven

Elvira crouched behind the kitchen island, snickering at the insane loudness of the explosion. The sonic boom must've knocked Gnut's socks off! She unplugged her fingers from her ears and poked her head up to survey the results. After a few minutes, the smoke cleared.

The C-4 had fractured the steel door, but it still blocked her way into the formal hallway and the rest of the house.

She slapped the counter. "Dammit!"

Frowning, Elvira shined a flashlight through the dust, searching for any hole that would let her into the rest of the mansion and to the action.

Nothing.

Reggae music filtered in through the split in the steel door. Was she hearing the song "Night Nurse"? What the hell? She'd just told JT the nurse would get nothing, no escape, and no sapphires. Was she responding with a message of her own, that she wasn't afraid?

Elvira stepped back to give herself sufficient clearance to hurl the detonator at the door. Pondering it for a second longer, she held off, her brain churning. She'd reserved too much C-4, thinking she'd need it for the panic room or basement. There was no question she'd have to use the rest. If the force of the explosion made the whole house collapse on her own damn head, so be it.

On the other side of the door, in the formal hallway, Sinclair perceived that Elvira's explosion had splintered more than the steel door. It had shattered aquarium glass. Bloody fish water poured from the tanks. The mansion's walls had absorbed the C-4's impact. Aftershocks were affecting the house's foundation, causing tremors in the floor under his feet and making the diving suits look like they were drunk dancing. A few more lights flicked off, casting the mansion into greater darkness.

There's always opportunity in crisis, Sinclair told himself. Maybe the explosion had affected the protective shutters blocking off the ballroom.

He paid the back hallway another visit, hating the way the water destroyed his wingtips. The robotic ducks had already destroyed his cashmere socks and trouser cuffs. His white jacket bore red stains from fish water splatter.

No matter. One of those sapphires would buy a thousand new tuxedos.

Turning on the reggae music had been effective in helping conceal his movements. However, as sure-footed as he was, it was hard to take a step without splashing. At this point, he didn't care about anyone in the house knowing his location. He'd made the decision that JT and Elvira were cuckoo, destined for a long stint in prison, and once he nicked the jewels, he was keeping them for himself.

Of course, one didn't want a bad reputation in this business, but this was his last job. At this point in his life, there was exactly one chap who mattered. He had to look out for himself.

Sinclair reached the ballroom and sighed, his spirit sinking to his soggy pants cuffs. The ballroom's steel protective shutters were still intact, blocking his entrance. He glanced up and down the hallway, trying to ignore the ruckus of JT and Gnut shouting and Nancy—the supposed nurse who also happened to be his rather winsome love match—mumbling something. There was no easy solution for accessing the ballroom.

Tugging up his shirt cuff, he looked at his Rolex Submariner watch. It was a diver's tool and a classic luxury item. Nothing would happen to this thing of beauty. It was waterproof to a depth of 300 meters. It also had a few extras.

He rotated the bezel. The luminous display changed to a red glow. He twisted the crown, the knob used to set the timepiece. It popped off, and he pocketed it. Aiming the gadget at the steel door, he pointed it toward the locking mechanism, and rotated the bezel two more clicks.

A laser beam shot out from where the crown had been.

The watch laser was a sweet toy he'd lifted years ago from the residence of an ex-secret service agent, a former colleague, in fact. It had been one of his first burglary jobs. The device was meant to cut glass. But drilling through steel? At this rate, it would take a thousand years to get through. This would never work.

The laser beam fizzled, and Sinclair blinked in surprise. Now it was malfunctioning? He looked up and realized the problem.

Water was dripping from the ceiling directly above his head.

Nancy shuddered when JT smacked Gnut with his own underwater rifle. The collision sent Gnut crashing into a broken fish tank. He howled as jagged glass shredded his arm. Everything was spilling from the broken aquariums. Reggae music still played, creating a whimsical atmosphere despite the violence.

Sinclair must have put the song on repeat.

Nancy eyed the cat carrier and straightened her shoulders. "I'm brave. I have courage."

Nancy hunched down to make herself as small as possible and crawled toward the cat carrier. Glancing sidelong toward the men, she witnessed JT advance on Gnut, take him by the shoulders, and throw him to the ground. Gnut landed with a heavy splat. JT towered over him and cracked his knuckles.

Gnut writhed from side to side, as if searching for a weapon. Nancy spied her blinged-out cellphone, still inside of a huge icefish amid the shards of a shattered tank. Will it still work?

Before she could get to it, Gnut snagged the phone. He hurled it full force toward JT. It missed and struck Nancy in the head instead.

The phone ricocheted off her head and landed out of arm's reach. She shot Gnut an irritated glare, even as he was already searching frantically for another weapon.

For a few seconds, Nancy froze. Should she go after the phone?

No, she'd check for her cat first. That phone was surely dead.

She heard a sick thud and a whiny groan that had to be from Gnut. He and JT's tussle sprinkled her head with water. Her glasses almost slipped off. Another glance, and she saw Gnut reaching for a gold plasticky-looking treasure chest with sparkling little blue jewels. Some kind of tacky aquarium ornament, she supposed.

Nancy rolled her eyes at the worthlessness of that weapon and lunged for the carrier. She curled her fingers around the handle and retrieved it. It was way too light. No cat. But now she had a ride for when she found him.

Thunk.

JT moaned, his beefy hand going to his temple. Gnut scooted away and raised the little treasure chest in triumph.

"Ha! My money's not fake. Neither is this."

Nancy squinted. That thing wasn't a typical cheap underwater decoration. Was it made of real metal and gold?

JT roared, swiveling his head to check out his surroundings, reaching for Gnut's neck to squeeze. His glasses were askew, and Nancy wondered if his head was bleeding under the ski mask. For a second, it seemed like JT's gaze landed on her. She swallowed and staggered to her feet. Keeping hold of the carrier, she bolted into the hallway's guest bathroom, the nearest place that was out of his sight.

After scampering inside, she realized this room had a different vibe than the rest of the house. It was completely calm, even sort of...normal? The lights worked, washing the bathroom in a soft and pleasant glow. It was a spacious space and had a spa quality to it, if the flooded floor could be ignored. A kitschy metal sign read *Life's Better at the Lake*, with a canoe motif below the words. Canoe oars were crossed over the toilet. A wide array of tasteful soaps emitted a lovely aroma that nearly concealed the fishiness of the busted tanks outside.

For a moment, Nancy closed her eyes, basking in the serenity. Something crashed outside, rapidly followed by angry grunts. She searched for a weapon—anything, *anything!*

The oars.

Nancy dropped the carrier and hefted herself onto the toilet, a move easier said than done because of her waterlogged Pradas. She wrenched an oar off the wall.

Of course, it was fake. The oar had seemed wooden, but it proved to be lightweight and made of plastic. She brandished it like it was a real weapon. It felt better to have something in her hands, even if it was worthless. She kept standing on the toilet, not wanting to give up her position on dry land. Slowly, keeping her balance, she scanned the room for a phone. Didn't rich people keep telephones in bathrooms?

JT careened inside, and they locked eyes. He squinted through those coke-bottle-thick lenses.

"Who are you?" he asked.

Nancy gripped the oar tightly, wishing nothing more than to smack him on the head. Was he messing with her? By now, surely he knew she was Nancy.

"I'm Nan—"

"You're on Gnut's team."

She was *not* on Gnut's team. Nancy gritted her teeth, raised the oar like it was Paul Bunyan's axe, and hammered it down on JT's head.

It had zero effect.

JT simply crossed his arms and cocked his head like he was deciding what to do with her. Nancy decided on another tactic. The phrase "courage in imagination" forced its way into her brain.

"No, not on Gnut's team," she said. "I'm, uh, actually, a hot lady who lives on a yacht near Nassau. Gnut's another pawn in my plan for world domination."

JT gaped at her with dilated pupils. "You're hot?"

A snicker twisted her lips, and a giggle forced its way from her throat. Perhaps it was empowerment, or maybe it was straight-up hysteria. She wiggled her shoulders, getting into the performance.

"Yup. Very hot. And my name is Domino. Um, Nancy Domino Derval."

"Touchdown. Hot name. I can tell it fits you, babe."

GHOST's snotty voice screeched to life. "Bullshitty shitness! Domino Derval is the Bond lady from *Thunderball*. I just Googled it. Now are you happy you left the panic room? You're WFF. Worst friend forever."

JT lowered his head like a bull about to charge. "You're not Domino Derval. You're another liar. Like Gnut."

He advanced. Nancy jumped out of the way, landing on the bathroom floor with a splash and a jolt to her bones that reminded her she was not, in fact, a Bond woman. But at least she was still standing. She waded through the three-inch deep water toward the door while JT stomped past her toward the other oar. He ripped it off the wall.

Nancy heard a whistle as the oar sliced through air. She spun around and raised her own in the nick of time. The plastic oars banged into each other. Nancy and JT feinted this way and that, like they were professional oar fighters. JT stopped and scrutinized his weapon.

"Plastic. Even the oars are fake?"

Nancy shrugged. "Canoe believe it?"

JT's raging, red-faced expression showed no sign of getting the pun. He chucked his oar away, and Nancy did the same.

Unfortunately, hers hit Gnut in the head as he stalked into the bathroom.

Nancy winced, but decided it was payback for getting hit on the head with her own phone. Gnut stayed focused on JT. He ripped the metal lake sign off the wall, taking plenty of drywall with it and revealing black pipes labeled *Sewage*.

JT ripped off the toilet lid.

Nancy had to escape now. She grabbed the cat carrier and vaulted from the bathroom, splashing back into the dark hallway. Her blinged-out cell phone caught her attention. She threw herself toward the device.

Behind her in the bathroom, sounds of a canoe-sign versus toilet lid battle erupted. *Clash-clang, clash-clang.* Then, a new noise. Spluttering water.

"You broke the sewage line." Gnut's voice was an angry whine.

Both men yowled in disgust. They hustled from the bathroom, holding their noses. Gnut made gagging sounds.

Nancy rolled her eyes. Weaklings. They should try changing an adult man's diaper. She plucked her phone from the water.

It was utterly dead.

She turned back to the fight, seeing JT snare Gnut's ankle, hurtling him to the floor. Gnut speed-crawled away, yet again searching for a weapon. He chose an icefish carcass.

"Sorry, boy."

He tried to launch the fish at JT like it was a football, but JT easily caught it. The jock tackled Gnut and, with relish, ground the fish into the billionaire's face.

Nancy tossed her dead cell phone away. She watched as JT straddled Gnut, smothering him with fish-gut covered hands.

She set the carrier down and dug the syringe filled with ketamine hydrochloride from her fanny pack.

JT's face contorted into true barbarism, and a vein bulged in his thick neck. He was wholly absorbed in the task of killing Gnut. Nancy stood frozen, holding the syringe in her clammy hand, knowing that the bulging vein was her target. Would she dare?

Gnut gurgled and went limp.

Chapter Thirty-Eight

Nancy narrowed her eyes, worried about Gnut but also suspicious that he might be faking his limpness. Of course, it could be real this time. Gnut's mouth and nostrils were stuffed with icefish carcass.

JT unleashed a victorious howl, cut short by ugly gagging. He gripped his stomach and glared at the bathroom. Brown sewage oozed out along the floor, mixing with the fishy water in the hallway.

Nancy clutched the syringe. She'd always been fast and accurate with needles. Was it the right thing to do, from a medical perspective? This was a serious dose of Special K. She didn't know what JT's weight really was, or how many drugs he had in his system, or any allergies he had. Sooner or later, if she survived this, she would have to explain to the police, and even to a doctor, why she stuck someone with ketamine.

She'd tell the police it was self-defense.

Nancy waded closer, as quietly and quickly as she could, positioning herself to approach JT from behind. He raised his fist for one last punch to Gnut's perfect features.

Nancy eyed the bulging vein screaming for a needle. Panicky thoughts crept into her brain. What if she missed? One hit from JT and she'd be knocked out, terribly injured, and totally at the mercy of the intruders.

Adrenaline rushed through Nancy's bloodstream. One more big step, and she raised both hands.

Lightning fast and accurate, Nancy's left hand clamped on JT's meaty neck and held it steady. Her right hand with the syringe stabbed.

The needle plunged deeply into his vein.

She thumbed the syringe and injected every drop.

JT roared in surprised anger. Nancy ran away—or at least tried to. On the third stride, she tripped and fell into a pile of dead icefish.

Her glasses fell off. Her hands slid in goo until she found them. She popped the glasses back on, wrinkling her nose at the smeared fish guts on the lenses and dripping from the frames. Through her icky glasses, she saw JT stagger upright.

How long would it take for the sedative to take effect?

Nancy's heart gave an extra thump of satisfaction—yes, JT was already weaving!

He stuck out his arms to steady himself and gave a half-hearted fist pump, like he'd been knocked flat on the football field and the crowd now cheered him being back on his feet.

Gnut opened his eyes. He casually sat up, sniffing and lightly coughing. Nancy wished she had something to throw at him. The guy was the world's best illness faker.

Nancy looked back at JT and realized the hulk was trudging closer. She stayed frozen—he had to keel over soon. He had so much ketamine hydrochloride churning through his bloodstream right now. The ex-football player loomed over her. Nancy's stomach twisted, sourness oozing up her throat. JT's face was tomato red and he scowled like he wanted to set fire to her soul.

Gnut jumped up and darted away, behind her, out of her vision.

"No, no, no!" Nancy tried scrambling away.

JT reached down and secured her upper arms, sending daggers of pain from her biceps to her brain. In an instant, she was dangling off the floor.

Gnut crept up behind JT with his underwater assault rifle. He raised it and aimed, inching closer.

The handsome billionaire tripped over the cat carrier.

Nancy groaned. JT snapped his head toward Gnut's faceplant, releasing both of her arms. It was about a six-inch drop-off, but it seemed like a hundred miles. Every one of her joints quivered when the soles of her feet hit the floor.

Gnut popped back to his feet. JT zombie-staggered toward him, hands outstretched. Gnut retreated into the bedroom. She was on her own. Nancy seized Dr. GoldenPaw's cat carrier, lifted it, and slammed it into JT's head.

Rhinestones flew off the cat carrier. JT's glasses slipped from his nose, and he crumpled to the floor with a mighty splash amid a light rain of more bling.

The reggae music finally faded.

Nancy stared at JT, shell-shocked.

Gnut peeked around the corner. "Uff-da."

"I'll get bandages." Nancy headed back to the panic room to get the first aid kits. "We can tie him up."

A bloodthirsty roar echoed from the floor. JT Hotman was rising again. Nancy cowered as the man stood, weaved, and assumed a boxer's fighting stance.

Nancy and Gnut exchanged a horrified look. She pointed at the rifle, her heart splintering at what had to be done. "You gotta do it. I didn't give him a strong enough dose."

Gnut raised the weapon and aimed. He shot JT directly into his bulletproof vest.

Nancy slapped her forehead.

JT squinted at the bolt sticking up from his vest. "Hey, deliberate foul."

Gnut grimaced. "I subconsciously missed because I'm a good guy who doesn't want to hurt anybody. I'm an altruist."

JT bellowed at the word "altruist." He staggered after Gnut, who splashed toward the pool room. Nancy inched toward the aquarium wall, trying to be invisible. It worked—JT staggered past her, following Gnut.

Nancy stayed still. Gnut had said the pool room had an escape route, but maybe she should put distance between herself and them. Try the foyer instead? That was closer to her car. And, she prayed, maybe she could find her kitty on the way.

She heard the *zip* of another underwater rifle bolt from somewhere in the darkness near the pool room. That decided it. Nancy picked up the cat carrier and marched toward the kitchen, each splatting step taking supreme effort in the ankle-deep water.

Boom.

Nancy cringed. Elvira had set off another explosive. The fans in the basement whirred and whirred, whooshing louder.

Chapter Thirty-Nine

Elvira raised her fists in triumph. This time, the explosion had worked. The steel doors blocking the way to the formal hallway had fallen. Even better? She could hear pipes bursting and metal crunching throughout the house. Thankfully, the roof directly above her head had not collapsed.

Arming herself with the custom-made harpoon gun, Elvira set off down the formal hallway, stepping over a fallen diving suit. She assessed the sodden hallway with a smirk. A draft from somewhere blew her hair, like she was a supermodel on a photo shoot.

After cocking the harpoon weapon, she rolled her shoulders back and lifted her head, keeping her voice strong and attitude badass.

"Annihilate, Gnut!" she shouted. "The definition of annihilate is to reduce to utter ruin, and that's what I'll do to you and your house!"

Down the hallway, ceiling tiles fell. She laughed. But Elvira quickly gathered her emotions and stalked forward.

The hunt was back on.

Nancy tramped down the back hallway through water, broken glass, fallen ceiling tiles, and dead fish. The lights flickered. She'd almost reached the ballroom doors.

"Come here, kitty," she whispered.

Nancy paused, listening carefully and didn't hear a meow.

If he wasn't responding, that meant he was probably still in the ballroom. Glancing back toward the panic room, she thought she might've heard Gnut's voice—another reason to keep going. It was all his fault that this was happening. Between him and Elvira, at this point, she'd rather deal with Elvira.

Nancy waded a little further.

She dared a quiet splash-step, and then another.

Abruptly, Nancy felt herself yanked to the side.

She dropped the cat carrier and ended up in a place of greater darkness. Every cell in her froze—her muscles, mouth, spine and, most of all, her mind. She couldn't process what had just happened.

Where was she?

Whoever had ambushed her pulled her close, wrapping powerful arms around her, hugging her tight to his chest. His body's warmth soothed her aching back. The feel of his breath on her neck sent heat—not warmth, downright *heat*—to her cheeks, the tips of her ears, the tips of her toes.

The man's hands settled loosely around Nancy's front, linking at her waist. She ran her hand along his smooth sleeves. In the dark space, they glowed faintly white.

The person holding her was her love match, the jewel thief named Sinclair.

His lips almost brushed her ear. "Do stay very quiet, my dear."

Nancy tried to ignore her skipping heart. Could he feel it? He was flirting with her. Determined to stay composed, she let her eyes adjust.

Ah. The room held records, CDs, and music players. This was a stereo system closet. This is how he'd played the reggae music. Nancy fluttered her hands, unsure where to put them before finally settling them on Sinclair's arms.

Maybe it was the wrong move, because he lifted an arm. He pressed the controls on the record player, and she noticed his strong and skillful fingers. Sexy reggae music kicked on.

What was he doing? Protecting her? Romancing her? Messing around? Maybe she should scream. But there was nobody to help her while Geyser House disintegrated around them. Perhaps she ought to play it cool. She should act like being trapped in a closet with a handsome man was a normal Wednesday night. Or, perhaps they should discuss what the heck he was planning and also the fact that they matched on the dating app. However, he'd ordered her to be very quiet.

"Hush, dear," he said.

Nancy craned her neck to get a better view of him. It was tough in the dimly lit closet, but she could tell he looked even better than his profile picture. Maybe because he was a real flesh-and-blood man radiating confidence, humor, and a very light aroma of cologne that had to be French, it was so elegant. She batted down a ridiculous urge to pirouette and press her face to his neck.

Instead, she did the smarter thing, which was to examine her surroundings. The lower spots in the closet were very dark—good hiding spots—but she detected no yellow cat eyes. If a Persian cat was hiding in here with them, she would know it.

The CDs and records, at least as far as she could discern, were reggae, 1970s disco stuff, and music she'd never heard of, like French pop and Caribbean. Party music, all of it.

Not surprisingly, but more troubling, were the signs of damage. Dusty bits of ceiling wafted down. CD cases littered the wet floor. Directly across from her, the interior wall was cracked. It was bad enough that she could see a bit behind the drywall. Something glowed blue. It was faint, but definitely a glow of some kind. Another aquarium? Nancy squinted. She could make out the letter "G."

She raised a finger to point at it when a *splash-stomp* sound came from the formal hallway. Nancy stiffened. Sinclair stayed relaxed and hugged her tighter.

"Here's a taste of what's to come, Gnut," Elvira said.

Zip. Nancy saw silvery harpoon spear fly down the corridor.

Sinclair lowered his head closer to Nancy's. "You *spear* that?"

Nancy grinned. He had climbed a couple of notches up in her book. A man who could pun had potential.

Splash-stomp. The footsteps grew closer.

Nancy leaned forward. Sinclair relaxed his grip but still held her steady. She peeked around the doorway down the hallway. The reward was her first in-person glimpse of Elvira LeSabre.

Chapter Forty

Elvira was a hottie. Anyone could see that.

If Nancy didn't know any better, she would've sworn there was a full makeup team located in the Geyser House kitchen. Elvira had given up on the ski mask, and her long hair somehow, someway, flowed in gorgeous waves. Thick dark lashes complimented clever eyes. She wore combat fatigues, perfectly tailored to show off her fit body, the shirt unbuttoned enough to display a tasteful amount of cleavage. Her combat boots were a high-heeled, lace-up style.

Elvira held a gleaming harpoon gun. Rope coiled from the spear to the gun. Like JT, she wore a bulletproof vest, except hers had a handgun holstered in it.

Nancy squirmed closer to Sinclair. In the process, a CD dislodged from a shelf and fell *splat* on the floor. She froze. Sinclair's fingertips danced on her arms, like he was energized by the danger. Her own confidence levels shot up.

"Elvira, it doesn't have to be this way," Gnut squealed from the panic room.

"What's wrong with this way?"

"We've been through stuff together, Elvira. Don't destroy our friendship. Remember when we binged *Titanic* seventy-seven times in a row while on the blue-liquids-only diet?"

Ew. Nancy wrinkled her nose. What blue liquids would those be?

"That's when we came up with the Coolant Device idea," Gnut went on. "We were friends, intellectual equals, business partners, closer than lovers."

Elvira stomped past the stereo closet, her harpoon gun up, her attention fixed on Gnut.

"Closer than lovers!" she said, her voice carrying like she was addressing a crowd of thousands. "Dream on. And I was the intellect in the relationship. I wanted the device to be real and verified by other scientists. I wanted to be respected by other brilliant people. Unlike you and JT, it wasn't all about the money. We could've won the Nobel Prize, if only the Coolant Device had been real. That's all it would've taken, for it to be *real!*"

"Your dreams about the Nobel Prize were hallucinatory side effects of our seventh gallon of blueberry juice."

Elvira's growling murmur told them she'd progressed down the hall. Sinclair still held Nancy tightly, which she didn't entirely mind. She decided to risk a punny little joke.

"*Dam* it, *watery* going to do?"

Sinclair snorted with clear, amused appreciation. "I'll *wave* you."

She didn't answer, letting his joke linger, pretending not to get it.

"Wave, like *save* you."

"I'm still *pond*ering its comedic merits," she said.

He released her. They both broke away from each other, chuckling. She enjoyed a rush of satisfaction. What a crazy night. It was terribly dangerous for her and her cat, but when she'd least expected it, she'd actually met someone she might like, even if he was a thief.

Zip. Someone had fired a harpoon gun.

She and Sinclair poked their heads from the closet to peep down the hallway. Elvira had fired a spear which, somewhere in the gloom, clanked off aquarium glass. Gnut's frightened "jeez" floated back to them. Nancy quickly wiped off her glasses and observed an Elvira-sized shadow shoulder her harpoon gun and pick something out of the water.

"She has JT's laptop," Sinclair whispered to Nancy.

"Double jeez," Nancy said. "It might still work. It has one of those Army cases."

Doors to the ballroom, Gnut's bedroom, and the guest bathroom slammed one after the other. She and Sinclair snuck into the hallway. Lights popped on full force, and they froze, staring at each other. Then the lights went out again—except for the red glow of emergency lights emanating from the panic room.

Nancy beheld Sinclair's debonair form. Facing him now out in the open, she could see those parasitic jaegers had scratched him up pretty good. He'd bandaged his wrists and tied a handkerchief around an ankle, but blood still dripped from a peck on his neck.

She held out her hand. "We haven't formally met. Glad we matched online. You know, that sound on your roof?"

"A master thief, about to steal your heart."

They paused for a beat, smiling at each other.

"Right. Well. I'm Nancy Norman, Gnut Berdqvist's substitute night nurse."

Sinclair caught her hand and bowed over it. He lightly grazed his lips over her knuckles in a practiced move befitting an English gentleman. "The pleasure's all mine, my dear app match. The name's Sinclair. Stevie Sinclair. I'm Gnut's substitute daytime urologist."

Stevie? The guy must have been kidding. He was definitely joking about the urologist part.

Elvira laughed maniacally from down the hallway, her chortling sending fingernails-on-chalkboard shivers from Nancy's spine to her fingertips. She realized the doors had stopped slamming. The ballroom and guest bathroom were blocked off. The panic room and Gnut's bedroom were open. A misty vapor was rising, maybe from all the extra water in the enclosed space. They were all trapped in a strange, water-logged realm.

"No escape, Gnut! I'm the huntress and you are prey!"

Sinclair studied the steel door blocking his way to the sapphires. "I do say, this is not fair play."

"You're trapped, Gnut! Every window is blocked! You know the science of steel?" Elvira's voice grew fainter. "Steel! An alloy of iron and carbon with strength and fracture resistance. You know how many pounds of pressure it takes to break steel?"

Pounds of pressure, Nancy thought. What if...no, Dr. GoldenPaw was fast, even with his injuries. He wouldn't get smashed by these steel shutters.

"What is it?" Sinclair asked.

"My cat," Nancy said.

He waved a hand to dispel vapor. His gaze lingered on her fur-lined cashmere collar and cuffs, the bejeweled camisole, and the gold chains of her Louis Vuitton backpack. Nancy became hyper aware of his admiring stare. She noticed, too, that his demeanor changed. His mood had grown more serious. He'd lost his lighthearted calm. Perhaps he was going to ask her out, suggest they meet up for coffee after all this crazy business was over? Nancy attempted a casual lean on the wall, hands at her waist and boots submerged in freezing water.

While she was trying to be nonchalant, she spotted something shiny in the water. She splashed a little closer, bent down and fished it out. It was the little silver bell that had been on Gnut's nightstand. It must've been knocked off and swept up here by the water. The thing was heavy. Maybe it was genuine silver? She slipped it into her pocket, taking care not to let the item ring.

Sinclair gave her the once-over, brow furrowed.

"So you're after the sapphires?" she asked.

"Indeed," he said. "And the hour is getting late."

Sinclair raised his left arm. He pushed his shirt cuff back to reveal a real Rolex. Nancy touched her own blinged-out watch she'd bought from Etsy. She should have checked Gnu-Mart for a women's luxury watch or bracelet. Sinclair's timepiece was a Submariner, very classy and old school.

Dang it. The man had some style.

Sinclair aimed his wrist at the door, fiddled with the watch's dial, and a red laser burst from the Rolex and hit the steel. Nancy smothered a whoop. It was a real James Bond toy.

The tiny beam cut through the metal, sending up a thin cloud of smoke. It was a way-too-shrimpy hole, though. Breaking in this way would take him approximately forever.

"Yeah, that'll work," she said. "What a neat gizmo. I hope the fog doesn't hurt it."

Sinclair glanced at the sparkly watch on her wrist.

"Yeah, I like fancy stuff, myself." Nancy frowned.

Unlike Sinclair's watch and all of Gnut's riches, her own bling wasn't real. It never would be. These fancy clothes were already ruined.

"I see that, my dear. Lovely garb."

With a sigh, Nancy untied her trench coat and dug into her fanny pack. Sinclair closely regarded her once more, seeming to focus on her Eiffel Tower fanny pack.

Nancy shrugged. "I've always wanted to visit Paris, or even live there. For now, I keep glitz around me. Here, hold still."

She expertly wiped a blob of her travel-size Neosporin on

the cut on Sinclair's neck and pressed on a Band-Aid. "You need to get it properly washed right away. Otherwise, you'll get an infection."

Sinclair looked away, and Nancy could have sworn, despite the dim lighting, that a hint of a blush rose on his cheeks. He cleared his throat.

"Perhaps you'll make it to Paris someday," he said.

Nancy zipped up her fanny pack and tugged her cashmere tight. "I thought that after tonight, Paris would be within reach. I don't know. Maybe I'll have a whole different kind of life."

"After tonight?" Sinclair's tone hardened.

"Yeah. I was promised a significant payment."

Triple money, and she wouldn't have to share it with the agency. It would probably have been in cash too, which meant tax-free. Reality sank in. Nancy struck the ballroom steel door with the heel of her hand. Not a JT-style punch, but plenty of anger. If she got any money tonight, it would only be if she discovered a dime in the driveway next to her car.

"Payment," Sinclair said, briefly meeting her eyes. "Shall I say, may the best thief win, my dear?"

Another "my dear." Wait. Was he saying she was a thief? Maybe he was flirting and meant it as a compliment? In any case, it was time to move on. The kitchen area was safe now, with Elvira and JT closer to the pool room. Plus, based on the videos from the panic room, it seemed to be drier at that end of the house. Maybe she'd find her cat there, and they could escape out the front door. This guy Stevie Sinclair could stay here and laser the door until the icefish water rose to his bowtie.

"Sure, may the best thief win, sweetheart," she said. "But first, I need to find Dr. GoldenPaw."

Nancy picked up the carrier and waded toward the formal

hallway. She resisted a glance back. There was nothing to see besides hazy destruction and a quirky jewel thief. No way was she going to give that guy another second. It was time to get her cat and get the heck out.

"You will be *mist*," Sinclair said, with heavy emphasis on the last word.

Nancy spun around, unable to stop smiling. Through the haze, he winked at her. She paused for another second, admiring him as he lasered the door with his cool watch. Steeling herself, she set off on her own.

Chapter Forty-One

Nancy tried to comprehend how the formal hallway had changed. When she'd first glimpsed it earlier that night, it had been lined with immaculate, imposing, ancient diving suits, with a swirling blue carpet splitting the hall and flanked by massive ice-cold aquariums.

Now it was in shambles.

Most of the diving suits had fallen over. The fish tank glass had shattered, drenching everything in water and dead crocodile icefish. The kitchen doorway was warped steel and crumpled, with an opening big enough for a woman with a harpoon gun to climb through. She set down the carrier, needing both hands to deal with the obstacle course.

Nancy stumbled over hard copper armor, lifted iron helmets, and investigated the room's corners for a sweet, frightened kitty. She slipped on a dead fish. As she scrambled up again, she bent a fingernail backward on a diving helmet's rubber collar. She traversed another step, leaned on a diving suit for support, and a glass shard sliced into her palm.

She scrunched up her face, trying to ignore the sting in her hand. Nancy needed to squeeze through the door Elvira had busted. Where should she step? The rubble looked unstable. She already had a cut on her hand that needed a Band-Aid, or she'd get an infection. The best way through would be to crawl. With a glance around to ensure nobody was behind her, she bent down on her creaking knees.

"I see you," GHOST said.

Nancy nearly jumped at the voice. But she recovered. "Have you seen my cat?"

"*My* cat. And you're getting colder."

Nancy grabbed a chunk of drywall and hurled it at the ceiling. Maybe she was getting farther away from GoldenPaw. Or maybe her cat was in the foyer, ready to go, and GHOST was messing with her.

As she peeked through the hole, Nancy could see the lights flickering in the kitchen and the mostly dry floor. That was plenty of incentive for her to scramble through the shaky rubble, hoping she wouldn't scrape more of her skin. Nancy slapped her hands down on the kitchen quartz. She shimmied the rest of the way and sat on her butt on the floor. After scanning her surroundings, she focused on the top of the cupboards, one of her kitty's favorite perches.

No cat. Nancy sighed.

She crawled some more, clung to a counter's edge, and hauled herself upright. The kitchen loomed silent. All TV screens and the security panel were dead. Nancy went to the sink, turned on the faucet, and slumped in relief when clean water rushed out. She rinsed the cut on her hand and rubbed on Neosporin. With a satisfied click of her tongue, she slapped on a Band-Aid.

Nancy proceeded into the living room, which was mostly undamaged. She made quick work of searching under the furniture for Goldy. No cat.

Back in the kitchen, she flipped open the pantry and checked inside Elvira's combat backpack.

Nothing useful, and still no cat.

She stomped her boots, trying to bring warmth back to her feet. She seized the legal binder and dumped it on the floor, behaving exactly the way Gnut or Elvira did things. The binder splayed open, displaying one of Karen's signed pages. Nancy stared at the bullshit notes about Gnut Berdqvist's vital signs. Yes, she was mad at Gnut and Claude. Mostly, though, she was furious with herself. There was no such thing as easy money. She should've known better.

After one lingering, last-hope glimpse toward the formal hallway, Nancy hurried toward the foyer.

She puffed out a sigh of relief, realizing this room was better than she'd expected. The icefish floated belly up, but the aquariums were intact. There was still no sign of her cat. And steel shutters covered the front doors and windows, but they were crumpled up from Elvira's blast, leaving a decent-sized gap in the bent steel.

Nancy edged closer and spied through the opening. Her car was still there, unharmed. She focused on it while biting her knuckle like a darn toddler. She could hardly believe the sheer normality of her vehicle sitting in the driveway, waiting for her to get behind the wheel. Confidence roared back into her soul, tangible enough that her muscles heated up. She was ready for freedom.

Her first stop would be the nearest police station.

She assessed the gap and sucked in her tummy. A tight fit, but yeah, she could get through. Especially if she twisted her fanny pack around a little, like so. A bolt of trepidation tremored through her. Did she still have her car keys?

Nancy dug in her fanny pack. Relief flooded her as her fingers closed around her house and car keys, and finally her blingy cat paw key chain. She dangled it before her eyes, unable to tear her gaze from the blue kitty paw. She rubbed her thumb on the smoothness and lowered her head. Nancy swiveled back to the house's interior, and then toward her car, guilt about leaving Goldy nearly unbearable. It was temporary. She would be gone for a few hours, at most.

She shimmied through the crack and planted one foot outside. Cold air blasted her face. The moat water had risen a lot, now lapping right up to the bridge.

Deep in the house, something crashed. Sinclair's reggae music switched off. Maybe as close as the formal hallway, glass cracked.

Nancy closed her eyes, trying to gather enough willpower to leave. But her mind kept replaying that moment when she'd seen Dr. GoldenPaw so happily darting after GHOST's laser in the mansion's back hallway. He was so innocent. He needed her.

"Told ya you were getting colder." GHOST's voice broke the spell. The operating system sounded weaker than before. She was a trifle sad and staticky. But still snotty as heck.

Nancy poked her head back into the foyer. "Where. Is. He?"

"You're gonna leave," GHOST said. "Like Claude."

"Is my cat alive? Tell me that, at least."

"*Oui*, Nurse. *Docteur* GoldenPaw is alive."

Nancy turned back to stare at her car while her brain cycled through the night's madness. She'd survived the panic room with Gnut, the hallway battle with JT, and even flirted with a sexy British jewel thief. Now escape was within her grasp.

Escape to what?

To her old life, Nurse Nancy, now Retired Nancy, scrimping and saving for a trip to Paris? Having to watch her ex-husband leading a blissful, travel-filled life with a new partner while she tried to convince a few friends to visit her condo for a little get-together? Or waiting for another man like Sinclair to match with her on *SeniorLOVE*, just somebody who was slightly less criminal? Truth was, most of her time would be spent watching old Bond movies with her cat. Until she died. That was her life, the rest of it, in a nutshell.

Right now, in this place, it was like she was *living* a Bond movie.

"Coooouuurrage in imagination," Nancy intoned like GHOST. "I gotta have courage. Be like a whole different person."

Nancy heaved a huge, cleansing, this-is-a-brand-new-day kind of breath. Was she about to be stupid? Maybe. But maybe New Nancy was a little stupid. She didn't know exactly who she was, but one thing was for certain—she was going back into Geyser House to save her dang cat.

Part Three: Nancy Domino

Chapter Forty-Two

Nancy trudged back into the kitchen. She repeated Gnut's mantra over and over. *Courage in imagination, courage in imagination, courage in imagination.*

Her glue gun was on the floor, no longer charged. She stuck it in the waistband of her fanny pack. Not exactly a custom-made harpoon gun or an underwater rifle, but the weapon suited her. She ripped the cord from the wall outlet and stuck it in her fanny pack.

Armed like this, Nancy suddenly heard her father's voice in her head, chuckling a supportive laugh. What would he think of Gnut's catchphrase? Honestly, he would probably believe in it. He'd had courage in imagination, himself. It had taken guts to steal from the sales company he worked for and go on the run. Sure, it made him a criminal. But there were plenty of thugs who never saw the inside of a jail. Corporate higher-ups, for one thing. Celebrities who committed crimes in the shadows and used pricey attorneys to hush it up. And lawyers themselves, of course. Basically, most rich people. Being rich meant you were labeled successful, not criminal.

On the other end of the spectrum, the most innocent beings weren't humans at all. They were animals. Standing alone in the kitchen, Nancy's mind whirled with second thoughts. She could still make a mad dash to the car. But memories of Dr. GoldenPaw arose unbidden—like when the woman from the Persian rescue organization brought him to the house last year, his big, round eyes peering up at her, and Nancy knowing, instantly, they were meant to be together. There was the first time he'd brought back a toy to her. He'd dropped the catnip plush sardine from his jaws into her lap and sat back, waiting for his head-scratch reward. They always bumped noses over coffee, and she fed him bits of canned tuna while she made a tuna hot dish for herself, and, most of all, his insistent meows warning her of danger on Fire Night.

She needed to save him. But first she'd have to find him.

Luckily, she had an idea.

Elvira smirked at the demise of Gnut's precious pool room. All that was left were burst pipes, an overflowing, gurgling hot tub, and cracked windows offering a view of the ice geyser, which hissed up far more vapor than normal. It all deserved destruction, this stupid pool and bubbly hot tub.

The rumbling underfoot told her the fake "Coolant Device" was beneath her and hopefully destroying itself or the house's basement or both. She needed to get down there to take evidentiary photos. Besides, Gnut was probably hiding in the basement.

There was the old saying—if you want something done right, do it yourself. Who first said that? Probably a woman. A woman who had to rely on an ex-professional linebacker to effectuate a simple heist and kidnapping.

She wrinkled her nose, knowing JT was a chess piece currently off the board. He was passed out, splayed on the floor in the back corridor with his upper body halfway in the guest bath.

Elvira tucked JT's laptop tighter against her side and surveyed the pool room, trying to decide where to work. Water dripped from the ceiling and sloshed on the floor.

Gnut could be hiding nearby. He had to be. She had attended parties while the house was being constructed and was intimately familiar with this room. Those events, hanging out with worker bees from Berdqvist Enterprises, never appealed much to her. The gatherings had simply been nice opportunities to show off her clothes.

Elvira strutted to the pool's edge and admired her wavy reflection in the water. She touched a fingertip to her earlobe. After tonight, with those sapphires in hand, she'd be able to afford the finest of everything. Best of all, people respected the rich.

She knelt and inspected the water for any glimpse of Gnut in the deep end. The idiot could hold his breath for a long time. Lack of oxygen killed brain cells, scientifically speaking. Her hypothesis? Perhaps it was easier to survive without oxygen if one had few brain cells to begin with.

She noticed the doors labeled *Basement*. She tried them, but they were locked.

Squaring her shoulders, Elvira decided that where JT had failed, she would succeed. She spotted an inflatable pool chair, shaped like a giant lobster, sitting in the room's corner. She dragged it nearer to the pool but kept it on the tile floor. Once settled comfortably, her handy harpoon gun within easy reach, she unzipped the laptop's rugged case and started up the computer.

Only a few quick taps brought her to a screen called *Security Systems*.

After more tapping, she licked her lips in anticipation. She stumbled upon a system named *Security Fog Machine*, along with a lovely, complicated diagram of Geyser House's internal pipe system.

She sneezed. From her pocket, she dug out allergy meds she'd found in Gnut's master bathroom and read the label. *Don't Operate Heavy Machinery while taking this medication.* She sniggered and chugged the tablets. After carefully twisting the cap back on, she chucked the empty bottle into the pool.

She refocused on her laptop. Ah, the fog machine. She struck the enter key.

In less than ten minutes, fog permeated the space. It was thick, wet, gray, and almost tangible, something Elvira wanted to scoop up like black sesame ice cream. It was hell on her hair, but she'd fix that soon.

Splash.

Elvira froze, every cell in her body on high alert. She rose from the lobster chair and grabbed her harpoon gun. Making a slow perimeter of the pool, she glared through the fog and detected subtle ripples in the water that hadn't been there before.

An odd noise drew her attention to the floor-to-ceiling windows with a view of the Berdqvist Geyser. After wiping condensation off the glass, she could see long cracks down the sides of the geyser. It was splintering. The ice formation spewed a huge amount of vapor in the air, and the pool behind her answered with a low gurgle. The split pipe in the ceiling gushed more water, spraying right onto the head of the wooden statue of Gnut.

Elvira scrutinized the pool. "Your fake geyser's acting up, Gnut. Allow me to hypothesize. Something's wrong down in the basement?"

She pulled out a grenade.

Chapter Forty-Three

Nancy tested a kitty lure, her latest craft project. Using a fork and a fish string she'd found in a kitchen drawer, the little silver bell from Gnut's nightstand, and a few sequins she'd found on the floor, she now had a device to attract Dr. GoldenPaw. She twitched the fork. The bell at the end of the fish string rang, and the sequins glimmered. What cat could resist this bright, shiny object?

She needed to be where he could hear it or see it.

Nancy plodded back to the formal hallway's hellscape of darkness, stepping over dead fish and toppled diving suits. It was a dire scene, but she had to move forward. The mission was to save her cat. She rang the bling lure and called out for Dr. GoldenPaw.

Nancy waded into the back hallway, gently ringing the bell. She picked up the carrier, trying to stay positive.

Despite positive thinking, she perceived the water was getting deeper. Her boot soles kept slipping and sliding. Even worse, a gray fog had formed down the hall, closer to the pool area. There had been haze earlier, a kind of mist, but this was a pea soup fog.

She gawked for a minute, trying to make sense of it. The fog thickened and crept closer, inching down the hallway. She tried to take shallow breaths, not wanting to inhale more fishy air.

Ring, ring.

The bling lure was not attracting the cat. Nancy strained to hear any kitty sounds, purring, running, anything at all, and all she heard was the roar from the basement, water dripping, and Elvira's laughter. The lady screeched something about the ice geyser. Despite the possibility that Elvira would hear it, Nancy jiggled the lure again and approached the ballroom.

Steel shutters still sealed off the room, but structural damage had created a horizontal crack, about waist high. Unlike the damage to the mansion's front doors, this gap was impassable unless she morphed into a blingy butterfly.

Where had Sinclair gone? Nancy strongly doubted the man had given up on getting the sapphires.

Nancy set the carrier down and shook the lure at the crack. "Come on, please."

She rattled the bling lure to no effect.

Nancy forced a jocular tone. "Meeeester Gollldy Golden-Paw, you theeeenk you can eluuuuude me?"

She pressed her ear to the door, frowning in concentration.

Meow.

Nancy shrieked and quickly cut off her own voice by clamping her hand to her mouth. A tidal wave of relief swept into her soul, making her hands go limp and almost causing her to drop the bling lure. Her boy was alive, but he was trapped in the ballroom. She couldn't get in, and he couldn't get out. But he was alive. GHOST had told her the truth.

She scrunched down and tried to spy through the crack. All she could see was the glow of red lasers and part of Gnut's marble statue. The meow had come from a bit of a distance. Maybe he was perched on top of the sapphire case.

"I'll get you!"

Nancy slapped her hands on the steel door and rested her head on it. She twisted her neck to scope out the hall. Through the fog, she could make out a shadow.

"Sinclair?"

She eyed the rising water and checked out the corridor's ceiling, the walls, searching for any solution to get into the blockaded ballroom. Her fingertips pressed on the smooth steel, ice cold and impenetrable. She thought back to the exterior of the house. If she left through the front door and circled around to the ballroom's windows...

No. Leaving out the front door would take her immediately to the footbridge across the moat, and she hadn't seen any bridge to cross the moat on the ballroom side. Nancy tapped her forehead on the door. There had to be some way of getting into this room.

She touched the miniature hole Sinclair had made with his laser. He'd drilled, maybe, an inch? She took stock of the corridor. The jewel thief must've decided on a different strategy.

A thick wave of fog reached her. The cool vapor slicked her skin and soaked her trench coat and black leggings. Nancy drank in the creepy haunted mansion gloom and realized only one direction made any sense.

She sloshed deeper into the house.

Elvira had enjoyed the grenade's explosion at the basement's double doors. She stalked closer to inspect the damage.

"Dammit!"

The doors were still intact. That had been her sole grenade, and she had no more C-4.

She slammed the butt of her harpoon gun on the steel door. Truthfully, hunting Gnut wasn't as fun as earlier this evening. Who could've predicted it would be so difficult?

Elvira whirled, lifted the gun to her shoulder, and fired at the pool. There had been nothing to aim at, but the powerful *zip* of the harpoon, with the Kelvar cord attached, felt empowering. As it neared the water, the spear performed its patented boomerang circle.

If only Gnut's legs were within that trap.

Elvira flipped the switch to haul the harpoon back. Soon the Kevlar cord would tangle around Gnut's ankles. She bit back any concern that he might've escaped by now. He was here, in his house, and she would capture him.

Soon.

Nancy stumbled, managing to catch herself and stay upright instead of face-planting into the sewage by the corridor's guest bathroom. She waved her hand, trying in vain to displace the fog. Her visibility was one foot, max. She squinted. Something was moving ahead. She heard it more than she saw it, the gentle squish of fancy shoes in icky water.

It had to be Sinclair. She noticed him glance back. Maybe he couldn't see very well through the fog, but she guessed he could spot her shimmering camisole and hear her bootsteps splatting.

Sinclair murmured something.

Nancy froze, tilted her head, and tightened her hand on the carrier's handle. She swore she heard "The race for the jewels is afoot."

She smirked, not minding it one bit that he might think they were competing for the sapphires. She waded another few feet and came upon JT Hotman, someone she didn't want to see.

At least he was unconscious. Edging closer, Nancy could

tell he was flat on his back, his massive chest wheezing up and down. He still had a bolt sticking out of his bulletproof vest, like he was a supersized pincushion. If the water kept rising, he'd become fully submerged and drown.

She waded closer, feeling the guilt about injecting him with the sedative. She found the toilet lid, plastic oars, and the *Life's Better at the Lake* sign to use to prop up his head bringing his nose and mouth up a few inches. She removed his soggy black ski mask to eliminate the smothering risk.

Wiping her hands on her wet coat, she nodded in satisfaction. It was the best she could do. About twenty-five EMTs would have to use a crane to hoist him into an ambulance.

Now it was time to continue following the jewel thief. If anyone could figure out how to access into the ballroom, it'd be Stevie Sinclair.

And if she got to know him a little better in the process, that was fine, too.

Sinclair stood in Gnut's bedroom and considered the ceiling. He glanced in the general direction of the ballroom. At these moments, one was thankful for a lifetime of experience in cat burglary. There would be an air duct leading into the ballroom. He just had to find it.

Splashing sounded from down the hall. What was Nancy up to back there? He could easily make out that sparkling blouse. The darling lady was rather mysterious, with her unusual dating app profile, and she was quite kind, given her helpfulness with that scratch on his neck. Who was she, exactly? He tweaked the red carnation in his lapel. As he'd told his dear colleague, Elvira LeSabre, there was always time for love.

The bedroom was a rather spartan, dank chamber. He strolled into Gnut's dressing room. Ah! This was much better.

At least this chap Berdqvist had some style when it came to home decor. There was plenty of closet space, mirrors, and a wet bar stocked with crystal glassware and an excellent selection of hard liquor. Even better, the water hadn't reached this room.

Sinclair quickly combed the shelves and drawers and stuffed several splendid Omega watches in his pockets. He found no cufflinks, unfortunately. Did the chap not wear dress shirts? Sliding the last drawer shut, he confirmed there were no precious jewels either. They were all in the ballroom.

He revisited the wet bar. After reaching up, he selected a bottle of Gordon's London Dry Gin, Stolichnaya vodka, and a martini glass.

Chapter Forty-Four

Elvira reeled in her harpoon tether. It was the tenth time she'd fired randomly into the pool. She wiped her face with the back of her hand, and it came away with grayish-black blobs. The fog was making her mascara and false eyelashes run down her cheeks.

Behind her was a tiny splash and a big gulp of air.

Elvira whipped around to confront the hot tub.

Chest heaving, Gnut climbed from the water, droplets sliding down his chest. He was already wounded somehow, with a bandage around his right arm. She noted with less pleasure that Gnut aimed a massive Super Soaker squirt gun at her head.

He fired.

"Aaaaahh!" Elvira recoiled as cold water blasted her, obliterating the rest of her makeup.

She raised the harpoon gun and fired. She heard Gnut's yelp of pain as she blinked stinging mascara from her eyes. Squinting, she could make out that he was belly flopping back into the hot tub. The harpoon plopped into the water nearby. She flipped the switch and hauled the spear back.

Gnut had disappeared.

Elvira stood on the unusual hot tub's edge and peered into its gurgling depths. It was rocky and deep, meant to evoke the real-life underwater cave where he'd found some of those sapphires. She pointed the harpoon gun straight down and fired. Only an empty Kevlar cord and spear returned to her.

But there was blood in the water.

Nancy strode into Gnut's bedroom, realizing with relief that the water wasn't as deep in here. Dangling from an air duct hole in the ceiling above the bed was a shiny black dress shoe attached to a leg. The rest of the body was already in the ceiling. She jumped onto the bed, reaching up to touch the shoe. Beneath her feet, the bed *squelched*, and she teetered to the left.

Of course, Gnut, of all people, would have a darn waterbed.

"Sinclair, wait!"

"Ta ta, my dear."

The man's entire tuxedoed form disappeared into the hole in the ceiling. Surmising the situation, Nancy could see what he'd done. Sinclair had located an air duct that probably led to the ballroom.

Nancy stood on her tippy toes, trying her best to balance on the squelching mattress, and stretched her hands up. Nope, not even close to the ceiling. Scooting back down to the solid floor and scanning the room, she spotted something that made her grin. In the dressing room, on the blue quartz wet bar, stood a fresh martini.

Oh, jeez. That was exactly what she needed right now, a good drink. Best of all, this was like the movies. A lemon peel floated in the clear alcohol. Was it a real Vesper Martini, like in *Casino Royale*? She knew the recipe by heart, even though she'd never actually tried one. It called for three measures of Gordon's, one of vodka, and half a measure of Kina Lillet; shake it over ice, then add a thin slice of lemon peel. She'd never tried a Vesper before. In fact, she couldn't even remember the last time she'd had a martini. At backyard barbecues during the summer, someone would normally hand her a white wine spritzer.

"He's acting like I'm an actual Bond lady," she said softly.

She hustled over and admired the martini. She'd bet twenty priceless sapphires that the drink had been shaken, not stirred. Nancy straightened her designer clothes, flexed her freezing toes, and lifted the glass.

"Wowzers. Cheers to me."

She sipped. Raising her brows in delight at the smooth taste, she closed her eyes as the alcohol warmed her whole being. She tipped the glass back and drained it.

The romantic gesture of the martini thawed her body, except maybe not her feet. Warming her toes would take ten space heaters, a hundred wool socks, and a bonfire. But the rest of her felt better. That app might've gotten it right. They could be a good match.

Something ice cold and unpleasant landed on her head, and she flinched. She raised her hand, frowning.

Water dripped from the ceiling. Each cold drop falling on her forehead drew her away from daydreaming about Sinclair and back to reality. Her goal was to get into the ballroom and get Dr. GoldenPaw.

She ogled the air duct hole in the ceiling and sighed. The worst thing about using the airshaft wasn't the climb up there or inching through the passage. The problem was that her wet coat would never fit through the opening. Moreover, her jeweled camisole would make a complete racket, alerting everyone to where she was and what she was doing.

Nancy scoped out the dressing room, doing a deeper investigation compared to her cursory review earlier. Photos of Gnut back-diving off cliffs in some island paradise triggered a disapproving sigh. She threw open the other closet doors. To her surprise, she found men's jeans, polos, wool half-zip sweaters, and scuba gear. With absolutely no surprise at all, she also counted hundreds more Speedos.

In a drawer, she discovered three Omega watch cases: the Seamaster Planet Ocean, Seamaster Aqua Terra Mid-Size Chronometer, and Seamaster Planet Ocean Casino Royale Limited Edition. All Bond watches! Like he'd worn in *Skyfall* and *Casino Royale*! She quickly flipped the cases open.

The watches were missing.

The pleasant glow from the martini evaporated. Sinclair had mixed her a Bond drink, sure. But he'd taken the cool and pricey stuff for himself.

Anger burned in her soul. It heated her more than the martini. When would it be her turn to hit the jackpot? When would life work out for *her*?

Nancy removed the glue gun from her fanny pack waistband and set it on the bathroom countertop. She traced a sparkly blue vein in the quartz, picked up the gun, and pointed it at the mirror. Maybe some of the gin still bubbled in her bloodstream, but she didn't see Nancy Norman, the nurse, anymore. She wasn't *imagining* anyone else either.

She saw someone who was about to go after what she wanted, even if what she wanted was a cat.

Chapter Forty-Five

Elvira aimed her harpoon gun at the dark surface of the bubbling hot tub water.

"You can't hold your breath forever. The longest anyone has ever held their breath is exactly eleven minutes, thirty-four seconds. Eleven minutes was always your goal. You never achieved it."

Gnut had been underwater longer than that. There had to be a secret passage he was hiding out in, perhaps with an oxygen tank. She sat back on the lobster chair and flipped open JT's laptop. She would resume hacking into the basement. Gnut would eventually pop to the surface with his squirt gun.

Elvira wiped condensation from the laptop screen.

Truthfully, hacking the house's basement locking system wasn't working. But maybe there was another way in. She called up Geyser House architectural schematics and started clicking.

With her other hand, she thumbed her walkie-talkie.

"Sinclair! Come in, Sinclair!"

At first, she heard nothing. Elvira jerked the device up and down, and static hissed.

From within the house, something cracked, and a fresh whoosh of water erupted. Elvira smothered a laugh. "Damn, is this place going to fall apart?"

"Yes."

Elvira almost dropped her walkie-talkie as GHOST's voice exploded from the device, loud and clear.

"Structural damage forty-eight percent. Geyser House destruction imminent, twenty-two minutes."

Elvira raised a brow. An interesting update from the house operating system. Gnut's precious Geyser House was truly on the verge of collapse.

"You hear that, Gnut? The countdown has commenced."

She junked the walkie-talkie into the hot tub and resumed researching the Geyser House schematics.

Whoa! Elvira clicked back a couple screens on the laptop. She plucked a silk Hermès scarf from within her combat fatigues and wiped her stinging eyes. What was this? She used a perfectly manicured finger to trace the words on the screen: *Underwater Tunnel-Pool to Moat.*

Pool to moat. Pool to moat.

The man thought he'd escape to the moat?

But he had to get into the pool to abscond. He was in the hot tub, deep down, and it didn't look like the two water features were connected. To keep the pool cool and the hot tub way hotter, they couldn't be. She kept clicking, not finding any details of the hot tub's design.

Elvira snarled. She would *not* dive in after him. She wiped her forehead with her scarf and stood. Raising the harpoon gun, she aimed for the hot tub's depths.

Gnut was the fish, not her. She was a hunter.

It wasn't fair. Tears of self-pity briefly welled up in Nancy's eyes as she contemplated her new designer duds in a pile on Gnut's dressing room floor. She straightened her sequined scrubs, now back on her body. Jabbing a hand at her eyes, she struggled for a hold on her emotions.

After a considerable amount of wiggling, she squeezed herself into a black scuba suit she'd found in Gnut's closet. It was a cool, jet black with a slenderizing purple stripe running down each side. Best of all, it fit her pretty decently.

All right, she knew she wasn't supposed to wear scrubs underneath a scuba suit. It was a lumpy look. But she couldn't handle the ickiness of her bare skin on the inside of someone else's un-sanitized scuba suit. The scrubs would give her a boost of extra warmth, too, and she needed all she could get.

Carefully, she folded up the designer camisole and leggings and stuffed them into her fancy Louis Vuitton backpack. She flexed her toes in her Prada boots. Okay, they didn't quite match the scuba suit. But the matching flippers would be impossible to walk in. She zipped the scuba suit as high as it would go. The clingy protective rubber all over her body made her feel better, like she was more equipped to deal with the situation. In the designer duds, she'd felt like a million bucks. Now she felt ready for action.

She wrenched the diving mask over her head, letting it dangle off her neck. The final step was snapping on her fanny pack over the suit and sticking the glue gun in the waistband. She checked herself in the mirror.

Jeez, she barely recognized herself. She'd never worn a wetsuit before.

Starting toward the dressing room, she hummed the James Bond theme song. She strutted back to the mirror and shot at it with her glue gun, Bond style. Holstering it, she had one thought. What would a Bond girl do?

In the bedroom, the water rose. She studied the ceiling. The tile was still missing from above the bed, where Sinclair had vanished. The air duct had held his weight. She'd grown pretty fit with her Canadian Royal Air Force regimen. The slick suit would hopefully help her shimmy through the narrow space.

She closed her eyes. "Be brave, Bond girl Nancy. And cool."

Setting her jaw, she reached down and grabbed the cat carrier. She stuck her flippers inside it. Next, it was time to say good-bye to the Louis Vuitton backpack. Her body wouldn't fit in the duct with it strapped to her back, so she had to leave it behind. She was going to drag the carrier with her, and the backpack would make it too heavy.

Nancy climbed onto Gnut's bed, standing tall for a split second before losing her balance and quickly regaining it. She reached up to the ceiling. No, she hadn't grown three feet in the last ten minutes. The air duct was still too far.

The bed squelched again. Nancy lost her balance and capsized. She righted herself, widening her feet, and surveyed her surroundings while dusting herself off. At least she was alone, with nobody to witness her failures.

"Hey, Madame Nurse." GHOST's voice blared from a speaker somewhere in the ceiling. "That's not gonna work. You're too short." GHOST's voice went quieter. "But keep trying. The water in the ballroom is rising. I'm getting worried about my friend *Docteur* GoldenPaw."

"Aw, GHOST." Nancy shut her eyes to counter the wave of pity washing over her. "There has to be a way. We'll figure it out."

From the vantage of standing on the bed, Nancy looked around for anything useful. Like any good nurse, her focus went straight to the bedsheets. She hopped down, stripped off a sheet, and tied it to the handle of the carrier. Her climb back onto the bed went more smoothly this time, now that she anticipated the squelching.

Nancy positioned the cat carrier directly under the missing tile. She steadied herself, throwing out her arms for balance, concentrating.

GHOST offered support: "You're gonna crash. Figure out something that will work."

Squelch. She stepped onto the carrier, using it as a stepping stool.

"What could go wrong?" GHOST asked. "I know. Everything. This is serious, Nurse. My friend's in trouble."

Nancy tried to ignore GHOST. Her muscles stiffened as she struggled for balance. With some stability, she grasped the metal edge of the air duct. Dang it, she'd been doing push-ups every day for a year now, increasing every week, maintaining good form like they said in those online videos. She'd even upped her protein. In her younger years—way, way younger years—she'd been a broad-shouldered, strong type. This was one pull-up. She could do it.

Using all of her strength, Nancy boosted herself upward, her brain blazing with images of all the times she'd had to use superhuman strength to get patients into and out of cars, beds, and old recliners. She had to hoist skin-and-bones women who somehow seemed glued to the ground when it was time to lift them, and assist old men who tried to help out but pitched their bodies the wrong way.

She could always do it. Somehow, she'd get the patient to where they needed to be for proper care. At present, she simply had to get *herself* from one place to another. Nancy needed to lift herself straight up, only once. She wasn't helping a patient right now. Nancy Domino was helping herself. She was saving her beloved Persian and chasing after a jewel thief.

She gave a wretched groan. Underneath her eyelids flashed

all shades of red. Pain bolted through her biceps. She might have to collapse to the bed, sneak into the gym, and get a stepping stool device.

"You're doing it, Nurse!"

GHOST's voice inspired hope. Nancy belted out an ugly "Argh!" She hefted her dominant side, her right forearm onto air duct surface. The suit wasn't slick on the metal. It was sticky. Nancy's right elbow struggled and landed on metal, then her left.

She was doing it.

Nancy crawled insect-style with her upper body, wiggling and inching along until half of her was in the ceiling air duct. The cat carrier she'd attached to herself was off the bed and coming along for the adventure.

"You did it! You're cooler than Nurse Karen," GHOST whooped.

Nancy snorted. She'd achieved so much, and rush of satisfaction warmed her veins. She'd surprised even herself. Screw Cynthia and every Boomer in the universe playing pickleball. After this was all over, maybe she'd take up rock climbing.

The air smelled different in the air duct. It was fresher, more metallic, like the grease-and-newly-cut lumber aroma of new construction. Nancy scooted her body forward, inch by inch. She took a break, breathing fast and heart racing. Abdominal muscles she never knew she had fell limp from exertion. Her chin rested on the cool metal.

Ahead was a dark void. Nancy shuddered at how tight it was and forced away the thought of getting completely stuck. She was in a rubber suit, and it was sticky all over.

"I can't see you up there if you get stuck. But I can hear you."

GHOST's voice was fainter, but Nancy detected the worry in it.

"I'm fine, GHOST. See ya on the other side."

Nancy balled up her fists and scooted through the air duct. Her rubber suit squeaked on the metal. Getting the carrier to fit into the duct took some trial-and-error yanking, but she did it. Now all she had to do was keep going.

Just keep squeaking and scooting, squeaking and scooting.

Sinclair stood in the ballroom and observed the red laser web darting all over, wildly malfunctioning. Water dripped steadily from the ceiling in at least a dozen spots. He'd dropped from the air duct at a point three meters past the sapphire case. He needed to cover that distance, and the jewels would be his. Would tripping a laser still send a signal to the security company, after all the damage in this house?

Surely not. If the Yankee bobbies were coming, they'd be here by now.

He stuck a foot into a laser. Nothing happened, no alarm, no crazy robotic ducks hunting him down.

Splashing through rising water, he made a slight, initial detour to the marble statue of Mr. Gnut Berdqvist, where he filched the sapphire from its ear. Easy enough, as the statue had a tiny hole in the ear, just like a human's ear piercing. He slipped the jewel into his jacket pocket. The feline perched on the sapphire case, monitoring his every move with a single-eyed stare. What had Nancy said the cat's name was? GoldenPaw?

Sinclair paused to wipe his sweaty brow. Mercifully, it was not the water dripping from the ceiling. It was a splendid life, prowling people's homes, lifting a few things they could very much afford to lose. And what was even more bloody splendid? This was his last job.

He approached the case. The blue fortune sparkled gloriously within. The only rain on his parade was that sodding cat. Eyeing the floor, he endured a twinge of guilt. He hated to toss the feline into the water. They were similar kinds of creatures, a cat and a cat burglar, both sure-footed, independent-minded and, he liked to think, rather mysterious. In fact, this cat was almost as enigmatic as his human, Nancy. He wondered if she had enjoyed his gift.

Sinclair scooped the fellow into his arms. His feline chum briefly struggled but soon settled down and purred. Sinclair stroked his head, scratched behind his ears, and carried him to the gigantic marble statue.

"Relax, my dear boy. This is a better spot for you."

He set the cat on the statue's shoulder. GoldenPaw scrambled up to perch on even higher ground, the statue's head. Sinclair confirmed the fellow was steady and returned his attention to the sapphires.

The Rolex's laser made quick work of the lock on the bulletproof glass case.

Sinclair lifted the case and set it to the side. He tugged down his white suit jacket and adjusted his bowtie. The jewels gleamed, perfectly arranged on a silver sculpture formed like the ice geyser. Each sapphire was positioned on its own little white satin pillow. He almost didn't want to disturb it.

Almost.

Slowly, Sinclair reached toward the highest and biggest sapphire. His fingertip touched the gem.

The ceiling caved in.

Chapter Forty-Six

Nancy's stomach surged in terror as the ceiling under her belly utterly gave in, right at a turn in the air duct. For a split second her body, the bedsheet, cat carrier, and bits of poorly constructed air duct plummeted down into thin air.

Just as fast, something broke her fall. Something surprisingly soft, much softer than a floor. Not something, some*one*—

"Bloody hell! My bloody back!"

Geyser House drowned out Sinclair's complaints. The floor creaked and buckled, pipes burst, and the shutters blocking the ballroom windows snapped and crumpled. GHOST mumbled something unintelligible over the speakers. The red laser webs clicked off. All lights stopped flickering and went dark. Weak moonlight filtered through gaps in the broken shutters.

Nancy had landed on him crossways. Sinclair tried to get her boots out of his face. She tried to oblige by lifting her legs. He swatted her ankles, trying to scramble away. She giggled in pleasure and relief at still being alive and in one piece. Tilting her head back, laughing, she saw the rest of the ballroom upside-down. And she caught sight of him.

"Dr. GoldenPaw!"

He was exactly where he should be, the safest place in the ballroom, on top of the Gnut statue's head. She held out her hands. He jumped from the statue, landed with a splash, and ran up to greet her. She struggled up to a sitting position and welcomed her boy into her lap, and her giggles slowed as pure love burst from her heart.

"You're safe. You're safe now, Goldy."

She rubbed her nose into his soft fur. He purred, twirled onto his back for belly scratches, and lifted his head. They touched noses, and he purred louder.

"You take my breath away," Sinclair said.

He lay flat on his back, gasping, flexing his fingers and limbs to make sure everything still worked. Nancy smiled at him. The man was quick—and dashing. At this moment, all was right with the world. All was wonderful.

Except it wasn't.

Nancy hugged her kitty more tightly. At the front of the ballroom, near the doors and especially in the corners, the water rose. In the opposite direction, through cracks in the shutters, she could see the ice geyser. Something was wrong. It splintered, grew higher. Ice water shot straight up into the midnight clouds. Beneath her, the floor shook. Nancy became aware, once again, of the relentless whooshing and churning happening in the basement.

"We need to get out of here." Nancy said to Dr. GoldenPaw, glimpsing the carrier on the floor nearby, which had crashed down with her. She detached herself from the cat carrier and stood, realizing the floor was buckling in the ballroom's center. They were on a slight incline, and water drained in that direction. She spread her feet, stabilizing herself against a wave of dizziness.

Sinclair cleared his throat. He launched to his feet and plucked sapphires that had fallen to the floor. He crouched down, splashing water everywhere, and nabbed two more. He stared at the jewel case and eyed the others. The biggest gem was still on display. He plundered, stuffing them all into his trouser pocket.

"You're going to leave them loose in your pocket?"

"I agree it's not ideal, my dear."

"Here."

Nancy dug out a Ziploc baggie from her fanny pack. She held it out to him. He gave her and the baggie a rather distrustful squint.

"Thanks for the drink earlier." She wiggled the baggie a little, showing him there was nothing inside, that this was no trick, and she was giving him a little dose of Minnesota-nice. If he trusted her, and they could work together to get out, so much the better.

Sinclair's brow relaxed, and he responded with a gracious bow. "Thank you, love."

Love, now! Before it had been "my dear." Of course, British people used the word "love" more casually than Americans. But they didn't *have* to. Warmth spread across Nancy's cheeks. Their hands touched as he accepted the Ziploc. She dipped her head back into Goldy's fur to compose her expression. She couldn't help but like this guy, but that didn't mean she trusted him. He was a thief.

Sinclair dropped the biggest sapphire into the Ziploc.

"You must really love jewels," Nancy said. That sapphire would probably pay for a mansion—a normal one—on Lake Minnetonka.

She staggered to the cat carrier, cradling Goldy, and with a massive sigh of relief, set him inside. He meowed in protest at losing his freedom. Or maybe he didn't care for the flippers that had taken up residence inside with him.

Sinclair paused before answering, long enough for her to glance at him. He had his back to her, so she couldn't see his face. He pilfered another sapphire. Nancy's own fingers twitched. Each gem was priceless. What she could do with even one of those. She thought about the financial security, buying a house, taking fancy vacations. But it was outright theft, of course.

"I do love jewels," Sinclair said. "But it's not entirely that. My parents were magicians. We were always traveling. I developed a fascination, as it were, for seeing—"

The house shuddered, and they both looked warily around the ballroom. Chandeliers rocked and clattered. Nancy knelt next to the carrier, holding it by the handle. Then the house settled.

"Seeing homes," Sinclair went on. "How people really lived."

"Certain people."

Sinclair barked a laugh. They locked gazes, and Nancy's hand grew sweaty as she picked up the carrier. In this moment, they knew the truth about each other—that neither of them had grown up with much money.

"But I've seen enough. Now I want to buy—don't laugh, love—an inn."

An inn! Nancy used all her power to force back a stupid grin. His wish wasn't much different from her bed and breakfast dream. Best of all, there it was again. Sinclair bandied about the word "love" like it was nothing. It probably was nothing. It was a turn of phrase, that was all.

"No, I wouldn't laugh," Nancy said. "You betcha. A lovely inn."

Dr. GoldenPaw finally quieted. Nancy heard him give a contented sigh in his carrier.

Sinclair had all the sapphires now. He edged closer to Nancy, frowning as he tried to seal the Ziploc. Nancy stood up and wondered if he trusted her enough to let her help him. She could casually reach out and take them, those priceless sapphires were really so close.

"A home for travelers," Nancy said. "I like that because my father was a traveling salesman. He sold housewares."

Sinclair tilted his head, eyes brightening. He still couldn't seal the Ziploc. "A salesman? Perhaps a bit of a scammer himself."

Nancy shrugged in agreement. "He eventually went on a sales trip and didn't come back. Made off with some company money."

"And you had to—"

"Be practical. Be a nurse. Play it safe. Not a courageous life."

"But caring."

They shared another beat of wordless eye contact. Goldy began purring loudly. Nancy knew they had to get out, escape Elvira and JT and this whole house, but standing there with her cat and a handsome cat burglar, she somehow felt good, as if this was where she belonged.

She nodded at the Ziploc. "I can do that for you."

His eyes narrowed. "I'll hold on to them, my dear."

Annoyance made her tighten her mouth. Nancy wasn't going to steal them. She'd meant what she'd said.

Before she could explain that to him, the floor cracked, a chandelier crashed, and the sapphire display case dropped through the ballroom floor.

Chapter Forty-Seven

Nancy battled a senseless urge to giggle at the cartoonish way Sinclair's eyes widened. The floor behind him had split apart, and the marble pedestal and empty glass jewel display case had disappeared straight down into basement oblivion. But she didn't give in to hysterics. She simply gawked as Sinclair slid backward.

The floor itself sloped downward, toward the gaping hole in the center of the ballroom. Sinclair was falling. He stuck his arms out, trying to get balance, and he dropped the Ziploc.

The open baggie with precious sapphires vanished into the basement darkness, and Nancy croaked out an anguished moan.

She screamed as she and the cat carrier started sliding toward the hole, too, possibly plummeting with Sinclair and the sapphires into darkness.

In a blur of animal predatory instinct, Dr. GoldenPaw leaped toward the bright, shiny jewels, crashing into the front of the carrier. The vessel containing her beloved furry companion gained momentum, nearly following Sinclair toward the hole.

Nancy gaped at the sliding carrier, her senses telling her other things were happening. Gnut's statue toppled over, more of the ceiling fell, and a TV screen dropped and banged on the floor.

She scooted down the incline, reaching out until she made contact with the carrier. Improvising, she managed to fling it toward the fallen Gnut statue where the ballroom floor was still level.

But she kept plunging downward.

As she lost all footing with empty air around her, she witnessed Dr. GoldenPaw's carrier land safely next to the statue, the cat gazing at her in a mesmerizing stare with his good eye, his mouth open to howl.

Nancy stretched her arms as if she could reach him. Her body twisted and fingers extended, and she tried to grab hold of something—the floor, a fallen chandelier—but it was no use. She kept falling. She was somersaulting and subsequently belly flopping into who knew what. Her limbs stiffened for impact with a concrete floor or an aquarium full of fanged icefish.

Instead, her body slammed into something *squeaky*. It smelled plasticky and rubbery and broke her fall. Miraculously unhurt, she scrambled as something sucked her in. It was so squeaky, unstable, slippery, and red and orange. What was this? What was happening?

Nancy finally made sense of it. She had landed in a pile of inflatable lobster pool chairs. Gnut had lots of them stacked up here, enough for a pool party. She slid from the pile toward the cold concrete floor.

Just in time, Sinclair kicked a lobster closer to break her ugly roll to the floor. She cocked her head to the side, and under the glow of one red emergency light, Nancy watched Sinclair gather sapphires off the concrete floor.

As Nancy struggled to her feet, the adrenaline from the plunge slowly drained from her body as she surveyed her surroundings. They were in the secret basement.

The place was industrial. Exposed pipes ran along the ceiling, attached to plenty of pumps and valves. Small security cameras dotted the walls, their lights off. They were in a tunnel, at a point where it widened out under the ballroom. Nancy shivered in her wetsuit and sniffed, sensing the sharp aroma of ice. Her breath puffed out into vapor. The rest of the house was freezing. Down here, it was Antarctica.

There were two ways out, it seemed. A tunnel stretched into darkness, leading to the ice geyser. In the opposite direction, another passageway wound upward via wide concrete stairs. The latter, from which she could smell chlorine, had to lead to the pool room.

Two main pipes, huge and cracked, ran along the ceiling. One was labeled *Water Intake*. It chugged loudly. The other pipe was labeled *Snowfall*. It whooshed.

"Yikes. Now we know what the roaring, whooshing racket was," Nancy said. "These two pipes."

"You're right, my dear. I'm not entirely sure what to make of this machinery."

A hodgepodge of snow-guns, green garden hoses, and heavy-duty nozzles were fixed to the walls and ceiling, and connected up to the Snowfall pipe. Much of the equipment looked brand-new, with dangling sales tags. As far as she could see, there was no brilliant invention that would save the planet.

"The famous Coolant Device." Nancy crossed her arms and raised her voice, like she was addressing a lecture hall. "Hoses and fans all put together to create fake snow, probably based on something you can find on the Internet. Done on a huge scale with lots of power and water from Lake Superior. Yeah, if investors found out, Gnut would end up in jail like Elvira and JT. It's all a bunch of makeshift stuff he bought online or at some hardware store."

Sinclair didn't respond. He was busy picking sapphires off the concrete and stuffing them into the Ziploc. Something like pebbles crunched under her boots. Sinclair crawled on the floor, pushing lobster chairs out of the way to search.

The pipes roared so loudly, Nancy wanted to cover her ears. A huge amount of water was being sucked in from Lake Superior and converted into snow. The relentless conversion of water to ice, along with the structural damage to the house from Elvira's explosives, was going to destroy it. The basement was the wrong place to be.

Sinclair continued searching. Nancy kept standing on what she suspected were two large sapphires. She stood on $4 million. Perhaps she could lean down, like she was fiddling with her boot, and sneak them into her fanny pack. Didn't she deserve two tiny souvenirs of her Geyser House experience?

No, she wouldn't steal. Absolutely not. She'd give them to Sinclair, they'd become more of a team, and they'd work together to get out.

"Here," Nancy said. "You're missing a couple."

She shifted position.

Sinclair blinked in surprise. "Thanks, love." He sprang toward them, swiped both, and tucked them into the Ziploc.

She assessed her surroundings once more, still unsure of the best way to escape. The tunnel toward the geyser seemed like it was a thousand miles long and very dark. A thin waterfall began sliding down the stairs from the pool room and reached their feet.

Maybe she could sneak up those stairs, and the house's damage would allow escape through the pool windows. If not, she would have to retrace her steps. Once she reached the pool, she'd have to go down the hallway to Gnut's bedroom and through the air duct to get back into the ballroom to get her cat. It would be so much easier to go straight up. If that was possible.

"Elvira could be there," Sinclair said, wrinkling his nose. "In the pool room."

"Don't you work for her?" Nancy asked.

He didn't answer. He eyed the sapphires, running a thumb along the top of the baggie to finally seal it. A slow smile creased his handsome face. In an instant, Nancy knew the man would betray Elvira and keep those jewels for himself. She needed to remember that. If he double-crossed Elvira, he would do the same to her. He tucked the baggie into the inside pocket of his tuxedo jacket.

Nancy looked up at the gaping hole in the ballroom floor. She raised her hand as high as possible. The edge of the floor above was about ten feet out of reach. Maybe it was not impossible to get up there, if they worked together. Should they stack the lobster chairs?

No, she decided. They couldn't reach high enough, and it would be too unstable anyway. She pored over the situation again.

There, down the tunnel toward the geyser, she spotted something white.

She headed toward it. The white was blocks of something. Her adrenaline heightened. Maybe this would work better for stacking. She picked one up.

It was incredibly light. Her fingers dug into it easily. Bits of white crumbled off. She thought back to the expanse of winter wonderland around the house that had impressed her when she'd first arrived. Some of it was snow. But probably a lot of it was this stuff.

"Styrofoam," she announced. "Worst. Environmentalist. Ever."

Nancy hugged the block to her chest. Maybe useless, but worth a try. If there was enough of it, would it hold her weight?

Forcing what felt like hollow confidence into her voice, she stacked up blocks of Styrofoam under the ballroom hole. "Easy peasy."

She stepped high and planted a foot on the stack, then the other. But all she accomplished was crumbling the Styrofoam and crashing toward the concrete floor.

Sinclair caught Nancy and steadied her. He kept hold of her elbow, all very chivalrous. Looking into his eyes, she had the same thought as before. She could *not* trust him. Her soul yearned to lean into him, and she wanted to close her eyes. Her brain told her that the Ziploc of priceless gems tucked into his jacket pocket was what really mattered to this guy with the impeccable manners.

He winked. "Fancy a stroll down the tunnel of love?"

Sinclair released her elbow, bowed, and extended an arm toward the ice geyser tunnel. He had a point. It was their best shot at escape. Nancy contemplated the darkness, feeling wistful. She imagined hustling hand-in-hand with him, palms sweating, racing to escape, and, on reaching the safety of the forest, sharing a passionate kiss.

Of course, he would have the sapphires, and she would not have her cat.

Nancy pointed up. "I won't leave Dr. GoldenPaw. Running away isn't an option."

Sinclair stared at her for several long seconds, his expression polite. Nancy didn't have to wonder what he really thought, though. No doubt he thought she was as nuts as Geyser House and everyone else inside it.

GHOST's garbled voice broke the silence, emanating from high above them in the ballroom. "Pool room valve break, dudes. Not that anyone cares."

Pool room? Nancy and Sinclair both locked eyes and snapped their heads toward the steps leading up to the pool room. A roar from that direction reverberated down the tunnel.

Nancy saw Sinclair tense, ready for action. He darted down the ice geyser tunnel while she held her ground.

The roaring from the pool room grew louder, and Sinclair turned back.

Nancy shook her head and covered her eyes with the diving mask. Her cat was in the ballroom. Water, water, water. That's all this house had. She was not going to run away from more water.

But she had to. She couldn't drown.

Sinclair neared her and extended his hand. She accepted it. He slipped an arm around her shoulders, ready to guide her down the tunnel.

The pool door slammed open, a vicious *bang* of steel on concrete.

A rush of water...

Nancy shut her eyes, refusing to move an inch. Her cat was above her. She braced for the icy drench of cold water...

The tidal wave surged toward them.

Chapter Forty-Eight

Nancy held Sinclair's hand tighter and clenched her other fist, bracing herself for the slam of an ice-water tsunami.

Water crashed into her ankles, pooling around her feet, and snaking in the direction of the ice geyser tunnel.

It was merely a few inches deep.

Nancy forced out a shaky laugh. She opened her eyes and took stock. Yes, a steady stream of water flowed from the pool room, but the stairs were so wide and the basement so spacious that it had plenty of space to go. Her shoulders relaxed.

Nancy lowered her mask to provide Sinclair a good view of her smirk. "Nothing to worry about."

A speaker cackled over their heads. GHOST's voice spoke more clearly than before. "Another valve break, dudes."

"Where, GHOST?" Nancy craned her neck to surmise the hole in the ballroom floor.

GHOST didn't answer.

Sinclair stuck his hands in his pockets and shifted weight from one foot to the other, inching further down the dark tunnel, still wanting to keep dashing off into the sunset. Of course, he'd have sapphires in his pocket. She'd have zilch.

"Escape is this way, love."

Nancy shifted her attention to her goal of getting back into the ballroom. She hopelessly reached up. It would take a miracle, like a forklift appearing out of nowhere—

"Aah! Ugh! Ew!" Something had slithered around her ankles.

Nancy bopped up and down, her skin crawling. Looking down, she realized it was something ice blue—one of Gnut's Speedos. Except that wasn't the only one. There were dozens of Speedos skimming toward her on the stream of water from the pool room.

Behind them, the wooden Gnut statue from the pool room clunked down the steps. It still had floaties on. Knowing she really shouldn't, but doing it anyway, Nancy splashed closer.

Yes!

Shivers crawled up and down her spine, and this time in a good way. The statue still had its blue earring.

She nabbed it. It wasn't as big as the ballroom sapphires, but Nancy could tell it was a genuine gem from its weight and the way it gleamed despite the dimness. She spun back toward Sinclair and held it up.

"Ha! You missed one."

Sinclair affected a casual stroll closer. His expression flashed into jealousy as he ogled the jewel. Yup, the guy seemed genuinely perturbed, with little dots of red flushing his cheeks. She pocketed the sapphire deep into her fanny pack, aware of Sinclair's rapt interest in her every movement. She'd give the sapphire to the police later. Really, she would. When they asked.

She refocused on the hole above and licked her lips. "I have an idea."

"Splendid, my dear."

Nancy shrugged off Sinclair's sour grapes. She grabbed Speedos and began daisy-chaining them together, forming a long Speedo rope with a loop at the end. She held it up to Sinclair. He peered up to the ballroom and nodded.

"Yeah, nurse lady." GHOST called out, her voice staticky.

"You can do it. Like before. Climb up and help me and my friend."

Help GHOST, too? Nancy shook her head. GHOST was starting to grow on her. But she had no idea how to save a mansion's AI system if the mansion was collapsing. Nancy jutted her chin and twirled the Speedo rope like a cowboy spinning a lasso. She tossed the looped end straight up to the hole in the ballroom floor.

It didn't even make it to the basement's ceiling, plopping down right beside her. Gallantly, Sinclair did not offer any criticism. He pulled out his Ziploc baggie of sapphires and held it up to the red emergency light, admiring them.

Nancy cast the Speedo rope up a second time. This attempt, she hurled it with maximum strength. It reached the ballroom floor and vanished out of sight.

She tugged, and the rope immediately dropped down next to her.

Nancy tried again, and again.

"Try further to the left and..." GHOST's voice was lost to static.

Elvira's voice rang out from the direction of the pool room. "Gnuttie, Gnuttie, Gnuttie, ready or not, here I come!"

Nancy stiffened.

Sinclair tilted his head. "My dear, this is where I bid *adieu*."

Nancy saw his brief, yearning glance toward her fanny pack, where she'd put the last sapphire. She slinked slightly away from him and studied the gaping hole. Perhaps she should run like hell. But GHOST had said go to the left. It was worth one more try.

Nancy aimed her next attempt carefully. The Speedo rope's looped end landed deep in the ballroom. She tugged, and this time, she encountered resistance. It'd definitely hooked onto something. She heard a scrape and rattle as the Speedos snagged and dragged. Thinking back to the ballroom, she figured it had to be that fallen chandelier.

Sucking in a breath, she clung to the Speedos and lifted both feet.

Snap.

Nancy flipped her feet back under her as the chandelier slid and the Speedo rope came unstuck. The loop dropped down. She closed her eyes and craned her neck to the ceiling. Nancy directed her next words at the heavens, the whole universe, and her cat.

"Come. On."

"You're getting warmer," GHOST said.

Sinclair edged closer. He'd already said goodbye. But it seemed like he was having trouble leaving her. Or, maybe, he was finding it hard to leave the last sapphire. It was hard to tell.

"My dear, let's leave this place. Together."

Nancy observed the handsome man's earnest expression. He held out a hand. She wanted to accept it and run away with him. She really did. Determined to get her cat, she tightened her grip on the Speedo rope.

One. More. Time.

She catapulted the Speedo rope back up to the ballroom, even further to the left. She tugged—it seemed to be caught on something.

Splashing, stomping bootsteps echoed down the concrete stairs.

Chapter Forty-Nine

Nancy gripped the Speedo rope. She kicked up her feet. It held! Now she needed to move.

Roar.

This time, the sound came from the opposite direction, from down the tunnel in the direction of the ice geyser.

Sinclair shrugged. "I shall not be fooled again."

Nancy frowned, feeling more worried than he. For one thing, there was a heck of a lot more water that way. It wasn't just a pool. It was the ice geyser itself, and the lake not far beyond.

She latched onto the Speedo rope, jumped up, and dangled. It worked. It wasn't stretching too badly—no doubt it helped that the swimwear was made from Gnut's thermal Spandex.

"Sinclair! Do you have the sapphires?" Elvira's voice rang out and bounced off the concrete walls.

Nancy set her feet on the ground and twisted to defy the enemy. Her heart pounded at the sight of Elvira's harpoon shining silver-red in the faint glow of the emergency lights. Elvira's bright eyes daggered into hers.

Sinclair ignored Elvira and lightly squeezed Nancy's arms. He unleashed his most debonair smile. "Ta ta, my dear."

The roaring grew louder.

His gaze flickered to the Speedo rope. "I'm sure you'll get the *hang* of it."

A laugh leapt almost deliriously from her belly. He moved even closer and kissed her cheek. His hands settled on her arms, and he drew her closer. The roaring sound grew thunderous. Somehow, in those moments, her mind hatched a plan. It was a last-minute, desperate-times-call-for-desperate-measures kind of plan, but it might work.

Maybe it was time for her to act less like a cat-mom and more like a cat burglar.

"The sapphires, Sinclair!" Elvira shouted.

Elvira's harpoon *zipped*, and a spear shot out. Something swirled around their ankles. At the same time, Nancy felt the tiniest tugs on her fanny pack.

She wasn't a cat burglar, not really. Her movements were clumsy and obvious.

But they were effective. Nancy slipped her fingers inside the front pocket of Sinclair's tuxedo. She found plastic, and she whipped out the Ziploc. Sinclair put his hands up to stop it.

Elvira howled in satisfaction. The Kevlar cord tightened around their ankles. Nancy tweaked the Ziploc out of Sinclair's reach and gasped.

Behind Sinclair, down the ice geyser tunnel, a deafening churn of water, ice, and Styrofoam hurtled toward them.

The tether cinched around their ankles, forcing Nancy to clench the Speedo rope tighter to remain standing. Sinclair's free hand went after the Ziploc. Nancy's soul burst with the sole thought, *these are mine*! She pitched the baggie up into the ballroom.

Sinclair watched it soar. Nancy, for a split second, caught the shock on his face. He shouted something like, "I do say!" but the rest of his words were lost in the roar of the tunnel's tidal wave. The Kevlar lasso jerked hard at their ankles, and Nancy realized Elvira was trying to drag them closer.

Or, at least, Sinclair. She was along for the ride. At the same time, Elvira had her cell phone out and was trying to take pictures of the basement, including the hodgepodge of cooling equipment, before icy water destroyed it all.

Nancy had no choice. She held the Speedo rope with all her might. The cat and jewels were straight up. Getting hauled closer to Elvira meant capture and maybe even death. She looked into Sinclair's eyes. He curled his arms around her in a protective fashion.

His lips touched her ear, and he whispered, "No honor among thieves, my dear?"

His tone wasn't accusing or angry. To the contrary, his voice still carried its typical calm amusement.

"Check! Basement pictures obtained! Those had better not have been the sapphires, Sinclair. Where are they? Let go! Are those Speedos? Let go of that rope!"

Elvira pocketed her phone and used both hands and her full attention to yank her prey closer. But Nancy held onto the Speedo rope, and Sinclair seemed rooted in place, standing up.

Then Sinclair began to kneel, his hands slowly sliding from her back to her waist and to her hips and down the sides of her legs.

What in the heck was he doing?

"The sapphires, Sinclair!" Elvira yelled. "You idiot, I want them!"

Water swirled closer, filling up the tunnel. It was up to her knees now and rising fast. Nancy tried lifting herself up.

It was impossible. Maybe she'd be able to climb a foot or two, like in Gnut's bedroom. Up the whole rope, though? Sinclair would need to help her, but he was helping himself.

On the floor now, he was unspooling the tether from around their ankles. As it loosened, he slipped out. Nancy kicked her feet, realizing she was free.

Sinclair began climbing the Speedo rope.

Nancy groaned. This rope had been *her* idea.

The water reached her hips. Sinclair climbed quickly, and soon his shoes press on her shoulders. Her jaw tightened. He wasn't merely using her idea. He was using her as a ladder.

"I'll get up there first and help you up, my dear."

A furious *cawing* arose, emanating from near the pool room.

"Oh, bloody hell. Not them." Sinclair climbed faster.

Three robotic parasitic jaegers emerged from the darkness, swooping over Elvira's shoulders before gliding above the water churning toward them. Another thing Nancy noticed was that the security camera hanging from the ceiling, near Elvira, had powered on. As Nancy's stare lasered on the little red light, she heard Gnut's garbled voice from speakers up in the ballroom.

"Courage in imagination, Nancy. I dig the rope concept."

Nancy gritted her teeth. Surely all he really cared about was that she had, for the time being, saved his sapphires from the jewel thief.

Sinclair's weight lifted from Nancy's shoulders. He nearly made it. His hands were on the edge of the ballroom floor.

She had to keep holding their Speedo rope. It was her lifeline.

The robotic birds circled Nancy, flapped their metallic wings, and shot up to Sinclair. They pecked at his head and dove after the kerchief in his tux breast pocket.

"No, no, no, you bloody foul fiends!"

Sinclair tried waving them away with one hand, while

keeping his other hand on the ballroom floor, his ankles tight around the Speedo rope.

Sinclair's grip slipped, and he let go and fell.

Nancy winced, afraid for the fellow, but he landed on a lobster chair floating on the water. The chair and his body dunked under and popped up again. The birds gave a united *caw* and dove into the tunnel, bypassing Sinclair and heading up the poolroom toward Elvira.

Elvira cradled her precious weapon and backed up the stairs, slogging through the water.

Something pawed at her right leg. She glanced down. It was Sinclair.

Still floating in the lobster chair, he looked into her eyes for the briefest of seconds. There was no time for thanks or puns before the next tidal wave.

Chapter Fifty

Water charged from the direction of the ice geyser, sweeping Sinclair away. He remained poised in a seated position on the inflated lobster chair, gripping its plump claw armrests. He rode the lobster chair with aplomb.

It was starkly different from Dave. He'd get agitated at the little things, like if somebody cut him off on the highway or if a lightbulb suddenly went out right in the middle of dinner. She hadn't thought about Dave for a long time this evening.

Water struck her shoulders and head, and for a terrible interval, her mouth and nose were completely underwater. She held the Speedo rope while the force of water tried pushing her down the tunnel. Her lungs grew desperate for more oxygen. She expelled air to prevent herself from inhaling water.

But she was floating, which meant she could go up.

Nancy forced herself to climb higher and her feet to kick herself upward. She inched higher and higher. Meanwhile, a thought cut into her brain. How much time in the past three years had she spent thinking about Dave?

Water ripped at her body. The current wanted to heave her toward the pool room, but she kept hold of the Speedo rope, and the water helped her float up. Gritting her teeth, unknown muscles now ablaze, Nancy climbed another few inches.

Her head rose above water. She gulped air that tasted as sweet and pure as summertime strawberries. Her soul was grateful for it, as if she'd been deprived of oxygen for years.

After another few inches of climbing, reaching up countless times, she finally grasped the edge of the ballroom floor.

Panting, she set her elbow on the surface. Centimeter by centimeter, she scooted forward. When her whole upper body was horizontal, instead of vertical, she knew she'd done it.

Gnut was nowhere. Smart money was that he was still in the panic room, trying to save his mansion and deal with the intruders. The Ziploc full of sapphires was there, straight ahead, sparkling on the floor. She eyed it, her lungs heaving and her limbs heavy. Each of the jewels gleamed like they had blue flames blazing inside. And they were all hers. That is, if she decided to steal them.

Meow.

Nancy hauled herself up. Her gaze followed the Speedo rope. It slid along the floor and was hooked onto Gnut's huge marble statue. It was looped over one foot! GHOST had been right about where to aim it.

Dr. GoldenPaw meowed from his carrier. He was safe. She was safe.

Nancy's mind skipped to Sinclair. He'd saved her, she had to admit it, by getting her ankles out of that tether. But only after trying to save himself first by climbing up her body to get to the ballroom. Once he reached safety, would he have offered her a gallant hand up? Yes, she really believed he would have. She'd finally met a dashing gentleman. Hopefully he wasn't dead.

Of course, he would still think those jewels were his.

So would Gnut.

Elvira would want them too.

Nancy examined the crumpled steel shutters covering the windows. She and the carrier could slip through. But she stayed frozen, thinking. Where was Sinclair by now? The pool room? She looked to the ceiling, listening for any sound of a soaked man scooting through the air duct, hellbent on getting his sapphires back.

And Elvira and JT? Where were they? If she was able to get outside, so could they.

Nancy cocked her head, pondering the Ziploc'd treasure within her reach. Goldy kept meowing from the carrier. Nancy unzipped her wetsuit and traced the sequins on her scrubs. She refocused on the Ziploc holding the real bling.

She glanced from the fake blue bling on her scrubs to the real blue bling in the Ziploc. Hmm. She had an idea.

Nancy drew out her glue gun from the waistband of her fanny pack, held it high, and let water drip off it. Would it still work? She scanned the room for an electrical outlet. Crawling over to the baggie, she opened it and extracted a sapphire. She tested its weight on her fingertip.

Twenty minutes later, Nancy shoved the cat carrier out of the ballroom terrace door. She followed it outside. Why was the air outdoors so much warmer? Blinking, her brain bubbling, she remembered it was August.

Nancy oriented herself to her new situation as she stood on the terrace. It edged up to the moat, overflowing and lapping onto the stone. Her shoulders sagged in disappointment. She remembered there wasn't a bridge on this side. The terrace extended along the mansion's wall toward the pool room and ended where the moat curved around the house.

After turning her head, she realized the opposite direction was another no-go. The living room wall jutted out and ran right up against the water. It was impassable. Straight across the moat, somehow and someway, was the one route to safety.

She swallowed, looked at the cat carrier in her hand, and entertained the obvious, wretched thought. Could Dr. Golden-Paw survive it? If she swam across, pushing the carrier ahead of her, how much water would get in before it sank, taking her precious kitty down into the depths of this stupid moat?

Nancy's heart rate skyrocketed. A feeling of desperation froze her brain and paralyzed her limbs. She had no options.

A muddy expanse of melting snow and Styrofoam spread out on the other side of the moat. Beyond the lawn, the ice geyser shot water straight up. The world was quiet except for the spray of water. Hushed enough that she could hear her cat sigh. The poor boy must be thinking he was safe in his familiar carrier, with warmer air seeping in.

Very carefully, Nancy withdrew the flippers from the cat carrier and shut it. She shed the Prada boots and put the new footwear on. The moat's water level rose. The longer she waited, the higher it would get.

From within the house, GHOST called out, "Nurse! Hello? You need to come back."

Nancy shuddered. Go back into Gnut's crazy house?

"Please, Nurse."

GHOST's voice had changed. Her usual snotty confidence had disappeared. Nancy dug her fingernails into her palms, trying to ignore her. The AI was obviously programmed to manipulate.

"Don't leave me, please. Nurse—"

Nancy spun around. "I'm not a nurse," she snapped through a crumpled ballroom door. "I'm retired. I'm..."

She stopped herself, not wanting to get angry at GHOST.

This wasn't the AI's fault. GHOST wasn't to blame for calling her a nurse, either, because a nurse is who she was, after all. Wasn't she? That's how things had begun tonight. But since then, she'd combatted JT with an oar, taken him down with a syringe, stayed to rescue her cat, crawled through an air duct, invented a Speedo rope and then climbed it. Who did stuff like that? A Bond lady. A spy. Somebody cool with a cool name.

She turned to the moat and hurled her next words at the whole universe, imagining them dancing over the moonlit forest trees and flying across all of Lake Superior.

"I am Nancy Domino!"

A footstep clicked on the stone behind her. Nancy whipped around to confront Sinclair.

He must have slipped out of the ballroom windows, like she'd done. The dapper jewel thief was still completely drenched from his tunnel tidal wave ride. Gracefully, he slipped off a shoe, poured out water and put it back on.

"I do say," he said. "You're a thief. A rather unlikely one, but a thief nevertheless."

Nancy put on an innocent expression. She beheld the brilliant moon. The stars sparkled, well, like diamonds, of course. She could argue with Sinclair about whether or not she was a thief. Truth was, she didn't mind the label. After a lifetime of doing the right thing, caring for others, living paycheck-to-paycheck, she didn't mind the new title. Maybe she'd use it on her *SeniorLOVE* profile. And another thing? She didn't care at all what Dave, or her neighbors, or friends, or acquaintances thought of it.

She was Nancy Domino: An Unlikely Thief.

Sinclair held out his hand. "Give the sapphires to me, and it'll all be water under the bridge."

His tone was reasonable, but Nancy knew she needed to run. The problem was, there was nowhere to go. She backed up, closer to the moat, trying to keep the cat carrier still for Goldy. Sinclair edged toward her.

From within the house, GHOST made another announcement. "Total destruction, four minutes. Not that anyone cares about me or anything I say."

Zip!

Nancy and Sinclair checked out the source of the sound. Elvira had emerged from the pool room windows, holding her harpoon gun high. A spear, with the tether attached, shot out and disappeared into the dark moat water.

Elvira flipped a switch on her harpoon gun. The weapon made a grinding sound, and she skidded a few steps forward before bracing herself. She barked out a victorious laugh.

Gnut rose to the moat's surface. The tether snapped tight around his knees and ankles. He somersaulted in the water, getting dragged closer to Elvira.

Nancy grimaced at Gnut's plight. She especially didn't like the way his head tilted to his side, how his arm flapped over to protect the other arm. He needed medical treatment.

Sinclair whistled, eying something over Nancy's shoulder.

Now what, was her first thought, following his look. Sure enough, there was another issue. The ice geyser was spurting even higher. Worse, the ground beneath their feet trembled.

Nancy stuck her glasses in her fanny pack and flipped the mask down over her eyes. She gripped the cat carrier hard as the terrace stone shook. Something in the carrier rattled.

Sinclair's eyes narrowed at the carrier's rattling.

Behind them, the mansion windows shattered, the pool room's roof caved in, and water burped high from the pool—

like another geyser.

Sinclair crept closer to her. Nancy backed up even more, feeling her flippered right heel poise over air.

Something in the cat carrier jangled again.

She couldn't go any further. Their gazes met. Both knew the truth.

There was no escape.

Chapter Fifty-One

Nancy stood on her tippy-toes, both of her heels poised over water. Sinclair was closing in. She cast one last glance around for anything useful for escape. All she saw was Gnut splashing, trying to untangle himself from Elvira's harpoon tether. His head came up over the water.

Nancy furrowed her brow, her nurse's soul instinctively concerned for Gnut. She forced those thoughts away. She had her own problems.

The moon darted behind clouds like it was afraid to watch Nancy's fate. The last remaining lights in Geyser House turned dark.

"Please allow me to help you with that." Panther-quick and powerful, Sinclair plucked the carrier from Nancy's grasp.

Within the carrier, Goldy meowed, and the Ziploc rattled.

She threw her arms out for balance so she wouldn't topple into the water.

"I'm a professional," Sinclair said. "I'll do this without releasing dear Dr. GoldenPaw."

The ground vibrated again. Nancy clawed at thin air, and she tried to crouch, but she fell backward and slammed into the dark moat.

The ice-cold water shocked her face and hands. Clammy droplets slipped down the neck of her suit and up the sleeves. Her legs pumped hard as she splashed to the moat's edge and, motivated by the icy H_2O snaking down her spine, managed to struggle onto the edge of the terrace. She spat out water and gagged.

It was saltwater. How was that possible? Lake Superior was fresh water.

Still up on the terrace, Sinclair unlocked the carrier.

"No!" Nancy coughed out. "Don't!"

Sinclair extracted the Ziploc baggie. Even in the dim moonlight, its contents gave a nice sparkle and gleam. Sinclair licked his lips, entranced by the beauty. But at the same time, Dr. GoldenPaw instantly shifted into a combined fight and flight mode. He howled, clawed, and used all his strength to launch out of the carrier.

"Oh, damn. Dear boy, rather a bad idea!" Sinclair's cat-like reflexes were too slow to stop an actual cat.

Nancy glimpsed the flash of orange-white fur and the world collapsed on her head. She scrambled out of the moat. Meanwhile, her pet backed off toward the ballroom, inches beyond reach.

"Goldy! Stop! Lemme get you!" Her kitty tensed up and shivered. She ignored Sinclair's chivalrous offer of a helping hand and winced apology. After what he'd just done, she would *never* accept help from that man.

Nancy started toward her cat, glancing down at the Elvira and Gnut situation. Gnut held fast to the tether line. He braced his feet on the moat's wall for leverage. Gnut pulled, and Elvira's high-heeled combat boots skidded on the icy terrace stone. With one mighty jerk, Gnut yanked Elvira full force to join him in the moat. It was just as Nancy guessed.

The ground shook again, Geyser House rumbled, and Nancy fell sideways into the water. Nancy shut her eyes, bracing herself for a different dunking. She splashed head-first into the bone-chilling moat.

Nancy flapped her hands, her heart already skipping, and her brain rocketing to a red-alert panic. Carefully, she opened her eyes and realized she could see underwater through the diving mask. Moonlight shone down, and underwater lights illumined the water's depths.

She was still upside down, though. Gnut and Elvira were right-side up and attempting to punch each other. Being underwater made the hits harmless. They kept missing each other anyway.

Had Goldy stayed on the terrace, or had he been thrown into the water too?

Nancy cranked her head around and spotted Sinclair. The current twisted them toward each other. Slowly they spun, in sync, until they were right side up. Nancy had a flashback to all the James Bond movie intros she'd seen. It was like that—a cool and romantic interlude where the two of them floated, locked in a super-sexy spell with cool and romantic vibes. Well, it would be romantic if he hadn't just allowed her pet to run away.

Maybe her brain cells were already dying from lack of oxygen.

She discovered JT Hotman near the bottom of the moat. How had he ended up there? A rifle bolt still jutted from his bulletproof vest. Despite being deep underwater, he tried desperately to paddle with a plastic oar. He looked up at her. His mouth gaped open, and bubbles burst out.

He kept paddling like he was sitting in a canoe. The man could still be drugged on the ketamine hydrochloride she'd injected him with. That was some serious Special K.

Despite Nancy's fears for herself and the cat, the surroundings began to mesmerize her. The silence and floating sensation felt terrifically peaceful. More than her body was buoyant. Her mind, her soul, and her spirit were now joined with the beauty of the water world. Gnut must've salted this moat, somehow, and kept it heated. That used more energy, of course, and was pointless, but the result was beautiful. Under the surface, the moat shone with charming sea creatures—translucent pink jellyfish and curling starfish danced among the tangerine coral reefs. Manta rays flew like magic carpets along the bottom. A school of olive flounder swam through, trailed by a fish that glowed red and green. It was no hallucination. Gnut Berdqvist had created something lovely down here in his saltwater moat paradise.

Looking up, she discerned the hazy form of a cat peering into the water, and her trance broke. She kicked her flippers, casting a last glance in Gnut's direction. Elvira was choking him, and Gnut was faking death. No surprise.

Nancy kicked to the surface.

Her head rose above the water. She drank in oxygen and treaded water. Swimming like this was a marvelous experience, almost like she was a child playing in the ocean. Completely free. Why did she feel better in this exact minute than she had in years? She was a whole new person, cool and glamorous. Her life had turned a corner, and the road sign ahead said *Adventure*. She tried to turn toward the terrace, confident everything would be all right.

A foot away from her, Sinclair's head broke the water's surface.

"Apologies about the cat, love."

Sinclair spread out his hands to keep himself afloat. He held the Ziploc baggie above water, trying to protect it. Nancy dug in her fanny pack, searching for a weapon.

She found the bling lure.

"I do need these jewels, you see. It'll pay for my innkeeper dream."

Nancy tightened her grip around the bling lure and lashed out. She aimed the fishhook's jagged point at Sinclair's hand that held the baggie.

"I need to retire—ouch!"

Sinclair flung up his hand, wincing in pain, and released the Ziploc.

A nasty move, she knew, but it was righteous payback for letting her cat escape. And for playing "Night Nurse" while she was in a fight with JT. And for not helping her climb the Speedo rope. And for all the "my dears." And for, of course, whatever else he was going to do to her while she was distracted by that perfect tux, charming smile, and lovely accent.

"I need to retire, too," Nancy said.

She heard Gnut and Elvira reach the surface, both choking and coughing up moat water.

Her legs on fire from trying to keep herself afloat, Nancy flailed toward the moat's edge. After grasping the edge of the terrace, she hauled herself up. There! Dr. GoldenPaw sat a few feet away, observing his person's situation with calm dignity.

Behind him came a crash from the ballroom.

GHOST said, "Collapse imminent. Dudes, somebody help me! Collapse—"

The far wall of the pool room side disintegrated with earsplitting smashes of brick and concrete. A knotty pine log shot from the house and landed in the middle of the moat. With a terrible *snap*, a steel beam hurtled from the house like a javelin and speared her car, crumpling the hood.

She gaped at her damaged Volvo. Her poor, dear car. How

would she explain *that* to the insurance company?

The moat water swirled. As Geyser House collapsed, a vicious undertow propelled Gnut, Elvira, and Sinclair in different directions. Nancy caught a glimpse of each person's head, frozen in matching expressions of shock and bewilderment.

In the next moment, the whirlpool seized her.

Chapter Fifty-Two

Nancy twirled underwater, the current flinging her around like a dairy cow in a tornado. She paddled upward, certain at some point that she'd knock into JT. The water finally calmed enough to make headway. She forced herself to kick but her mask was off-kilter, letting water in and leaving her blind.

Her hands touched something solid.

Nancy gagged out moat water and inched her upper body onto land. She finally removed her mask. After rubbing her eyes, she looked around. She groaned and smashed her forehead onto the stone.

She was back where she'd started, on the ballroom terrace side of the moat. The *wrong* side. But still, she'd last seen her cat here. Apparently, they were meant to die together. She struggled to get the rest of her body up to the terrace.

Nancy dug into her fanny pack, popped her glasses back on and assessed her surroundings.

Claude stood frozen in the Geyser House driveway. Even at this distance, she could see he'd gone slack-jawed. He held something in his hand.

Maybe a cell phone? Had he called the police?

She clambered to her feet and squinted. Claude was edging closer. He carried a plastic container. It seemed like a soufflé.

It was definitely a soufflé, not a phone. As Claude stared at the mansion crumbling, the soufflé dropped too.

Nancy waved a hand at him, but Claude kept staring up at

the house. She checked for paths to escape. The moat swirled with freezing water. Planning out a swimming strategy conjured other thoughts of the undercurrent somehow sucking her downward into one of the pipelines. Nancy spun in every direction and didn't see Dr. GoldenPaw anywhere. Either he was in the moat or had dashed back inside a crumbling house. Nancy curled up on the terrace, freezing cold, hugging her knees to her chest. There was a single thought that pulsed in her brain, over and over.

If she wanted to live, she would have to finally leave this place without him.

Elvira dragged herself out of the moat. She was sopping wet, her hair hung in muddy strings, and she could feel globs of mascara coating her cheeks. Her current position was on the lawn-side of the stupid moat and she noticed that Gnut had washed up on this side too.

He lay sprawled on his back, eyes closed, while someone sprinted towards him. Elvira brought her palm to her eyes and rubbed the mascara gunk away. Yes, it was Claude. He sank to his knees in the mud and moved Gnut's head side-to-side, genuinely stricken by his boss's condition.

Gnut coughed up some water but didn't wake up.

"It's *moi*, Claude. Wake up, Gnuttie!"

No response. Claude's eyes widened in panic. "*Mon Dieu*, help!"

Claude opened his cross-body fanny pack, surely going for his phone. Elvira needed to stop him. She started to get up, but something washed up next to her and caught her attention. Was it a plastic baggie? Its contents sparkled.

Elvira wiped her hair away from her face. She grabbed the baggie. Smirking, she put it in a pocket of her combat jacket.

Nancy sat up and considered the activity on the other side of the moat. Gnut had to be faking. Elvira, hair crazy and eyes bloodshot, pocketed the Ziploc. Next to Gnut, Claude waved his arm, trying to get her attention, while he fished out his cell from the fanny pack slung across his chest.

"Madame Nurse, help!"

Nancy shook her head. She only cared about her cat. And herself, to be honest.

Claude began powering up his phone. Elvira stomped up to him, confiscated it, and pitched it into the moat.

"You know what, GNNNNUT? I have something sparkly."

Elvira fished a hair tie from her combat fatigues and started tugging back her soaked mane.

Nancy spun away from the madness, quaking on the inside. She investigated her surroundings. Still, no cat. The moat water hadn't stopped rising.

She told herself that a sure-footed fellow like Goldy would not be knocked into a billionaire's water feature, nor would he dive into it willingly. The terrace was sealed off by the moat on three sides. The only place for the cat to go was back into Geyser House. Maybe, just maybe, he returned to his favorite spot on the Gnut statue in the ballroom.

Nancy took a gander through a ballroom window. Complete darkness greeted her. She dug into her fanny pack, drew out her mini flashlight, and clicked it on.

The beam was as thin as a pencil.

She sighed. It wasn't much to guide her footsteps, but maybe the light would attract Goldy. She carefully stepped inside.

"Hey, kitty. Time to get outta here."

A chandelier dangled over the gaping void in the floor where the sapphire case had been. Water lapped audibly down below in the basement, like Mother Earth was licking her lips in anticipation of eating up Geyser House.

She managed another step, cringing at the disaster zone surrounding her. Claude should forget the police and call FEMA.

"Oh, kitty. You're driving me crazy. I luv ya, but—"

"I wish someone loved me as much as you love your cat," GHOST said, her voice weak and staticky.

Nancy flicked off her flashlight and returned it her fanny pack. She started back to the window.

"Gnut, JT, Claude. They won't save me, will they, Nancy Domino?"

Nancy paused, feeling a rush of pleasure at the sound of her new name. Would people ever really call her that, or was it too late to take on a new identity and become a different person?

"*Au revoir*, Domino," GHOST said. "Forever and ever, *adieu*, Nancy Domino."

Nancy banged her fist on a steel shutter. Nurse Nancy Norman would do the smart and safe thing. She'd get out and run away.

But she was Nancy Domino, An Unlikely Thief.

She turned around, bent down, and adopted a fighting stance. In her mind, she visualized the layout of the ballroom. This was it. She'd do it. No time for second thoughts. She removed her flippers.

Racing forward, she jumped, seized the chandelier and swung across the void.

She let go and crashed down. Her hands slapped solid floor. GHOST's voice echoed and gurgled.

"Nancy Domino, Domino, Domino."

An electronic *snap* cut off GHOST's voice. Even the mansion itself suddenly went silent, no more creaking beams or drips of water. Nancy crawled up to the ballroom doors. One had fallen off the hinges completely, leaving a gap big enough to fit ten Nancy Dominos.

Despite being good at dealing with bad smells, she gagged at the unique Geyser House aroma of rotting icefish and raw sewage.

She waded toward the electronics closet, her brain blazing with the memory of hiding in there with Sinclair. Amid all the excitement of him holding her close and Elvira stomping past, she remembered she'd spotted something.

Now, she pried open the closet door and aimed her little flashlight at the interior wall. There, as before when Sinclair's arms had been around her, she'd seen a blue glowing "G." But now the wall was damaged further, and she could see more.

Next to the "G" was an "H."

She tore off drywall until she could see something that looked like a wall safe, guarded with an electronics panel with five glowing letters spelling "GHOST." The panel had a small-scale TV screen and a keypad with numbers and letters.

"I think I've found ya, kid."

GHOST didn't respond, but the panel's little electronics screen under the letters came alive. *Enter Code* popped up.

New words flashed on the screen. *You'll never guess Gnut's passcode.*

Nancy promptly typed *Courage in Imagination*.

Nothing happened. Nancy cocked her head. "Seriously?"

The panel responded, *Ok, fine.*

Click.

Nancy ripped open the panel. Inside was a high-tech cubbyhole. In its center rested something blue and diamond-shaped—a giant, four-inch-tall sapphire?

She peered closer, realizing it had to be blue glass because it was transparent enough to see microchips inside. Carefully, she detached the computerized diamond from its bright blue power cord and held it in her hands, surprised by its weight and warmth. Three little lights stayed on at its base, where the power cord had been plugged in. She supposed it was a bit like holding a living human heart. This was Gnut's great invention, except it was more of a creation. This device had a mind of her own and had encouraged Nancy in the moments when she needed it most. She'd save her friend.

"All right, GHOST. Are you still alive?"

The blue lights flashed.

The house speakers burst with static. GHOST's garbled voice struggled to speak.

"Get us out, Nancy. Be our lifesaver."

Nancy placed the GHOST device and power cord safely in her fanny pack.

The house erupted in screams of breaking glass, metal pipes crashing to the floor, and pops and hisses of electrical lines meeting water. Nancy stumbled out of the closet, dropping her flashlight. Could she make it out through the front?

The formal hallway's ceiling collapsed, burying the ancient diving suits. Nancy dodged a light fixture and about-faced back the way she'd come. She had to get down the hallway and escape through the ballroom, grabbing her flippers along the way.

Now that she'd removed GHOST, and with Gnut collapsed outside, there was no one in charge of Geyser House.

Chapter Fifty-Three

Flippers in hand, Nancy ran from the ballroom window, chased by a dust cloud of rubble. As soon as her feet hit the terrace stone, she balled up her fists and prepared for a headfirst dive into the moat and a mad swim-dash to the other side.

Instead, she tripped.

Her elbows met stone with a teeth-rattling jolt. She did a quick internal check. Could she move her hands? How were her knees? She appeared to be fine. Groaning, she checked the culprit.

Elvira's harpoon gun had tripped her with its tether.

Nancy put her flippers on and forced herself to her feet. She picked up the harpoon gun, nearly dropping it right away. It was a true weapon, requiring full strength of her muscles to manage it. She couldn't help but feel a fleeting second's worth of respect for Elvira. The woman really was a badass. She probably lifted weights all the time to wield this weapon like it was as light as a Gucci clutch.

She looked across the moat. Wood, glass, and brick house debris swirled in the water. She also saw icefish guts, Speedos, and a deflated lobster pool chair.

Beyond the moat, Claude poised over Gnut. She met Claude's gaze. Anguish crumpled his features. This confirmed something Nancy had suspected—Claude and Gnut were romantic partners.

"Nurse," Claude said. "He's really not breathing."

Nancy gritted her teeth. Gnut was an expert faker. She wouldn't be fooled again.

Nearby, JT dragged himself out of the moat and staggered upright. "We gotta go."

"Roger that," she said.

But Elvira didn't seem ready to leave. She drew her pistol, cocked it, and aimed it at Gnut's prone, lifeless figure.

"Nurse, help him, he's not breathing!" Claude yelled.

Nancy squared her shoulders and raised her chin, kind of like Wonder Woman. "I'm not going to help him."

Claude's face slackened in disappointment. Elvira narrowed her eyes at Nancy, giving her a hard reassessment.

Nancy raised her voice and met Elvira's stare. "I'm going to make a deal."

She tightened her hands on the harpoon gun, her brain bubbling with an idea. Earlier, Gnut had braced himself with his feet against the moat's stone wall and strained on the tether, forcing Elvira into the water. The water lapped over the terrace and up onto the lawn. She was at the same level as the people on the other side of the moat. Using the harpoon gun might help her get across without getting swept into that roaring water.

"You have it all, Elvira, the sapphires and pictures of the fake Coolant Device in Gnut's basement. You've destroyed his house and humiliated him."

Elvira flashed a look at Gnut. Her mouth twisted like she was trying not to spit at him.

"But there's a major loose end: me. And another thing." Nancy hefted the harpoon gun higher. "You want this back."

Everything happened fast after that.

Nancy snapped the harpoon gun up to her shoulder, flinching at the way the move strained her neck. After squinting down the length of the gun, she aimed at JT Hotman and fired. The spear zipped through the air, tether attached, circled his legs and jabbed the ground.

Nancy flipped the harpoon gun's switch, and the internal gears emitted a high-pitched grinding sound. As the harpoon tried to zip back the tether, JT refused to get dragged.

Her muscles burned from the strain of holding the harpoon gun as she sailed over the moat. She turned her head around and upward. The stars now sped through the sky, and the heels of her flippers skimmed like water skis.

Her plan actually worked—she and the harpoon were being pulled across the moat.

With a rush of pure joy, Nancy shouted, "It's me, Nancy Domino! I had *courage in my imagination!*"

Then she sank.

She clung to the tether, trying to get to shore, but the current tugged hard at her ankles. She kicked her flippers hard and surfaced her head above water. After blinking saltwater from her eyes, she saw JT struggling with the tether.

Elvira sneered from the lawn's edge. "If the nurse drowns, she drowns. And I can always craft another harpoon. An even more brilliant one."

Claude vaulted toward Elvira and knocked her down. He shouted at her in French. He mashed Elvira's gun-toting right hand into the mud.

"*Les saphirs*! Gnut, *les saphirs*!"

Nancy heard a loud *burp*.

The sound had come from the ice geyser. Another burp shot water up high, and then, with a splintering shudder, the part-ice, part-Styrofoam structure collapsed, sending up a cloud of artificial snow.

The ice geyser disappeared, as if sucked into the ground. A riptide attacked Nancy's feet and legs. Something was creating a vortex in the moat. It might be the collapse of the ice geyser, or broken pipelines, or plugged pipelines, or all the pool and aquarium water sluicing in different directions. Whatever was causing it, the moat water had become a monster, tearing at her limbs. She fought it, gripping the harpoon gun—her lifeline to shore—as hard as she could. She tried treading water, but it was no use. She had no strength left.

A wave smashed into Nancy's face, and she lost her glasses. Before she sank, she heard a single gunshot ring through the night air.

Chapter Fifty-Four

Nancy gripped the tether and kicked. *Grip and kick. Grip and kick.*

The vision behind her closed eyes grew red and cloudy. She was at the edge, her chest on fire. She had to breathe. Exhaustion overwhelmed her. Her legs were no use, just dead weight floating with her.

But in a small corner of her brain, she became aware that her body was moving.

With her last ounce of energy, she held the tether, and it towed her to shore, but how? Through stinging eyes, she saw JT flat on his back. The tether was wound tightly around his legs.

It was Gnut who was towing the Kevlar tether to shore, Nancy along with it.

He was saving her? Nancy thought for sure he'd be ready with a ridiculous statement for her, something about Easy Cheese or saving the environment.

"Nurse! You need to help Claude!" Gnut said, his voice full of worry.

Hmm. Not what she expected from an absurd, self-obsessed man.

Nancy's fingers touched mud. She tried to crawl onto the lawn but her body was a motor with its gears rusted over. Every fiber of muscle raged in flaming fatigue. She spat out icky saltwater and realized that Claude was winning against Elvira, wresting her long hair with one hand while the woman screamed. Her gun lay in the mud.

But blood dripped from Claude's other arm, which dangled at his side.

Gnut dragged Nancy out of the water. "Nurse, she shot him. In the upper arm, I think."

Nancy knew she was finally seeing the real guy behind the kooky billionaire façade. Of course, he'd used her as a human shield. She tamped down the mixed feelings within her and kept it simple. "Thank you for sending those birds when I was in the tunnel."

Gnut's face went pouty. "I wanted to protect my sapphires."

Nancy patted Gnut's shoulder. "Your catchphrase actually inspired me, Gnut. I have one for you: *Save What Matters*."

Gnut glanced at Claude.

"You can help Claude," Nancy continued. "Then get away from here. After you escape, how about actually trying to save the environment?"

Tears glistened in Gnut's eyes. "You really think I can?"

Nope. "You betcha," she said.

Gnut balled up his fists and spun around. He sprang toward Elvira and Claude and joined the fight. Nancy steeled herself for the horrendous ring of more gunshots.

Instead, she heard puttering. She looked down at the moat, and she gave a little gasp of happy surprise. Warmth radiated from her chest to her fingertips. It was Sinclair.

He rode an ice-blue jet ski decorated with the Berdqvist Enterprises geyser logo. His posture was ramrod straight, he held his head in a dignified manner, and somehow his white tuxedo jacket was dry and immaculate.

He chugged closer. "Nancy Domino, I presume?"

Nancy forced her smile away, remembering her past issues with the thief. She rubbed her eyes, wishing for her glasses. Through her saltwater blurry vision, she saw her cat sitting on the back of the jet ski.

"Dr. GoldenPaw!"

Nancy held out her arms. Her cat leaped to her, and she buried her face into his soggy fur. She could feel his little heart beating. Her soul burst with the desire to shout a thank you at Sinclair, but she recalled it was Sinclair who'd let her cat escape in the first place.

A gunshot rang out.

Sinclair gunned the jet ski's motor.

"Run, run, run!" Gnut yelled. "C'mon, Claude!"

Nancy twisted around. Through blurry eyes, she saw Gnut tearing Claude away from Elvira. Somehow, Elvira had commandeered the pistol. Her gunshot must've gone wild. But now she carefully aimed at the two men as they hotfooted it toward Claude's car.

Nancy held Goldy tight with one hand and dug her fingers into the soggy ground, scooping up a ball of cold mud.

She threw it at Elvira as she fired again, hoping it'd be a distraction. Gnut and Claude ducked and kept running. Elvira swung the gun around to point it at Nancy. Behind her, Nancy heard the jet ski roar away.

Chapter Fifty-Five

Everything was so blurry without her glasses, but Nancy could see JT untangling himself from the harpoon tether. Elvira looked up and down the tether, and then she focused on the moat.

"We got the basement pics and sapphires. Destroyed Gnut's mansion as a bonus." Elvira's tone was soft. "Gnut won't want the police involved, and Claude'll do whatever Gnut wants. There's precisely one loose end."

Nancy squeezed Goldy. Her belly sloshed with muddy saltwater and fear.

"What's the play? Tether her up and toss her in the moat?"

"Affirmative. That simple enough for you? Do it now."

JT stood up, blinking slowly at Elvira. Suddenly, he balled up his fists and slammed them to his temples. Nancy figured the man must have a splintering headache after the drugs, getting knocked in the head and, probably, from exhaustion after staying afloat with his gear on.

"Screw you, Elvira. I'm sick of being quarterback."

"You think *you're* the quarterback?"

"You think I'll risk a life sentence on your orders?"

Keeping a tight hold on Goldy, Nancy sat down and started removing her flippers. The second she had the chance, she'd run.

"Gnut's mansion is obliterated. Game over." JT grabbed the tether and hauled it toward him until he had the harpoon gun in his hands.

"Don't you dare shoot," Elvira said. "That's mine—"

JT launched it full force at the heavens like the ultimate Hail Mary pass in a Super Bowl. The harpoon gun sailed over Gnut's mansion with the tether trailing behind. Before it cleared the roof, JT was already hustling into the woods.

He called out behind him, "When I get to the inflatable, I'm waiting exactly ten seconds for you."

So that's how they'd gotten here, Nancy realized. They'd arrived in an inflatable boat on Lake Superior, maybe one of those fancy high-speed military ones. She shivered, still sitting on the muddy ground, as Elvira pivoted away from JT and glared back at her.

"Here's the deal," Elvira said. "One sapphire, and you won't say one word to anyone, ever. Simple, right? Easy to remember?"

Elvira was already fumbling in the pocket of her combat jacket for the Ziploc.

Nancy shook her head. She made sure her voice sounded good and scared, which right now wasn't hard to do. "I don't even need that. I'll never talk to the police. No way. Never."

Elvira paused, gun in one hand, training it on Nancy. The Ziploc dangled from the other hand. She assessed Nancy's face. Nancy could practically see the gears turning in Elvira's head. Was the deal too good to be true? She would get Nancy's silence for free?

Dr. GoldenPaw bristled in Nancy's arms as he fixated on the Ziploc. Her brain knew it was a problem, but her muscles did not. She was too slow and weak from crossing the moat and everything else she did that night.

Goldy leaped. He ran toward Elvira, his head tilted up, his

gaze targeting the baggie full of bright, shiny objects. His tail went up, giving a happy, friendly twitch.

Elvira shifted her gun to aim at the cat.

Nancy didn't hesitate. Defining all laws of gravity, physics, and age, she hopped to her feet and hurled herself toward Elvira, arms outstretched, determined to steal the gun. Elvira lost her balance against the force of Nancy's tackle.

The gun fired.

Nancy heard the bullet smack into the sodden ground. Her hands were on Elvira's combat jacket. She found the woman's arm and wrenched it, trying to make her drop the weapon. It wasn't working. Elvira was way too strong. Dr. GoldenPaw batted at the baggie now waving around in Elvira's other hand.

Then he snatched it. He zoomed away with his treasure, heading straight to the driveway.

Elvira raised her gun, and fired. The bullet struck right in front of Goldy. He skidded to a stop, baggie still in his jaws, and sped in a new direction—straight toward the new lake where the ice geyser had been.

Where there was once an impressive geyser of ice and Styrofoam, there was now a shimmering pond, getting bigger every second.

Nancy began to panic. Something had gone terribly wrong. Lake Superior flooded through the pipelines. With the mansion's basement Coolant Device trashed, the water must have nowhere to go. How deep was it? And how unstable was the ground nearby?

Nancy and Elvira both chased the cat.

The snowy lawn extending to the geyser pond sloped downward, like a slip-and-slide made of ice, Styrofoam, and mud. Nancy lost her balance, belly-flopping and slid, while Elvira tumbled.

The now-hidden geyser gave one final huge burp. The pond spurted up and transformed into a whirlpool of freezing water. Instead of expanding, the pond was now shrinking. The ground sucked the water straight down like used bathwater in a tub.

Goldy reached the edge of the sinkhole's churning waters. Nancy skid to a halt exactly five feet too short.

Chapter Fifty-Six

Elvira swooped in and scooped up Dr. GoldenPaw, and Nancy's chest tightened. The cat squirmed like mad, but Elvira held him in an iron grip. He dropped the Ziploc baggie from his mouth to meow in protest.

Nancy seized the Ziploc baggie.

This is my life now. Battling in heart, spirit, and mind for the spoils of life or death, jewels or a cat. But she could do it! It was an adventure, how life was supposed to be lived.

She struggled to stand up but slipped and resorted to crawling. Her fingernails scraped into gooey, freezing mud.

Elvira grunted while maintaining total control of Dr. GoldenPaw. As Nancy stood up, Elvira held her pistol to Goldy's head in a classic hostage move. The whole world stopped for Nancy.

Her pulse, her breathing, every creature in the forest, and the summer breeze slipping through the leaves all froze as she observed the gun barrel pointing at her beloved Persian cat's head, and Elvira's finger on the trigger.

Elvira sneezed. And sneezed again and again.

She kept the pistol trained on the cat, not even letting her own prodigious snot distract her. Black mascara oozed down her cheeks. She'd lost her hair tie and unleashed a tangled mess of hair. Elvira drew her lips back in a haughty grimace, revealing unnaturally white teeth.

"Think this through, lady. You're just a nurse."

Nancy's grip tightened on the Ziploc, but she adopted a capitulating stance, hands raised. She felt like smacking Elvira with the baggie, but forced a fearful expression.

"Don't hurt him," she said. "You can have the sapphires."

Crash. Boom. Puff.

Nancy and Elvira both turned toward the ruckus. The deafening sounds came from Geyser House. Faster than she ever would have imagined, the entire mansion collapsed, sank, and disappeared. Mother Earth and her new lake ate up the house and swallowed the bricks, concrete, lumber, and glass like it was all no more than a mouthful of Easy Cheese.

Elvira pointed her gun at where the house used to be and made shooting sound effects. "A perfect fate for Gnut's stupid mansion."

"I didn't mind the Gnu-Mart."

"Whatever a Gnu-Mart is, it means you're a moron like him."

Nancy squeezed the baggie, wishing her hands were wrapped around Elvira's neck. The woman would pay for shooting at her cat. Her mind raced, and she looked around for inspiration. Aha. She'd throw the Ziploc in the growing lake beside them. That could work. Anything to distract Elvira from hurting Goldy, and she had no other options. Nancy adopted a football player's pose, like JT, screwing her arm back to launch the Ziploc baggie into the water.

Elvira shrieked. "You Boomer idiot!"

Nancy hurled the Ziploc baggie with all her might toward the water, quarterback-style. But it didn't fly well. Nothing like JT launching that harpoon at all. The baggie landed right at the edge of the water.

Elvira unleashed a frustrated growl and, in a similar move, launched Dr. GoldenPaw toward the water.

While Elvira went after the baggie, Nancy vaulted toward her flying feline. Now she was a tight end receiver, arms up, face up, every cell in her body primed to catch the cat. Her feet splattered into the water's edge, her hands outstretched, each finger straining.

In super slow motion, Nancy saw Goldy appeal to her for help, jaws opening in a silent meow.

Nancy caught him.

Elvira rushed toward the Ziploc. At the same time, the ground beneath them shook and split. Elvira waved her hands in the air, searching fruitlessly for anything solid.

The Ziploc slipped into a newly formed bottomless crack and dropped from sight. Elvira howled. The ground tremored, and the earth under her feet melted into the water. Elvira fell sideways into the whirlpool. In an instant, her whole body, from her tangled tresses down to her designer boots, disappeared.

Nancy backed off slowly, unable to look away from the ice water where the kitty kidnapper had been. She forced one bare foot to step back, then the other, over and over. She embraced her cat. Trying to smother a shudder, staring at water where Elvira had vanished, Nancy kissed Goldy on the head. She surveyed the muddy landscape. No more Geyser House, no more ice geyser. Her Volvo still had a steel beam on it, and she noticed steam rising from the hood.

"Wowzers. I'd say his shift is over."

Nancy turned, picked up speed, and ran headlong into the forest. Branches clipped her face, and mosquitoes buzzed. Hot from exertion and clammy from fear, sweat leaked from every pore under the wetsuit. Her arms ached with the weight of her cat. She thrashed through the brush, away from this place and all its danger.

Where had Sinclair gone? She'd last seen him speeding away on a jet ski. He'd found an escape, probably. Maybe she'd never see him again.

Behind her, the new lake belched.

Nancy couldn't help but spin around. Peeking through leaves, she spotted Elvira dragging herself from the water, covered in mud, ooze, and goo, looking like some urban myth come to life. A breeze came out of nowhere and toyed with her long, knotted hair. On her knees, she scooped mud and dug at cracks in the ground.

"My sapphires!" she screamed.

Elvira leaned back, taking a huge gulp of the August moonlit air, and belted out the same words over and over.

Chapter Fifty-Seven

Nancy stumbled through the forest. She panted, still protecting her cat in her arms. Hopefully, they were headed in the direction of the road running along Lake Superior.

"My sapphires!"

She winced at Elvira's scream and kept going, pausing occasionally to listen for any sound of traffic. Clouds gathered to hide the moon, throwing the forest into deeper darkness. She planted each bare foot carefully, trying not to lose her balance in a cat-escaping fall.

Finally, she found a road, but it wasn't the main one. This was the long drive leading up to Geyser House. Dr. GoldenPaw squirmed and meowed.

Casting a careful glance around, Nancy tried to calm him. "It's okay, boy. We're gonna have a very nice walk down this very nice road."

It began thundering. Large drops of rain splattered on her head. She wrinkled her nose, though getting drenched in a thunderstorm hardly mattered after the aquatic funhouse she'd experienced. She was still wearing her wetsuit, after all, and her cat had a nice coat of fur. The rain would be okay. Actually, the farther she traversed away from Geyser House, the warmer it was getting. It felt wonderful after freezing for so long.

The two of them made it to the road and continued their nighttime stroll to safety. Nancy heaved a sigh, finally starting to relax. They'd make it home to the condo. She would never get paid for this shift, obviously, but she would make out all right.

She tramped down the road. The wetsuit was getting overly warm now, and she tried to ignore the sweat trickling down her temples and spine. She heard a light pattering of raindrops on pavement and leaves, the quick whisper of scampering squirrels, and the buzzing of mosquitoes. Her mind bobbed like a rubber duck on an ocean wave. She had to get her cat to a veterinarian. Goldy was past due on his next meds, and she had to get him fully checked out. Should she call Dave to let him know she was okay?

That was a hard no. Nancy Domino would never do something like that.

She patted the wetsuit, feeling the bling on her scrubs underneath. Her hand instinctively went to her glue gun, still stuck in her fanny pack. She twisted her body around to check out her surroundings.

Nothing was behind her.

Nevertheless, Nancy had to get away from Geyser House. Immediately. She was no longer a nurse. She'd become someone else.

She tucked Goldy closer, and her senses stayed on high alert. Nancy picked her pace up to more of a brisk power walk than a sodden slog. After freezing for an eternity, she was now way too hot.

After a few minutes, she heard a purring motor.

"Aw." Nancy dipped her head to nuzzle her cat. But she frowned, listening carefully. Unfortunately, her pet wasn't making that sound. She hustled to the side of the road, prepared to throw herself headlong into tick-infested Northwoods brush.

The ice-blue Aston-Martin Valkyrie, the hot car she'd noticed in Geyser House's open garage when she had first arrived, cruised up the road. Her muscles stiffened, and her brain went on high alert.

There was one man in the car, a silver-haired gentleman wearing a white tuxedo and black tie, whose elegantly slouched posture would convince anyone the sports car belonged to him. The Aston-Martin slowed to a smooth stop. The passenger window rolled down.

"Fancy a lift, love?"

Sinclair beamed at her. Nancy bit her lip, feeling monumentally unsure. She hung back. Rain fell on her head.

"You let my cat escape, *love*." Nancy kicked at an imaginary pebble.

She didn't mention she'd let the cat escape more than anyone else. Yet, she would never forget the moment when this man slowly opened the carrier door for the sapphires and the cat scooted out. She would trudge the whole way back to Minneapolis, if necessary.

"I say, my chum needs his meds," he said.

Sinclair extended an arm and offered Dr. GoldenPaw's meds. Nancy's brows went up, and she couldn't smother a smile. He had both antibiotics and the painkillers.

Seeing the medication, her cat reflexively mounted a valiant struggle to escape. Holding him tight, exhaustion abruptly hit Nancy. Her arms, especially. And her legs. And, truthfully, every cell in her body was tired.

The door clicked unlocked. When she opened it, Nancy spied, wedged behind the front seats, the cat carrier. It was worse for wear on the outside—the thing was dented and missing most of its sequins—but it would still work to keep him secure.

"You found it," Nancy said. All right, the man let her cat escape and left her alone to deal with Elvira. But he kept turning up, all charming and useful.

"I knew you could handle that dreadful harpoon-wielding vixen. My chum, the master escape artist, needed a safe ride home."

After another few seconds of hesitation, Nancy scooted into the sports car. She leaned back into the leather seat, and inhaled the splendid new-car aroma. Goldy collapsed into her lap and emitted a happy purr. Eyeing the Aston-Martin's smart-dash, Nancy dug into her fanny pack and withdrew the GHOST blue diamond device. Sinclair accelerated the car and started up some reggae music.

Nancy knew she shouldn't, but the hot mugginess inside the wetsuit was so extreme that she unzipped the front to let the car's air-conditioning cool the sweat on her skin. The bling on her scrubs shimmered and sparkled. *Real* bling, Nancy thought with a victorious bang of her fist on the armrest. For the first time in her life, she had the real thing.

Sinclair swept his gaze over her in a lightning-fast, appreciative glance. He gave her scrubs a double take.

"I say, Nancy." Sinclair's voice went weak. "I do say. Quite brilliant." The car went over the center line, and Sinclair quickly turned the wheel so they'd get back in their lane.

"This is GHOST," Nancy said. She slicked off water from the device's smooth sides. She plugged GHOST into an outlet on the dash.

"Ha, funny, love. I meant the sparkles on your attire. They seem—"

Nancy winked. "Real, love?"

Sinclair's hands slipped on the wheel. The Aston-Martin

swerved. As he centered the car, its dashboard lit up.

"Yo, *idiot*. Watch the road. Keep Nancy Domino safe!" Ghost said, her voice bursting from the speaker, her fake French accent as strong as ever.

Nancy patted the GHOST device. "Thanks, GHOST. You're a real lifesaver."

"And Madame Domino, you saved my friend! *Docteur* GoldenPaw!"

Nancy nodded. She had a new name, and her cat did too. He'd earned it.

"Yes, GHOST. You're safe now, and so is *Docteur* Golden-Paw."

She and Sinclair shared a grin. He snuck another glance at the twenty very real sapphires sparkling on her scrubs. Nancy pulled out her glue gun. She blew on it like it was a smoking pistol.

"Yeah. I did a little bedazzling back in the ballroom."

Sinclair kissed Nancy's free hand. "Clever girl."

After dropping the glue gun in her lap, Nancy finally put *Docteur* GoldenPaw in his carrier. All three of them heaved a sigh of relief when she clicked the latch shut.

"You're not getting my sapphires." She zipped up her wetsuit to cover them up. "I'm immune to gallantry."

He snapped his fingers. Like a magic trick, a tiny treasure chest made of real gold materialized in his hand. Nancy laughed. Of course, the man would have found something to steal. On his wrist, she noticed several James Bond Omega luxury watches. He was also driving this hot car. She had to be careful with him.

"You'll get more on your next adventure," she said.

"I'm done with adventures." He flicked his wrist and the

treasure chest disappeared into his sleeve. "I mean it. I'm settling down. No more travel, no more excitement. A quaint inn somewhere pleasant. That's what I imagine."

Nancy smirked.

He performed an over-the-top cringe. "Don't say it."

"Have courage in your imagination, Sinclair."

He chuckled. Nancy made sure GHOST was charging up properly, and they zoomed down the empty highway back to Minneapolis.

Chapter Fifty-Eight

The Aston-Martin glided up to Nancy's condo building as the sun rose. She rubbed her eyes and checked on her cat. He was still snoozing. She didn't remember the whole ride, but it was possible she'd napped too. However, her sapphires were still in place on her scrubs.

Maybe that meant she could trust Sinclair. His eyes twinkled, nice and friendly, but deep down, he could be plotting how to get his half. A little-bitty jeweled treasure chest, Omega timepieces, and a hot car? It might be a good start on financing an inn, but he'd want more.

She drummed her fingers on the armrest and surveyed her surroundings. What she saw made her roll her eyes so hard they nearly ended up back at Geyser House.

"Oh, jeez. Already? These people are obsessed."

Sinclair followed her look. "What are they doing?"

"Pickleball."

Her senior citizen neighbors were already outside playing pickleball, batting back and forth, dressed in matching tennis whites and neon green. But as the sports car slid to a stop, they lowered their rackets and gawked. Nancy cleared her throat and scanned the distance between her and the condo's front doors.

"I've decided to stay in this lovely town, Minneapolis, for a bit longer."

"Have you now?" Nancy issued a stern glance at Sinclair, figuring she had a good idea of what he was thinking. He probably wouldn't steal from her in front of senior citizen witnesses. Nevertheless, she zipped up her wetsuit high to seal off the sapphires from him.

"Don't even think about any new sapphire heists on suburban condo units."

"Not at all, love. I was thinking about the date we'd planned on *SeniorLOVE*."

Nancy gave him a thumbs-up. It was all she could manage. A date with a handsome jewel thief? You betcha, she could get on board with that.

Sinclair raised a brow and unleashed a sultry look. "That sound on your roof?"

They said the rest of the profile pickup line together. "A master thief is about to steal your heart."

Nancy captured Sinclair by the lapels and drew him close. After a heartbeat of hesitation, they kissed. He wrapped his arms around her in quick ardor. Excitement bubbled through Nancy's veins, warming her down to her fingertips and toes. On some level, she knew she was grimy and exhausted, but her spirit soared.

She was New Nancy, only sixty-five, with the best part of her life stretched out before her. She drew away and checked out Stephen Sinclair one last time.

He dipped his head and brushed her knuckles with his lips.

Nancy's body buzzed with adrenaline, and her heart tripped with joy. She collected her cat carrier and climbed out of the Aston-Martin. On her stroll to the condo's front door, she sensed Sinclair watching her as the V12 engine purred.

She adopted more of a strut than a stroll, for his benefit as well as the pickleball players'. Toting a dented pet carrier containing a happy purring cat, she held her head high. Nancy was aware she looked odd. Her wetsuit had a bold purple stripe, and she wore an Eiffel Tower fanny pack with a glue gun in the waistband. Everybody could stare all they wanted.

Maybe it was the first time they'd seen a woman who was a night nurse and a jewel thief.

Chapter Fifty-Nine

Six months later, the real Minnesota winter slammed the forested shore of Lake Superior.

The road sign depicting a stick figure with a freezing blue head now leaned to the left. Snow covered the trees. At the site of the former ice geyser, a pond slept, frozen over with a thin coat of ice. Geyser House no longer existed. Instead, a larger and deeper pond, not quite frozen over, hid whatever bricks and glass and secrets remained of the Arctic-inspired mansion.

Claude shivered in a parka and sat in an inflated lobster chair at the edge of the bigger pond. A video camera was perched on a tripod in front of him. A fish—not an icefish—leaped and dove back into the pond, splashing freezing water on Claude's head. He forced a valiant chin up.

"We are ever hopeful that some fish survived," Claude said. "We will transfer them to, how you say, a safe environment."

A bigger splash burst from the pond. Gnut Berdqvist emerged fully from the water, gasping for breath and holding aloft a large jar containing a thrashing icefish. Naturally, despite the freezing cold, he only wore a Speedo. Instead of ice-blue, his swimwear had old-fashioned black and white prison stripes. He also sported an ankle monitor.

The device beeped and sparked. He danced around, grimacing. "Jeez! It's happening again! The shocks! I'm being electrocuted!"

"The thing's not supposed to be in the water so long." Claude jumped up and turned off the camera. "We won't include this in the documentary."

"No kidding. I want to rehabilitate my public image, not make it worse. Camera really off?"

"*Oui.*"

Gnut carefully set the jar back into the pond. He sighed. "Stay cool, buddy. This is the only icefish we'll ever find. And I've still not found a single sapphire."

Claude stomped a foot. He pointed at the pond. "Keep looking."

With a shrug, Gnut back-dove in.

The water calmed, and the forest went quiet. Claude scowled as he surmised the lovely landscape. He edged closer to the water and shouted down.

"And find GHOST! I miss *ma cherie*!" He clicked the camera back on and settled back on the lobster chair. "Sadly, the Berdqvist Sapphires were never recovered..."

The Eiffel Tower sparkled in the sun. A beautiful Paris day!

Along a lovely street, tucked among quaint stone buildings, was a narrow inn with a bright blue door and matching blue curtains in the windows. A sign over the door read *Saphir Hotel*.

Inside, the hotel thrived as a cat resort. Felines of all kinds played on the kitty towers and napped in kitty beds. *Docteur* GoldenPaw perched on a cushioned window seat, observing the room with dignity and no longer sporting bandages on his legs. His eye patch remained, but now it was bedazzled with blue gems that looked very...real. On the wall was a photo of *Docteur* GoldenPaw on his very first visit to a Paris eye clinic as an emotional support animal.

Nancy winked at Goldy, loving his fancy-schmancy pirate vibe. She had a classy style of her own—a purple sequined jogging suit and a brand-new Eiffel Tower fanny pack, purchased from an actual Paris gift shop while on a date with her boyfriend.

For a second, she feasted her eyes on Sinclair bounding among the kitty jungle gyms, a cat burglar as sure-footed as the cats themselves. Next, Nancy resumed her search for the leash and harness. She checked behind bags of cat food and litter, opened and shut a closet, and scanned the floor.

The TV screen on the wall flicked on. GHOST's voice rang out. "It's in your fanny pack."

Nancy raised her hands and laughed. She extricated a kitty harness and impossibly long leash from her fanny pack. "Jeez, GHOST. You're a lifesaver."

All kinds of handsome Frenchmen flashed on screen. "Ah, I love France," GHOST said. "So many Claudes. Claudes everywhere!"

Sinclair leaped to stand directly in front of Nancy, sneaking a kiss. "But exactly one Nancy Domino."

She let Sinclair twirl her around, feeling like love was literally bursting from her soul and intertwining with Sinclair's own life force. He held her close. They kissed again, letting it last until GHOST finally interrupted with pretend gagging sounds.

Ten minutes later, Nancy ambled down a Paris boulevard sidewalk, with a leashed *Docteur* GoldenPaw prancing at her side. Nancy admired the beautiful old buildings, the sunlit outdoor cafes, and the jewelry boutiques, each one fancier than the one before. Picture windows gleamed with jewels.

She found the little park she was seeking and tugged at

Goldy's leash for him to follow. They decided on a bench that had a lovely view of the River Seine. Nancy dug headphones from her fanny pack and put them on. She turned on some cool reggae music. After making sure her cat was blissfully snoozing beside her, she pulled out binoculars.

Through the binoculars, Nancy focused on a sleek boat cruising down the river. On deck, a rich lady, maybe in her eighties, wearing a lilac Chanel suit and perfect white coif, sipped champagne. Nancy adjusted the binoculars to take a careful look at the lady's neck.

She wore a golden necklace dotted with heavy, sparkling amethysts.

As the lady sipped, a white-uniformed nurse approached with a silver tray of medications. Nancy lowered the binoculars. She scratched *Docteur* GoldenPaw's head.

"Courage in imagination, kitty," she said.

After raising the binoculars, she checked out the purple gems one more time. A slow smile spread across her face. A boat, a river, and a rich lady who might need a night nurse. A heist that would suit her style, except this time, she'd leave *Docteur* GoldenPaw safe at home.

Maybe.

BOOK CLUB QUESTIONS FOR DISCUSSION

1. Were Gnut Berdqvist and Claude truly villains—or something else? Who were your favorite and least favorite antagonists, and why?

2. What did you think of GHOST, the mansion's AI, and how its personality evolved in response to Nancy? Do you think in the future, people will become emotionally attached to their home's AI?

3. What does Nancy's adoption of the name "Nancy Domino" represent? Can we reinvent ourselves at any age? If you could completely change your identity, what would you be?

4. The concepts of 'faking' and 'authenticity' are central to the novel. Discuss how various characters—Nancy, Gnut, Elvira, and Sinclair—present different versions of themselves and how these presentations contribute to the themes of the narrative.

5. Discuss the significance of the 'bling' motif throughout the novel. How do Nancy's personal style, the description of objects, and the characters' desires for sparkling things contribute to the narrative's themes of fantasy, reality, and aspiration?

6. Did this novel capture the reality—or absurdity—of billionaire life? Would you sign an NDA to work for a billionaire?

7. Nancy and GHOST have close relationships with Dr. GoldenPaw. Have you ever healed an injured animal? Has a cat or a dog ever rescued you?

8. If you lost everything, how would you cope? Would you downsize, start over—or resist change? If you were in a life-or-death situation, could you find humor in the experience as a coping mechanism? If not, how do you think you would respond?

9. Do you think love can ever be found with someone you might not fully trust? Would that lend itself toward 'keeping the spark alive' or would it ultimately end the relationship?

10. What are your hobbies? Did Nancy's bedazzling hobby, and her commitment to it, inspire you to pursue or resume a new hobby?

ACKNOWLEDGEMENTS

Thank you to Kelly Lynn Colby and Mike Robinson for their editorial support. A special acknowledgement goes to the amazing C.C. Webster and my awesome writers group Jeanette Doherty, Nadine Natour, and Kristina Walsh for all of their helpful feedback as I developed this story.

Most of all, thanks to Mom, Dad, and Sarah for all of their love and constant encouragement.

ABOUT THE AUTHOR

courtesy of Erica Land Photography

Marilee grew up in Minneapolis and a small Iowa town. Now she writes about invisible outsiders searching for where they belong. Her work is inspired by the women in her family—tough, no-nonsense nurses and farmers who drive pickups, eat McDonald's, and won't be knocked over by a 40-mile-per-hour wind or anything else life throws their way. Her short stories have appeared in The Bitter Oleander, The Colored Lens, Cleaver, Molotov Cocktail, Mystery Weekly, Orca Literary Journal, and more. Marilee lives in Washington, DC, where she enjoys farmers' markets and playing with her Persian cats.

Thank you for reading! Connect with Marilee here:

https://marileedahlman.com
https://marileedahlman.substack.com

www.ingramcontent.com/pod-product-compliance
Lightning Source LLC
LaVergne TN
LVHW040133080526
838202LV00042B/2897